ALLISON'S AWAKENING

He picked up a thin crop and swung it from side to side. It cut through the air with a soft hiss. He bent it to test its flexibility, then he nodded slowly.

'This looks just about right. Do you think that would sting, slave?' he asked in a normal tone of voice. A man in the next aisle of the shop looked up and she blushed and turned her face away.

'Do you?'

'Yes,' she whispered.

'Maybe it's too lightweight. You're a very bad girl sometimes.'

ALLISON'S AWAKENING

Lauren King

This book is a work of fiction.
In real life, make sure you practise safe sex.

First published in 1997 by
Nexus
332 Ladbroke Grove
London W10 5AH

Copyright © Lauren King 1997

The right of Lauren King to be identified as the Author of
this Work has been asserted by her in accordance with the
Copyright Designs and Patents Act 1988.

Typeset by TW Typesetting, Plymouth, Devon

Printed and bound by
Caledonian Books Ltd, Glasgow

ISBN 0 352 33191 7

*All characters in this publication are fictitious and any
resemblance to real persons, living or dead, is purely
coincidental.*

This book is sold subject to the condition that it shall not,
by way of trade or otherwise, be lent, resold, hired out or
otherwise circulated without the publisher's prior written
consent in any form of binding or cover other than that in
which it is published and without a similar condition
including this condition being imposed on the subsequent
purchaser.

One

Allison Miller stepped carefully but quickly along the stony downward path to the beach. The land was hilly and uneven, but long familiar. As she picked her way around a hillock the vast panorama of the Atlantic Ocean came into view and her eyes moved to the horizon in an artist's appreciation of nature's beauty.

Grey-blue waves rolled to the shore in endless procession, the sound a soothing rumble. Seagulls wheeled overhead, their distinctive cries rending the air as they searched for their morning meal.

The sun had not yet risen, but the sky was light. On the horizon the sky and clouds reflected a growing orange tinge.

She reached the beach and her flat-heeled boots sank into the soft pebbly sand. Mist shrouded much of the beach and stony hillside, and she shivered a little in the morning chill.

The wind blew gently in from the sea, and her soft, blonde hair quivered and shifted, stray locks flipping across her face. She tossed them back unconsciously as she made her way along the beach. She tilted her head back, eyeing the lightening sky, then gazed out over the Atlantic, imagining what lay beneath its neverending motion: the darkness, the unchanging landscape deep below.

She sighed, gripped by a deep melancholy that had been growing on her for some months now. She had thought to leave the strife and unhappiness behind her when she left the city and came here; and she had. She had found a calmness, a serenity that had lent inspiration to her painting, giving it an uplifting tone that none who viewed it could clearly understand even though they were moved by it.

Jennie, her business agent, had waxed poetic over her work and had little difficulty finding eager buyers. At first, as the popularity, and thus the price of her paintings, grew she had badgered Allison unceasingly, trying to get her off the coast and back to town to attend showings. But her reclusive personality had actually driven her status higher and created more demand for her work.

People liked to imagine artists as moody and different, and the thought of her living alone on the south coast seemed to inspire them to part with more and more money.

That used to be important, she thought. Then again money was always more important when you didn't have it. Now she did and didn't know what to do with it.

'Just me, the sea and my painting,' she whispered, quoting Jennie.

But there was something missing. She felt there was a hole in her life, a hole that was growing week by week, month by month, an emptiness she didn't quite understand but felt nonetheless. She had an ideal life, or at least she had thought so once. But now, well, she missed people.

And who'd have bet I could ever do that, she thought.

Flashes of memories passed before her eyes in a dizzying blur: the teasing and taunting, the jokes that made her turn inward and throw up a wall around herself. She had been a tall, gawky, flat-chested girl with a face full of freckles and hideous-looking strawberry blonde hair. She was smart and she was shy and all of that had combined to make her a target.

In response she had ignored them, building a tall, strong wall around herself, a wall of indifference, of superiority. What importance would an eagle place on the taunts of worms, after all?

An eagle, she thought derisively, as if she had ever been that. More like a quiet sparrow.

The sun peeked over the horizon as she moved under the cliffs. The beach was narrow here, the water washing ashore only a few feet away from her boots. She found a large rock set back from the water and sat down. Leaning back, she watched the sunrise, unmoved, remembering how rare this pleasure once was, and how much it had meant to her.

She berated herself as stupid and ungrateful, thinking of all those mornings when she had cursed the alarm, hoping one day to have time of her own to do as she wished. Now she didn't have to wait for buses, didn't have to go out when the weather was foul, didn't have to get up early if she didn't want to, and didn't even have to work if she didn't feel like it.

She was completely free.

But not happy, a small voice said.

She had her joy in painting still, and there was the brief sense of satisfaction each time she completed one; but she remembered the shock and delight she had once felt when she had sold a painting. Now she expected them to sell, and paid little heed to whom or for how much they sold.

All her dreams had come true; all except one.

She had never really wanted to be alone.

She had told herself she was a loner; others called her a loner, in fact. She had been pretty much alone most of her life; for that wall she had built up had not evaporated when her hair shifted colour to its current bright gold, nor when her body softened into womanly curves, the freckles all-but disappeared, and her breasts finally arrived, plump and high and firm.

She remembered long ago looking at herself in the mirror and thinking with some surprise that she looked – OK; that she didn't look like someone others would taunt and tease. And as time passed her looks, which seemed all-important in school society, had shifted upwards, as these things were measured, to the point where boys actually asked her out.

But on the inside she hadn't changed. Too wary of being hurt or embarrassed, suspicious of being the butt of a joke, she hid behind her wall and remained separate. Alone.

In college, socially inexperienced, uncomfortable, confused and feeling inadequate, she had done what she'd done at school and avoided anyone's company but her own.

Most of the time.

It was dark in the car, and hot, and her mind was in turmoil as Eddie's hands fought hers as they raced over her body. He was handsome and, she thought, sweet, and she truly wanted to lose her virginity. But she was filled with alarm and anxiety, certain she would be inadequate, that he would be disappointed.

His hand shot up under her skirt, deftly slipping into her panties, and she gasped in alarm and wicked pleasure as she felt his fingers against her sex. The pleasure started to roll upwards, yet her mind fought it, filled with concern.

What should I do? How should I react? Should I move? Should I push his hand back? Will he be mad if I do? Will he think I'm a slut if I don't? Will he tell everyone tomorrow? What will he think of me?

She wanted to be seductive and sexy, sensual and sultry. She was terrified of doing the wrong thing but had little certainty as to what was the right thing.

And then his weight pushed her over on to her back and his weight was on her, her legs apart and his lips on hers. She felt his hand tugging her blouse upwards, then yanking her bra down, exposing her.

She blushed, glad of the near darkness, embarrassed even as she was excited. She felt his fingers on her nipples, blushed even more at how obviously hard they were, how they thrust upwards as his fingers, then his lips, slipped around them.

And then his hand tore the crotch of her panties aside, and to her shock she felt his erection against her. Again she was filled with alarm. Should she allow it, and what would be his reaction if she did?

She wanted to. For years she had dreamt of losing her virginity, of doing lewd, wicked things with boys and men, but her fears held her back. And even now, on the verge, still her fears stopped her from taking full part in it.

And then he was in her. Just like that. She grunted as his solidness filled her. There was no cherry to break, for in her secret enjoyment of her body she had long ago slipped her fingers and other objects deep inside herself.

His breath was hot on her face, his hands groping at her naked breasts. She sought for the eroticism that her fantasies contained but found none. His heavy hips ground against her thighs as he pumped furiously inside her. His erection stroked across her clitoris infrequently, yet she felt her pleasure starting to rise, felt the heat begin to take hold.

And then he collapsed on top of her with a loud groan and an exhalation of breath.

No; her few sexual encounters had been disappointing and nothing like the lewd fantasies she played out when she masturbated. Nor had the pleasure been there, the shuddering orgasms to which masturbation led.

She took a deep breath then stood up, unconscious of her grace. She reached down cross-handed and peeled her shift up and over her head, arching her back briefly. Her breasts thrust out towards the sea, round and firm, the nipples already stiffening as the breeze caught them.

She folded the shift neatly and placed it on the rock,

feeling the slow wakening of her inner heat, the arousal she always felt whenever she took her swims in the nude. It was wicked, being out of doors like this, where any man might see, might desire her body.

She kicked off her boots, placing them beside the rock, then gripped the sides of her trousers and slowly pushed them down, bending over as she stepped out of them.

She folded them and placed them on top of her shift, then ran a hand through her hair. She was wary in her nudity, yet proud of it and growing slightly more excited with each passing moment.

No one was there to see her trim stomach, her soft, ivory skin, the proudness of her full, upturned breasts with the eagerly erect pink nipples. No male eyes could ravish her softly rounded hips, her long, well-sculpted legs or the roundness of her curving apple-shaped buttocks.

They'd love to see you now, she thought, imagining the men were there, looking at her, gasping in delight and approval.

They'd all get erections, she thought, with more than a little pride.

Her bare toes dug into the loose sand as she stepped towards the lapping waves, and she felt a chill as the ground became soft, then moist, her feet sinking into it, the water lapping around them.

Allison had a deep sense of the erotic, perhaps due to her imagination and her long denial of the erotic within herself.

She stood there by the sea, nude, back straight, hair blowing softly about her face as she exposed herself to the Atlantic, imagining she could see right across it to the lands beyond.

She arched her back, sliding her hands up through her hair, then up above her head, imagining herself as a sculpture, arms extended, breasts thrust out tautly.

She almost wished some man were there, peeping at her. The idea excited her even as it made her wary. She looked round again, then gazed back at the sea.

What was it with her, she wondered. The idea aroused her, but she was ready to run like a rabbit at the faintest sound, at the least sign someone, man or woman, might be near by. She had nothing to be embarrassed about, after all.

She stepped forward then, into the water, the cold waves licking higher and higher until she dived in with a gasp, her long, lithe body slipping below the waves to glide through the chilled water.

She felt a surge of excitement inside her as the water skimmed across her bare flesh. She felt alive and free, and arched her back, turning upwards and surfacing, gasping for breath.

She swam out a short way, diving every few yards, then surfacing. She didn't like exercise, but didn't like how soft and plump her body got without it; and this at least was less boring than jogging.

The water was invigorating, but cold, and she could not stay in long. She headed back to the shore, then climbed, dripping wet, out on to the beach, her chest rising and falling rapidly as she reached up and twisted her wet hair.

Droplets of water cascaded down around her shoulders, striking the top swells of her cold breasts and dribbling slowly down. One caught at her right nipple and held there a long moment before dropping off.

The sun had risen higher and began to warm the air around her. She sighed and sat down on the shore, feeling chilled. She lay back, letting the sun paint her body a soft golden hue. She spread her arms and legs, closing her eyes briefly as her chest rose and fell, fantasies spilling over her, dreams and desires and fears intermingling.

The desire that had been throbbing softly inside her

since she had undressed began to grow, and she drew her hands in and cupped her breasts gently, squeezing in a soft, rhythmic manner, her thumbs seeking her nipples and rolling them against her fingers.

You're so wicked, she thought.

'Slut! Nasty slut!' she whispered.

And how she wished she was. She'd dress in tight, short, leather skirts and tight, low-cut blouses, wear heavy make-up and saunter as all the men looked at her with lust and desire.

She let her hands move over her breasts, kneading them gently, pressing them together, then apart. One of her hands slipped down between her thighs and cupped her pubic mound, again squeezing softly and rhythmically as she rolled her head to one side and gazed along the empty beach.

She wanted a man with her, a man to cover her with his body, his hard flesh against her, his lips on hers as his hands roamed over her, a gentle man yet one with steel inside him.

She let her middle finger press down harder than the others as it lay along her cleft, then began to rub slowly and gently. Her finger sank between her pubic lips and into the warm crevice between. She felt the excitement welling up with more power both from the physical sensation and the lewdness of what she was doing.

Her feet drew back slowly, her knees rising into the air, spread wide. She felt her clitoris as a soft bump behind its hood and hissed as her finger came closer and slipped along the edge.

Her breath was coming faster now as she stroked harder. She curled a finger and dipped it inside herself, feeling the tightness of her vaginal opening. She pushed deeper, feeling the pressure around her finger as it pushed through the soft pink folds of her sex. She closed her eyes, a soft sigh escaping her parted lips.

His body rippled with muscles along every inch of flesh. His face was beautiful, almost girlish, as his soft blue eyes held hers. He pushed against her, his hands slipping around her waist. She groaned as their lips met, as her full breasts pushed against his bare chest. He kissed her gently, his lips caressing hers, then sliding down her body.

Then in an instant he changed. His hair disappeared. He was bald now, his face taking on a cruel streak, hardening, leering. His hands were rough as they caught at her hair. He growled like an animal, his jaws parting, coming down on her exposed throat as he licked at her flesh.

His hands raced over her body, leaving a trail of fire behind as he sneered at her weakness. He stripped her, then flung her to the ground, standing over her, hands on hips. He was clothed in – no, now he was nude, his magnificent body there above her, his hardness thrusting out, so long and thick and threatening as he looked down at her.

He dropped to his knees between her spread legs as she gasped and dug her hands into the soft earth below her. Then he was on top of her, crushing her with his weight, his heavy chest flattening her breasts as his lips caught hers and his tongue drove into her mouth.

She felt his powerful hands on her thighs spreading them apart, then felt his hard erection. She moaned, whimpering in anticipation and denial as she felt its head against her opening. Then it thrust into her, sharp, hard and deep, filling her, making her cry out in wonder.

He growled again, thrusting in harder still, burying himself inside her, ravishing her as he began to stroke, as he began to pound his torso into her.

Allison groaned, her body writhing slowly, her fingers working feverishly at her sex. Her thumb stroked across her clitoris as two fingers pumped inside her tight, hot opening, sliding easily through the slick heat of her sex as she squeezed one of her breasts.

Her eyes were closed, her head rolling from side to side as she moaned in pleasure. The waves licked at her feet but she ignored them, her buttocks grinding into the soft sand as her ragged breaths puffed out of her open mouth.

She arched her back as the pleasure grew, burning like fire now, flooding through her body as her orgasm neared.

She knelt naked, on all fours, like a bitch on heat as he mounted her. She groaned as his fullness thrust deep into her body, as her pussy lips were pulled wider than they had ever been before, straining to encompass his mighty girth.

She braced her hands forward and apart as his powerful fingers dug into her flanks and he jammed the last inch of his erection into her overfull sheath. She felt cramps inside her, a bloated feeling in her abdomen.

He threw himself against her, his hard hips and pubic hair grinding into her delicate flesh, his cock twisting around inside her, making her gasp and moan in pleasure.

His hands moved up her sides, over her ribs, up along her spine to her shoulders, slipping over them and pulling her back against him, as if he could push himself even deeper into her hot belly.

'God!' she moaned.

He pulled back, his flesh rubbing across her sex with stunning results. She shuddered as the searing pleasure rippled along her spine. She felt every inch, every ridge and vein on his manhood as it slid through the clutching folds of her hot pink flesh and tugged free from her taut pubic lips.

Then he thrust in again. Hard. Deep. His hips jammed into her buttocks, hurling her forward even as his hands clutched her tightly and pulled her back to meet his next stroke.

Again. Again. Again. His mighty organ thrust into her

with powerful strokes. His hips slapped brutally against her upturned buttocks. Her breasts swung and jiggled below her as he used her, used her like an animal, like a whore.

She closed her eyes, grunting with each thrust, gasping and moaning as pleasure swirled inside her, as her head throbbed. Waves of heat and desire poured over her dazed mind, tossing it like a cork in a high sea.

He pistoned inside her, his hard shaft pumping furiously. Her nervous system was a blaze of energy as the orgasm towered higher and higher. Then it hit.

Her mouth opened wide and her head jerked back violently. Her back arched and she gurgled in helpless release, her chest locked, unable to breathe, unable to make a sound but a soft whimper of mindless delight.

Then the storm of pleasure eased and she collapsed with a great gasp, both sorrow and release hitting her simultaneously, and fell back unmoving, chest heaving, panting for breath.

Two

The sea birds continued to wheel and circle overhead, not interested in any sight but what fish they could see in the grey waters below. She lay there for long minutes, then sat up with a groan, shoving her hair back from her face.

She looked around her worriedly, knowing that one day she would be caught and suffer horrific humiliation.

She stood up with a grunt and began to dress. Then she halted. It was not far back to the cabin, and the idea of walking there naked was lewdly appealing.

She turned, gathering her clothes in her hands, and started to head back along the beach, feeling odd as she walked naked. She rounded a turn in the cliffs. Ahead lay more troubled waters, the waves crashing among rocks, some hidden, some thrusting their sharp heads above the waters. She looked out to sea casually, then paused, frowning at something out on the water.

She raised her hand to shield her eyes from the sun, squinting as she faced into it. It looked like some debris at first. Then she realised it was too large, that it was a boat. She thought at first it was a fishing boat. It was of a size of the local boats she had seen, but it seemed too sleek.

What really caught her eye, though, was the way it was bobbing up and down in the water as though uncontrolled. She sat down and watched it curiously. Any break in her routine was worth seeing to these days.

It was drifting on the water, moving closer. She could see the water foaming and splashing around the reefs and rocks that sat offshore. She wondered if it would hit one and sink, and caught herself hoping it would. It would be something interesting to see. Whoever owned it no doubt had insurance anyway.

As it moved closer she saw it was a fibreglass sail boat; rather a nice one, too, about sixty feet long. And she felt sad now that it seemed headed for destruction.

She winced as it struck a rock and heaved over to one side. It ground along the rock, its stern swinging around to face her. She raised her hand over her eyes again, trying to make out the name on it.

Wanderer.

She mouthed the word speculatively, thinking what it would be like to wander the waves, wander the oceans, go from place to place.

The boat was drifting further north as it came to shore, and she got up, walking towards it along the beach. She had the time. It was something novel, and she felt sorry for the little boat, felt as though she could, if nothing more, at least witness its sad fate.

Something shifted on its deck as it ground over another rock, something that rolled over, then over again, coming to rest against the rail. Allison's jaw dropped and she gasped in shock; she was certain she was mistaken and had let her imagination run away with her.

The boat heeled over in the opposite direction and she saw the thing roll back a little. There was no mistake. Not with the way the arm flipped out. There was someone on the boat, someone unconscious.

Or dead.

Maybe he or she was still alive, though too weak to leave the wallowing boat.

Allison looked down at the waves rushing ashore, waves which no longer seemed as friendly and peaceful as they had a few minutes before. She looked up and down the beach in growing desperation, hoping to find someone there. A policeman would be preferable, but almost anyone would do.

But there was nobody. Only her.

She looked out at the boat again, saw the figure slide sideways as a large wave rolled the ship. She gasped, her hands against her mouth as the figure was almost thrown overboard. The boat managed to right itself, but ground roughly against the rock with a horrible noise.

It didn't look as though the sail boat was going to come ashore. It was going to break up out there on the rocks, and the person on board drown.

It was at least a ten-minute run to her house, presuming she could actually run for ten minutes. It would take the police at least another fifteen or twenty minutes to arrive after that. Any help was at least half an hour off, more probably closer to an hour.

The *Wanderer* was not going to last that long. Already she could see water sloshing from side to side, could see the boat settling lower as it filled with water. Soon the person there would drown.

Allison was a fairly good swimmer. But the waters here among the shoals were generally unswimmable, with vicious undercurrents and strong, unpredictable riptides. Then there were the rocks, some just above the surface, many just below. She could easily imagine herself being flung against one and drowning.

And what if the figure was dead already? Should she risk her life in a doomed effort?

She closed her eyes and shuddered, and knew that if she did nothing she would wonder for ever, that for the rest of her life she would feel shame at not even trying to help another person in deadly peril.

She took a deep breath, then another, and, before she could change her mind, she gingerly made her way to the edge of the water.

A wave swept over her feet and ankles, then rose over her knees, then up to her hips.

Another wave, and this one ploughed into her, soaking her from head to toe and almost knocking her off her feet. She shoved the wet, matted hair back from her face and continued to move forward, then as another wave rushed forward she dived into it.

She emerged, sputtering, on the other side, and began swimming towards the boat. She swam awkwardly, using the breast stroke. There were too many rocks around to try swimming normally: she'd bring her arm down on one and break her wrist, that's if she didn't ram into one head-first.

She made poor progress. As she moved away from the beach the waves no longer fell over her; but they did throw her backwards, eliminating much of the progress she made. She was tiring fast, pausing to gasp for breath and look around her. It was hard to even find the boat at her level. She had to wait for a wave to raise her up to catch sight of it and make sure her direction was right.

A deadly chill was creeping through her body. Her hands were getting numb. Her feet already were. She began to think of the boat, sinking as it was, as a haven, longing for the moment she could pull her body up out of the water.

She cursed as her sweeping hand scraped her knuckles against an underwater rock, but kept moving. She angled ahead of the rock, then as she passed, gathered her legs in, pressed her feet against the far side and used it to lunge forward.

She did that several times again, then saw the boat ahead of her, off to her right. With renewed energy she swam towards it, watching the side rise and fall. Sometimes it rose almost out of the water, so she could see the bottom of the boat. Sometimes it dipped so low it almost disappeared under the foaming grey water.

Luck was with her, briefly, for the side closest to her dipped almost to the water as she reached it. She threw herself over it just before it rose quickly upwards, and was yanked clear of the water. She tumbled off the rail and on to the deck below, gasping for breath, grunting as her body thumped into the hard wood with bruising force.

She lay there for long seconds, feeling a deep relief at being out of the water, grateful at last to rest her arms and legs.

Her relief did not last long, though. The boat was rolling from side to side with alarming force, threatening to throw her right back out into the sea. She caught hold of the underside of a seat and clung to it as the boat rolled deeply in one direction, then back again.

A plastic water jug rattled emptily along the deck from one rail to the other, clattering and bouncing as the sail boat rolled, and up ahead, against the other rail with his legs partly wedged under another seat, lay the reason she had put herself in such deadly peril.

Allison sat up, still clutching the seat next to her, then got her feet beneath her. She knelt, and as the boat rolled to one side and reached its peak she let go of the seat and tried to crawl quickly over to the other side of the deck.

It was not a long distance, perhaps ten feet, but it seemed a mile as the rail rose up higher and higher, the deck tilting with alarming speed. She scrabbled forward on the wet deck, hands clawing for the seat as she felt her knees sliding backwards.

She caught it barely in time, her knees slipping out from under her and she dropped on to her stomach. She pulled herself up, almost screaming as her hand felt something soft and clammy: human flesh.

The boat tilted back and she quickly crawled to the other side, bracing herself with one foot jammed against the rail and one arm hooked round the bottom of the seat. Finally she looked down at the man.

He was, she guessed, about thirty, though it was hard to tell given his condition. His handsome face was pale, his long hair and clothing soaked. He was a large man, heavy and muscular, easily twice her weight. And her heart fell as she considered the impossibility of dragging him ashore.

She touched him with great reluctance, almost, though without admitting it to herself, hoping he was dead. But her questing fingers found a steady pulse at his throat. She tried to lift him up, grunting with effort, then let to in frustration.

The boat tilted alarmingly again, this time water pouring over the far side before it rose again. Now a couple of inches of water sloshed back and forth on the deck, and Allison's fear and frustration rose. The man was simply too heavy. She couldn't possibly move him, and even if she did how could she keep him afloat in the turbulent waters as she pulled him ashore?

She looked round wildly, then, as the boat tilted back again, released her hold on the seat and let herself fall towards the other end. She hooked her arm round a lever of some kind and used it to swing herself towards the opening of the cabin.

She almost didn't make it, but caught the edge, and all but fell down the steps into the cabin. The water there was chest deep, and there was little light coming in from above. She peered into the jumble of things floating around, everything from loaves of bread wrapped in plastic to newspapers and light bulb packages.

But the distinctive orange colour of a life jacket caught her eyes, hanging on a cupboard.

The boat continued to roll from side to side, and the water in the small cabin malevolently threw itself against the walls of the small cabin.

Allison could feel the front of the boat dropping, and her heart pounded as she realised it might go under at any moment. But she had to reach the life jacket if she were to have any hope of saving the man above.

She pushed deeper into the cabin, grabbing hold of whatever her scrabbling fingers could find for support to keep from being flung from side to side.

Abruptly the floor fell out from under her and her head dropped below the surface. A portion of the floor was open, a hatch of some kind lifting to expose the engine below. She cried out in pain as she banged her ankle against something hard, arms windmilling briefly as she fell into the water. She was able to pop to the surface almost immediately, arms splashing furiously to pull her another foot forward and back over the solid floor.

She reached the life jacket at last, panting desperately as she pulled it away from the cupboard. She turned, putting it under her chest as she kicked away, swimming now instead of walking, back towards the hatch. The boat wasn't rocking nearly as much now, but was listing sharply both forward and to one side.

The water was deeper. It was three feet from the roof when she had come down but now the top of her head was almost touching the ceiling as she desperately made for the hatch, for the light.

She dragged herself through, her feet coming down on a firm surface again. The deck was awash, one rail completely below the surface, the other high in the air. The man was draped over the seat legs he had been wedged under, held out of the water by the steep angle of the deck.

To reach him Allison had to climb up out of the water, put a foot on the steering wheel and grab at the far rail.

Then the boat, as if finally giving up, gave a hard lurch. Water foamed and bubbled at the hatch as it sank down into the water. The upper rail slid almost smoothly into the sea as Allison tried frantically to hold on to the man's arm.

Then the boat was gone, all but its broken mast, and

the water bubbled around them as she tried to keep him out of the water. Sudden fury leant her strength, and she clamped her bare legs around his body, yanking and twisting him up and around with her numbed, freezing hands until she could force the life jacket over one arm, then the other.

She eased her grip, gasping and coughing as the water surged round them, then turned him over, put her arm around his chest and began swimming to shore.

She was far weaker than she had been on the way out, but the waves were pushing her in the right direction this time. She had to be more careful of rocks, though. One wave slammed her back against one with such force she cried out and let go of the man, her fingers clawing at the back of his collar in desperation and grabbing it just in time.

He let out a weak groan, and she gasped in surprise, then redoubled her efforts, her legs and one arm sweeping against the water, pulling them inch by inch towards shore.

She realised the life jacket was keeping both of them afloat. For all her weak kicking and splashing she knew that if she let go of the man she would sink before he would. She had never felt so utterly exhausted, so drained of energy in her life. She found her will to continue fading, and every wave that rolled over them sent water into her gasping mouth.

Then she felt firmness below her, felt her back scraping against solid ground. A wave fell over them and she choked and gasped, but dragged herself backwards. She was on the beach, and a brief but powerful burst of relief sent energy surging through her system.

She got to her feet, still holding grimly on to his collar, and stumbled backwards, dragging him through the now hip-deep water towards the shore. She somehow pulled him clear of the water then collapsed on to the hard pebbly ground. She lay on her side, coughing out water, gasping for breath, then rolled on to her back and lay there for long, long minutes; just breathing, feeling with infinite relief the cold hard stones pressing into her back.

She would have been content to just lay there for ever, but she was trembling with cold and exhaustion.

Then a sudden movement caught her eye, and she saw him slowly sitting up. He swayed and almost fell back, but used his hands to support himself. He looked dazed, his eyes unfocused, and then he groaned as he slowly raised one hand to his head and winced.

Allison sat up as well, not without effort, and the man looked at her, squinting as though to focus his eyes.

'Who – where . . .' he gasped.

'Y-your boat . . . sank,' she panted.

Then, suddenly recalling her nudity, she crossed her arms over her breasts, closing her thighs together.

He turned his head slowly, looking uncertainly out at the cold waters of the sea, then groaned again, his hand pressed more firmly against his head.

He lurched to his feet and Allison rose instinctively, trying to support him even as she attempted to cover some portion of her body from view. She herself was tall for a woman at two inches shy of six feet, but he was much taller, perhaps six and a half feet, and with a large, powerful body.

'T-take me . . . somewhere – away,' he gasped, lurching forward and grasping her shoulders for support.

She had little strength and the two almost tumbled to the ground, but the downward pressure of his hands suddenly turned into a hard upward pull that kept her on her feet.

'Where? Where – can we go?' he gasped.

'I – my house. Can you . . .?'

His arm went round her shoulder and they stumbled down the beach, supporting one another like a pair of drunks, now one stumbling and the other supporting, then the second tripping and being held up by the first.

Only her own exhaustion kept her mind from twisting away from him. It was incredibly odd to be so close to this man, to be naked, utterly naked with him as they staggered down the beach. Yet she felt not a hint of sexuality, and was too weary and hurt to care about much of anything beyond getting to her cottage.

Allison was almost crying with fatigue by the time they made it up the winding path that led to her house. They fell towards the door, both of them leaning heavily against the wall. She opened it, for it was seldom locked, and they both lurched inside.

She collapsed on to the sofa while he tripped across the coffee table and hit the floor with a grunt.

But they were out of the wind and the heat was glorious compared to the chill outside. They lay there panting, and Allison's eyes closed.

When she opened her eyes again her body was stiff and aching. The cold had left her, and she was dry, but she was still exhausted. She moaned weakly as she shifted and looked round her.

She was on the sofa, and that puzzled her. Then it all came flooding back and she felt a deep, wonderful relief that she was here: safe, warm and dry, out of the frigid churning water.

There were several blankets on her and a pillow under her head. She wondered at that, certain that she hadn't done anything once she came in but collapse.

She sat up slowly, gasping with the bruised flesh and overworked muscles. The room was dim. It was dark outside, and rain was pelting strongly against the glass of the sliding doors as the wind blew against them. There were no lights in the living room but a small table lamp was on in the hall.

Then she saw him. He was sitting, sleeping, in an overstuffed chair in the corner. He was wearing her oversized green terrycloth robe. On her it fell to her ankles, the arms very wide. On him the top hung open, revealing a well-muscled bare chest beneath.

She studied him briefly, with an artist's eye, noting his finely chiselled features. He had a strong chin, a blunt, Romanesque nose and lush brown eyebrows. His lips were slightly parted in sleep, full and sensual. His skin was deeply tanned and weathered. He had shoulder-length nutmeg brown hair that was mostly straight, and swept back to either side from the middle of his forehead. His features, relaxed in sleep, gave him an almost boyish look of innocence.

Yet he filled the big chair to overflowing, only partly clad in her robe. Despite her tiredness and aching body she felt duel interest in that powerful male body. As an artist she had done some nudes, and appreciated the beauty of a well-maintained body, male or female. As a woman – as a woman she flushed at the nearness of him, both embarrassed and wanting to see more.

She felt a slow rush of embarrassment at realising he must have seen her naked, must have covered her with the blankets. What had he done, she wondered, while she lay helpless.

No. That was foolish. Surely he had been as exhausted as she, and as little interested in such silliness.

She winced and groaned softly as she stood up, clutching one of the blankets around her. She gazed round, briefly noting the dirty plate and glass on the kitchen table that hadn't been there that morning. Her stomach rumbled and she looked at the clock on the wall. It was mid afternoon. The dark was due to the storm outside.

Still, she had slept for hours and used up so much energy her body demanded replenishment.

She padded into the kitchen, grabbed an apple from the fridge and bit into it, savouring the sweet juice as she swallowed. She propped herself on a stool, studying him from across the room. She glanced at the plate and glass, frowning. He had obviously woken before her and helped himself to a meal. He had put blankets on her and then . . .

She wondered why he hadn't woken her and called the Coast Guard; surely someone official had to be called under such circumstances?

She opened the refrigerator and poured a glass of milk, then drank thirstily. Her skin felt itchy, and she knew the salt water had left its mark on her skin. She wanted to have a shower herself; or a bath, a long, long, very hot bath.

But not with a strange, half-naked man in her living room.

He was attractive, very attractive. She was more and more aware of her own near nudity as she sat there, and a small flutter of excitement hit her stomach.

She stood up and moved across to the living room, standing next to him warily, eyes fixed on his face. She felt her nipples tightening against the blanket she held against herself, and licked her lips uncertainly.

She looked down at his bare chest, so broad and powerful, the robe open almost to the waist.

She looked at his bare legs, so strong and thick, sprawled to either side. He had seen her, hadn't he? No doubt he had feasted his eyes good and hard on her nakedness as she lay there.

It had been a long time since she had been with a man, a long time since she had even seen one.

And she'd had few opportunities to actually study that particular portion of the male anatomy in peace and quiet.

Don't be ridiculous, she thought, her pulse racing.

It was childish, yet Allison was aware that a part of her *was* childish, had never quite grown up.

She bent over, reaching for the robe and lifting it slightly, eyes flicking to his face, then down, then up again, her heart pounding as the fear of discovery filled her.

She raised it higher, and there it was. His manhood lay curved downwards between his thighs, thick even in its softness, pressed in against his large testicles. It looked simultaneously threatening and erotic, and she stared at it with her lips slightly parted for a long moment.

This was wicked, she knew, absolutely wrong. Her mother would have beaten her for even thinking of it.

Yet her hand moved slowly forward as if it had a mind of its own, fingers trembling slightly.

Her mind was spinning with denial and excitement. She argued with herself as she held her hand in check. This was madness! What was wrong with her? Was she insane? Was she a deviant? Who did she think she was, taking such advantage?

And yet she had saved his life, so surely he ought not to complain when all she wanted was – to touch him.

She felt his soft warmth against her fingers and gasped. She swallowed repeatedly, then, as he continued to sleep, eased her fingers in further, running her fingers deftly along his cock at first, then slipping them around the soft organ, squeezing it gently.

And then she wanted more. He was so beautiful!

She let her fingers slip off him as she straightened, then dropped her blanket, shivering as it fell to her ankles. She stood before him naked, the tension inside her making her tremble. She swallowed repeatedly as she watched him, then eased down on to the floor between his legs, bringing her face in close to his groin. She fought to keep her breath silent as she reached out and ran her hand gently along his manhood, then caught it between her fingers again.

She let it lie in the palm of her hand, fingers open as she examined it. She drew her fingers in slowly, squeezing it, then tilting it upwards, pulling, stretching it out.

She leaned in, shocked at her own lewdness, and kissed the tip of his cock, then let her small moist tongue slip out and caress the underside of the head.

It seemed to quiver in her grip, and she drew back, looking up at him again. She leaned in and licked at it a second time, kissing the tip once more, testing its reaction. Her heart pounded in fear and excitement. She knew what she was doing was insane, but somehow couldn't bring herself to stop.

Her tongue trailed slowly up and down his rapidly hardening manhood, tracing, lapping and tasting him. She lifted him higher and examined his testicles, then kissed one and licked at it.

She licked wetly straight up the length of his shaft, paying extra care to the head, her fingers squeezing ever so carefully as her eyes continued to flick up and down between his sleeping face and very much awake cock.

She opened her lips, taking him inside her mouth and gently sucking. Her tongue caressed the underside of the head, and she felt him hardening still further, becoming rigid inside her mouth.

In the back of her mind she still shouted at herself, appalled by her own actions. But something deep had taken control of her, something that went beyond curiosity, beyond mere sexual desire, something deep and hungry that would not be denied.

She slipped her lips further down his erection, letting her saliva moisten and slick his skin. She raised her head, eyeing him, looking at his sleeping face, then lowered it again, sliding her lips along his hardness as he groaned softly above her.

She held still, hardly daring to breathe until he quietened and relaxed. Then her lips bobbed up and down once more before she pulled free of him.

As she examined his cock, she could feel a raw, barely controlled power within it. She used the sides of her arms to press her breasts in against each other as she let his slick flesh ease between them, then groaned silently as she squeezed them around it.

She drew back, her long hair sliding along his thighs

as she licked at his balls again, then rubbed his spit-wet cock across her face before once again taking it into her mouth.

She began to slide her lips up and down its length, moving slowly so as not to wake him, her mind spinning and twisting with lust and desire, fear and alarm.

One of her hands slipped down between her trembling thighs and she groaned softly as her fingers wriggled up inside her moist sex, pumping in and out as her thumb caught at her clit and rubbed it against them.

Her lips bobbed faster as her tongue worked with more pressure. His head fell back against the top of the chair and he groaned again, his legs shifting slightly further apart.

Allison's head continued to rise and fall in his lap as she ground her buttocks back and down against her own plunging fingers, riding them with greater and greater excitement, alarmed at the power, at the intensity of the need within her, at what it was forcing her to do, yet burning with a desire she had never known.

Her body was trembling, her nervous system spitting sparks as she continued to thrust her fingers up high into her sex, continued to stroke her thumb feverishly across her burning clitoris.

Then he came and she felt his sperm spitting into her mouth in a hot, salty gush.

The realisation cut across her roiling senses and she moaned in wicked delight. She pinched her thumb against her clitoris, her lips still locked solidly around his cock as her behind bounced wildly up and down.

His hands fell away as his cock softened, and she fell back on the floor, legs splayed, fingers plunging into herself. He sat there oblivious, head back across the back of the chair, breathing deeply, still asleep as she writhed there between his legs, gasping and whimpering.

Her legs were spread, her heels almost under her buttocks as she gasped and groaned, her fingers plunging again and again into her hot centre.

And it was those small, unfamiliar sounds which finally woke him from his deep slumber. His eyes fluttered open and he tiredly raised his head, at first not even noticing the girl before him.

Her movements caught his attention and his eyes widened slowly, incredulously, as he took in the eroticism of her desperate, heaving movement; the soft gurgling sounds emerging from under her tangled hair.

Three

Allison did not notice his open eyes at first. She was too intent on the vastness of the pleasure gripping her and came with an explosive release of pressure and heat. And even as it faded, even as her momentum eased and she started to settle back – legs splayed and bent back, back arched, lush breasts heaving – her eyes remained closed, her mind gripped by the soft, luxurious post-orgasmic languor.

Finally her eyes flickered open. She saw his eyes were upon her, dark and intent, and his excitement was clearly growing, the organ between his legs beginning to stiffen.

She blinked in sudden shock, gasping as he leaned forward, slid off the edge of the chair and on to his knees between her legs.

He reached down and grasped her under the arms as she gaped at him in shock and alarm. He smiled broadly down at her, then lifted her upper body as if she were weightless, holding her in front of him as he sat back on his own heels.

She continued to stare in stunned amazement as his eyes bored into hers.

'Been having a little party without me, hmmm?'

'I – I didn't!' she stuttered.

He raised his eyebrows, then loosened his grip, sliding his hands over her shoulders, then up through her hair.

'You have very soft hair,' he whispered.

She trembled, caught between fear, embarrassment and lust.

'Fingers are fine but wouldn't you prefer the real thing?'

She gasped, head jerking down as she felt his hardness against her, then back up, eyes caught by his.

He leant forward, lips brushing hers, then pressing down more firmly. She moaned softly, mind spinning, stomach churning. He pulled back again, tongue sliding along his lips.

'Wouldn't you?'

She could hardly think, could hardly move, yet somehow her head bobbed briefly.

His hands moved quickly, his right around her waist, his left behind her head, clutching her firmly as he pulled her against his body and his lips moved hungrily down on to her own again.

Allison gasped helplessly as he slipped his tongue into her oral cavity, stroking it along her own, then up along the roof of her mouth, then down again, flitting it around against the insides of her cheeks. Her hands moved up feebly against him as he lowered her back on to the floor, coming down on top of her.

Already his hardness was pressed against her sex, and she knew he could feel the moisture there, could feel the hot, seeping results of her self-abuse.

He ground himself against her as his mouth continued to move with voracious hunger against her own small, dainty lips, his tongue a live thing as it whipped around inside her.

He gripped her hair, pulling her head back. She cried out in alarm, then gasped as his teeth found her exposed throat and he bit down, sucking passionately, his other hands down below her now to cup and squeeze her shapely rear.

He reached down for his erection, pulling it up and centring it against her throbbing cleft. She felt its softness against her inner flesh as it eased her pubic lips apart. Heat escaped, rushing up around his sensitive cock as he pushed himself inside, then thrust hard.

She cried out, shuddering, her mouth opening and closing soundlessly. He thrust in again, and again she shuddered, eyes closing, body trembling. Her head fell back and he released it, sitting back on his heels and letting both hands slide up her.

Allison's mind was reeling with shock, humiliation, fear, and desperate excitement. She was naked! She was naked and he was seeing her, touching her, and more. How much, she wondered, had he seen when she was stroking herself?

'Oh God!' she whispered.

His fingers danced across her soft flesh, stroking her belly then riding up along her ribs before squeezing her breasts together. His fingers pinched and pulled at her nipples in a way that was both stinging and intensely arousing. She winced and moaned, a maelstrom swirling through her mind.

He ground his pelvis against her and heat rolled up her body, making her mind swim.

'Is this better than your fingers?' he whispered. 'Is it?'

He pulled back sharply, then thrust in again, and her eyes fluttered weakly.

She could not remember feeling so intensely aroused and could hardly believe what was happening. It was a dream and a nightmare; a fantasy come to life.

The instant horror she had felt at his first touch was fading. For he was now a participant. They were together.

She lay back as he began to maul her body, his hands and lips moving with astonishing speed, roaming over her body as he took her in with his eyes.

His eyes. She still couldn't face them. Even if he was delighted to find her there acting like a nympho at his feet, even if he was reciprocating and showing his desire for her, still his eyes were filled with something that shamed, thrilled and alarmed her.

She grunted as he began thrusting, for his cock was thick inside her and her sheath was straining wide around it, the thin pink walls of her sex taut as he began to slide his powerful organ up and down its length.

She looked up at him, then closed her eyes, turning her head away from the determination on his face.

He ran his hands down her hips, then up her legs, pulling them into the air, his big hands encircling both legs behind the knee as he pushed them back against her upper body, forcing her into a lewd and vulnerable position.

She blushed anew as her behind was raised and he began to make full use of her body. She had had few sexual experiences, and they were slow, uncertain, fumbling things, nothing at all like this.

She grunted each time he thrust into her, his hips striking her upraised buttocks hard and fast.

She opened her eyes again, looking up fearfully, and his eyes caught hers, staring down hypnotically even as his lower body rose and fell, rose and fell, moving faster and faster.

She continued to gasp with each hard thrust, her mind swirling as he rode on top of her. His hips slapped against her buttocks each time he buried his manhood inside her belly, and she began to understand for the first time the difference between making love and fucking.

For that was what he was doing to her, she realised. He was not making love. What he was doing could not be described in such a way. He was fucking her.

This was an entirely new experience for her, but she quickly found herself revelling in it. Her face was still scarlet and embarrassment clung to her, yet something deep inside her body and mind relished what was happening.

Her legs were thrown back against her shoulders again and again, pushed back by his powerful grip, by his heavy weight. She looked up to see her feet high above, toes twitching, smoothly tapering ankles looking so pale and distant even as they jerked to and fro in response to his motions.

She had never realised how wonderful a man could feel inside her. Her fantasies had been just that. But though her insides ached a little, unused to such vigour, the sexual haze which had gripped her earlier was surrounding her again and was growing more powerful by the second.

She had never made love before with anyone she did not know well. Yet there was something terribly freeing about not having to behave or act in a correct way, about not having to do anything but lie back as he controlled it all. She was being used, in a sense, as a masturbatory toy. Yet not only did this not bother her, she was excited by it.

Allison was shy by nature, but not in the normal course of events submissive. Yet sexually she felt her inhibitions dropping away in light of her lack of control, lack of responsibility. It was all his doing, and in that sense she felt no guilt.

Guilt had always been a constant companion. She had become so used to it that it was like a pain one hardly remembered.

Until it disappeared.

Now she gave herself fully to his use with the awareness she could do nothing else. She let her mind go and gave him her body to do with as he chose.

The sexual haze strengthened, a wall of heat radiating from her body as he continued to thrust himself into her clasping sex.

His powerful hands moved up her legs until he gripped her ankles, and then he leant forward, folding her body in two, forcing her ankles back harder, his weight unbearable as she groaned and whined, her back aching.

He was fully on top of her, supported by the hands gripping her ankles, and his feet far below him. The pressure on her legs and back was enormous, yet she hardly cared. She felt drawn into a raw, carnal act, as though she were being mauled by an animal; or perhaps a caveman, a force of nature that could not be controlled.

His thick organ was sliding back and forth through her swollen pubic lips, caressing them in that most intimate of touches. She felt compressed into a tight ball, and his furiously pumping cock was like a steel spear inside her as it thrust deep into the centre of her again and again.

She shook helplessly as an orgasm rolled through her, gurgling as her chest, squashed down by her legs, struggled to expand. Sexual electricity crackled along her nervous system like sheet lightning.

She trembled below him, hardly aware of anything beyond what had become the centre of the universe, that hot throbbing pit within which his cock was so furiously pumping.

Each thrust sent her mind spinning anew, and her eyes rolled back in her head as the fury of her sexual release overcame all but the most animal instincts within her.

She was hardly even aware when he stopped pumping, when his manhood was withdrawn and the pressure let up on her ankles. She cried out as he let her legs go and they fell to the floor, her back unfolding in an instant.

Then she lay there, gasping, groaning, body covered in sweat as she sought to catch her breath and fit her shattered mind back together.

When she finally pushed herself up on her elbows he was sitting back in the chair, the robe closed, staring down at her. She felt a mixture of shame, guilt and fear, yet also a strange sense of hot sexual delight. She had abandoned any pretence of propriety, and that left her with no sense or need of dignity to cling to.

That, of course, had always been a major problem with her sexual relationships. And with it gone she was free to ... well, to do anything he wanted, to act the slut he no doubt already thought she was.

For she had already done that, of course. His opinion of her could not possibly go down. Nothing she could do would shock him.

And there was a world of freedom in that, especially since he was a stranger.

'What's your name?' he asked.

'Allison,' she said, her voice a whisper.

'Allison. You're a hot, sexy girl, Allison.'

She found herself blushing, yet felt pride along with the embarrassment.

'You've got one hell of a body there, too. Very firm. Very soft.'

She sat up slowly, fighting the impulse to cover herself even as she closed her legs together.

There was an awkward silence, then she stood up, grabbing the blanket and pulling it around herself.

'I was ...' Her voice trailed off into confusion, wondering what she could possibly say to a man who had woken to see her masturbating.

'You have a lovely place here,' he said.

'Thank you.'

She licked her lips awkwardly, then turned away. But he caught her wrist and roughly pulled her back.

'Tell me, Allison, what were you doing before I woke up?'

She blushed anew, and looked down at her feet.

'You were a very bad girl, weren't you, Allison?'

'I'm sorry,' she whispered.

She should have been mortified, yet she wasn't. She

knew he was not upset, knew he was taunting her. Yet this time, the taunting didn't hurt.

'Next time I'd be pleased if I was awake to enjoy it.'

She blushed more deeply as he smiled.

'My name is Sean,' he said. 'In case you were wondering.'

She bobbed her head weakly.

'I think you owe me that, don't you?'

She bobbed her head again.

'What about now?'

She blinked her eyes. 'Now?'

He nodded.

She felt an instant's amazement that he could want yet more sex. They had just engaged in a raw, powerful sexual experience that had left her drained and shaken, yet he still wanted more. She wondered if men were always so insatiable or if he was simply oversexed.

He reached up and gripped the blanket, pulling on it. She held it for a moment, then with a breathless sensation of release she let it go and he pulled it free, exposing her again. She trembled briefly, her arms moving to cover herself, then she straightened.

He smiled and reached up lazily, hand sliding along her inner thigh. She jerked briefly, swallowing as he palmed her still damp sex and squeezed it softly.

'Get down on your knees, Allison.'

She opened her mouth to protest, then felt a need inside her, an unfamiliar desire, not to please him but to give in to him, to submit to him, to let him make the decisions.

And with it came a vast sense of relief, of freedom, even elation.

She sank to her knees before him, eyes wide.

He spread his legs slowly apart and opened his robe to reveal himself.

Her eyes flickered down to his cock, then up at his face, waiting. Their eyes met, and an understanding seemed to pass between them.

'Now,' he said. No – ordered.

She leaned in, her breasts brushing the chair, her nipples rigid, sparks seeming to flicker in them at the touch. Her hair slipped along his thighs as she reached for him.

'No.'

She halted. Instantly.

'Don't use your hands. Put your hands behind your back and keep them there.'

She wondered why, but briefly. She didn't have to care. He was making the decisions. She was free not to care.

She brought her hands up behind her back and clasped them together, then licked along his manhood, at the head, then along the shaft to the base. She had little experience in this, and had always been timid, hesitant to give her lover the impression she was loose.

But that didn't matter now.

Again she felt a sense of freedom, a wildness.

She slipped her lips around one of his testicles, feeling a delight at his intake of breath. She took it into her mouth, sucking softly, rolling it inside her mouth, licking as her cheeks rubbed against his cock.

She looked up at him, then down at his cock again, raising her head, letting his testicle slip slowly from between her lips. She licked at the other one, then sucked that into her mouth as well.

His hands slipped on to her head, fingers combing through her hair, stroking and caressing it as she moved her lips down his cock and sucked the head into her mouth. It was still soft, and she drew it into her mouth until her lips were pressed against his groin, then began to massage it with her tongue.

One of his hands moved down and cupped her breast, rubbing and squeezing, and his fingers pinched at her nipple.

Sparks flew again, her nipple burning, throbbing. She

moaned around his cock, feeling it hardening. Her lips slipped slowly back until only the head was inside, then she licked at it, rolling her head.

Before she had always been awkward, embarrassed when doing this, but now she felt alive, sensual. She slipped her lips back down its length, instantly feeling a new sense of hardness. She bobbed her lips now, sucking and licking over the glistening shaft as he watched.

His hand tightened in her hair suddenly, pulling her up and back. She gasped, feeling her scalp ache, but offered no resistance as he leant forward, pulling her head back so her chest thrust out. She continued to clasp her hands together behind her back.

'Stand,' he said, his voice gravelly as he released her hair.

She stood up, panting for breath, licking her lips.

He closed his legs and gripped his now hard cock, holding it up.

'Get on.'

She felt a thrill of excitement and moved forward, her hands coming around.

'No! Keep your hands behind you.'

She felt a flutter of confusion, but then instant release. It didn't matter. He was in charge.

She obeyed, awkwardly straddling him, her knees pushing into the sides of the chair as he held his cock up. She edged in against him, her breasts pushing against his face. Then she sank down, feeling his hardness against her, feeling the pressure against her cleft, then her lips pushed slowly in and back as his cock pierced her.

She groaned as she slipped down around him, the slickness of his cock and her sheath letting it slide up into her tightness with the sensation of feathers slipping over her skin.

His hands caught at her buttocks as his lips slipped around one of her nipples, and she threw her head back and moaned in bliss as she sank down fully and felt him lodge high inside her.

His fingers kneaded her flesh as she began to work herself up and down, the pleasure and energy growing inside her, the heat burning at her mind as she moved faster. He started to thrust up as well, and her buttocks slapped against his thighs as she repeatedly impaled herself on his thick girth.

She felt his fingers clutch at her as he groaned, and knew he was coming, knew his cock was spurting deep inside her. She half sobbed in joy, grinding desperately, feverishly against him, and moments later her own orgasm flashed through her nervous system.

Four

She lay against his chest for long minutes just trying to fit the shattered pieces of her mind together and catch her breath. When her heart had eased its frantic pounding she groaned, then slowly and awkwardly sat back.

Their eyes met and she blushed slightly, then licked her lips.

She stood up slowly, then picked up the blanket and wrapped it round herself. She stood there awkwardly for a moment, then backed up a step.

'Well, I need to take a shower, I think.'

He nodded and grinned boyishly.

'You'll be all right here?' She felt silly asking it, considering.

'For a while,' he said.

She backed away another step before turning and going down the hall to her bedroom, wondering what in God's name she'd done.

Something that should have been done long ago, perhaps, a part of her answered.

She felt little shame; probably, she decided, because he seemed to feel none. Certainly she had bared her body to him, and behaved in a lewd, sluttish way, but his own behaviour had equalled hers.

His name was Sean. It was a nice name. She wondered what he did for a living, what kind of a man he was, and what future the two of them had.

Now don't start getting sentimental, she thought

sternly. Just remember that people do that kind of thing all the time and then go their separate ways. He doesn't owe you anything because of what we've just done.

Her behind was a little sore, or more precisely, felt a little hot as the water pelted her body. She soaped herself up quickly, wincing a little as she recalled how dirty she had been. She had sweated mightily getting him up to the cabin. And then there was her hair. It was a bedraggled mess, and she thought it a wonder he had wanted to touch her at all.

She washed herself quickly, then her hair before rinsing off. She stood naked before the mirror, brushing her hair out as the blow dryer blew it back. She leant forward as she did, and felt a little flush of excitement.

In fact, every time she moved she felt a little ripple of eroticism, and she kept thinking about how Sean would react if he saw her in one pose or another.

She finished as soon as she could, filled with a thousand questions and a fear that he would be gone when she emerged.

Clasping a towel around her torso she eased out into the hall, then up to the corner, peeking round the edge. He was sitting on the sofa now, his back to her, watching television.

She backed away and hurried to her bedroom, then gazed at her clothes in despair for anything sexy.

Then again, she thought, it was a bit late to start thinking about seducing him.

She opened her lingerie drawer. In it were the soft cotton bikini underwear she usually wore and the more intimate, seductive wear she had purchased through catalogues and mail-order. It always made her feel sensual when she wore them, even though no one had ever seen them.

She felt her mind cringe a little in regret and shame. She hardly knew him at all, and felt amazement at herself for engaging in such shameless activities. It had, without a doubt, been the most shocking, erotic experience of her life. Nothing else could begin to measure against it.

She pulled on a lacy white thong, the strings cut high on the sides. Then she took from the drawer a matching bra which would thrust her breasts up and out invitingly.

She turned with it on, examining herself in the mirror as she had done many times before.

But this time a man is going to see me like this, she thought.

She drew her arms back, then crossed them behind her back, letting her eyes go wide and her lips push out helplessly.

A soft thrumming excitement began to set her insides quivering.

She shuddered weakly, then stepped to the wardrobe. Something simple, she thought, but attractive. I don't want him to see me as a total slut. Let him see me as an attractive woman. We'll get to know each other and . . . and who knows what then?

Soft, loose white trousers then, and a big blue and white checked blouse to tuck into them. Yes, it set off her hair nicely. She pulled on white socks, then dabbed a bit of her best perfume under each ear.

She stared at herself, knowing she was delaying going out there, embarrassed again as she remembered what she had done. She closed her eyes briefly, trying to convince herself he hadn't really seen her masturbating.

'Can't put it off for ever,' she whispered.

She walked to the door, gripped the knob, stood still for a long moment, then braced herself and jerked it open. She fixed a smile on her face as she walked down the hall and out into the front part of the house.

He turned to look at her, smiling lazily, and she got an instant mental image of his type.

Oh, you know you're cute, don't you, she thought. You're very cocky and very confident.

'Hi,' she said.

'Hi. I'm amazed.'

'At what?'

'You look almost as stunning fully clothed as you do naked.'

She blushed, and he grinned widely, showing white teeth.

'Do you, uhm, need to shower?'

'Did earlier. Hope you don't mind how I helped myself to the facilities, love.'

'No, of course not. Did you call anyone about your boat?'

'No. Who would I call?'

'I don't know.' She shrugged. 'Whoever you call when your boat sinks.'

'Normally the insurance company, but I wasn't insured.'

'Oh. I'm sorry.'

'Don't be. I'll have her raised. I'm not altogether penniless.'

She slipped into an upholstered chair across from him, then crossed her legs beneath her.

'What do you do, Sean?'

'When I'm not ravishing helpless maidens?'

She nodded and blushed, and he laughed.

'You blush a lot, you know.'

'Well, it's not like I'm usually involved in such things,' she said defensively.

'You mean you don't attack every man who comes near?'

'No!'

'But I was so gorgeous you just couldn't resist. Well, I understand that.'

'You are incredibly arrogant.'

'I know,' he said, 'but then I've reason to be, don't you think?'

'I think that I wasn't in my right mind. No doubt

exhausting myself saving your miserable life took something out of me.'

'I did mean to ask how I'd come to be here with you laying on the chesterfield naked.'

'I was out for a walk and I saw your boat going under. So I stripped off my dress and jumped in. It wasn't easy getting you to shore, you know, nor getting you home. I almost drowned myself!'

'What does one say? Thank you seems embarrassingly insufficient but, well, thank you.'

'You're welcome,' she said, blushing again.

'How long have you lived here, Allison?'

'Several years now.'

She tried to put across the image of happiness and self-content she usually did when everyone asked but he didn't seem to buy it.

'All alone?'

'I like my company.'

'I like your company too but still. Don't you get lonely? I know you get frustrated. Oh, wait. I apologise for that. I don't mean to make you feel embarrassed.'

'That's all right,' she said, only a little embarrassed. 'I think what I did today, well, I don't think anything will ever make me as embarrassed again.'

'Don't be silly. You woke up and saw me there half naked, all helpless. What else could any healthy woman do but have at me?'

She rolled her eyes, then jumped up and went into the kitchen.

'I'm going to make something to eat. I'm starved.'

'No, no, no. I'll make dinner,' he said, getting up and following her. 'I owe it to you. I shall be your slave for life.'

He took her wrist and lifted it to his lips, kissing it delicately. 'And you won't even have to tie me up,' he said with a wink.

'Well, if you're sure,' she said, hesitantly.

'Of course I'm sure. I'm a man. We men are always sure of ourselves.'

She rolled her eyes again and backed up behind the counter, then leant over on her elbows, watching him. He filled the room like a bear, not by his mere size but by his brazen charm, wit and personality. She wondered what it would be like to be so outgoing.

'If you don't mind my saying so, my girl, you have a miserable selection of food,' he said, after exploring the fridge and freezer.

'I'm kind of lazy about food,' she admitted. 'I usually just stick something frozen into the microwave.'

'No discipline,' he said. 'You should have been spanked more often when younger.'

He caught her look and laughed. 'Yes, I know. I'm arrogant. Also a male chauvinist pig.'

'I should be throwing things at you,' she said.

'Women are always much calmer after they've been given a good, solid ride,' he replied.

She gasped indignantly and threw a spoon at him.

'Men too! Men too!' he protested.

She settled back on her elbows with a mock scowl.

'You didn't say what you did for a living.'

'Do? Why must one do anything? I am comfortably supplied with money, courtesy of dear old dad, who was considerate enough after working himself to death to leave his accumulated fortune to me. I am not a chip off the old block. I dislike work intensely. I do my very best to avoid it.'

'Doesn't that get boring?'

'As compared to what?'

'Well, I don't know. I mean, don't you have any, uh, any goals.'

'What are your career aspirations, love?'

'I'm an artist.'

'So you have none?'

'Well, I'd like to become more respected, more . . .'

'Wealthy?'

'It's not just money.'

'Come on, love, this is boring. Oh, I suppose painting is interesting work for artistic types. God knows it's better than being an accountant or something. But living up here alone? No parties? No nightclubs? No sex? I think not!'

'I have sex,' she said weakly.

'Masturbation doesn't count.'

She blushed. 'I wasn't talking about ...'

'You live up here alone with nobody and you don't masturbate?'

'That's none of your business! What kind of a man asks a woman if she masturbates!'

'What kind of a woman opens a stranger's robe and begins fondling his body?' he asked with a wry grin.

'Well, you liked it!'

'I certainly did!'

'Anyway, I'm sorry. I shouldn't have done that.'

'I'm delighted you did. Otherwise we most likely would have had a polite little conversation, I would have gone on my way, and you would have returned to reading those silly books I see piled up in every corner.'

'I like reading.'

'I like it too. But there is more to life than reading about other people's exciting times, you know. You ought to have a few of your own.'

She laid her chin down on her arms with a sigh.

'You're right,' she said. 'I came up here to get away from it all but lately I've been realising I don't really want to get away from everything. I miss some things.'

'Like sex?'

She growled and he laughed.

'What are you making there anyway?'

'It's an old Scottish recipe.'

'What's it called?'

'I don't know for sure. I haven't named it yet.'

'I thought you said it was old.'

'It will be old, some day. Come here.'

She moved round the counter and he pulled her in front of him, took her hand and set it on a spoon in a large pot of meat, tomato soup and vegetables.

'Stir slowly and evenly,' he said, moving her hand round for a few seconds before releasing it.

He turned to the cupboard, humming to himself as he took down some spices.

He came back behind her, so close she felt his breath on her head as he poured some garlic salt into the stew.

She felt a few of the hairs at the top of her head sting and yelped, reaching up as he pulled back with a hair between his teeth.

'Stop that! You're weird!'

'I most definitely am weird. But you'll have to get used to me.'

'Why?' she asked cautiously.

'There is an old Indian proverb, you know, that says if you save a man's life you're responsible for him thereafter.'

'You're not Indian.'

'No, but we Scots are a lot quicker to take advantage of things like that than the Indians ever were. Free room, board and sex for the rest of my life is irresistible.'

'Forget it,' she said, though at the moment it didn't sound unattractive to her at all.

'Well, I suppose you're right. We in western society tend to believe the savee should be more grateful to the saver, as it were. Perhaps I should be responsible for your life.'

'No thank you.'

His hands massaged her shoulders and he bent in to kiss her on the side of the throat. 'Someone should,' he whispered.

'I'm doing fine.' Her soft voice belied her words.

'Oh balls, as my father would have said. You need to go to nightclubs and parties. You need to ride a Porsche at a hundred and sixty miles an hour down the autobahn. You need to walk along the Champs-Élysée on a sunny spring day, and lie on hot sand on the Riviera during the winter.'

'How do you know I haven't done all that?'

He made a disrespectful noise.

'A lot of people haven't done all that. Your crime, my dear, is that you can do all that and don't.'

'I have to paint,' she said weakly, still stirring the pot.

'Perhaps. But you don't have to spend all your free time reading soppy romance novels, watching television, and then go to bed alone every night.'

'No.'

'After I get the boat raised, why don't you come with me?'

'With you? Where?'

'I don't know. Wherever. Somewhere fun.'

'Don't be silly.'

'You can't think of a single reason why not.'

'I hardly know you.'

'So? You afraid I'll tie you up and ravish you senseless?'

He slipped his arms around her, then brought his hands slowly up to cup her breasts. 'Or are you afraid I won't?' he taunted.

She started to talk, then hesitated.

'What I'm afraid of is, well, awkwardness.'

'Awkwardness!' he exclaimed.

'Awkward people. Awkward situations. Awkward things that I can't just leave from. Awkward and embarrassing things. I know that sounds odd. I'm not sure how to explain it better.'

'I thought you said you could never be as embarrassed as you were when I woke up and found you on the floor naked, fingering yourself.'

She blushed and looked down, biting her lower lip.

'That turned out OK, now didn't it?' he said jovially.

'You wouldn't understand,' she sighed. 'I doubt anything would embarrass you.'

'Precious little, my sweet.'

'I'm not like that. I've always been shy.'

'Well, considering I owe you my life, I will endeavour to solve that problem for you, provide you with good, healthy sex, and show you what an interesting place the world can be, all at the same time.'

'You don't owe me anything,' she said.

Why was she fighting him, she wondered angrily. His invitation sounded so exciting she ought to be jumping at the chance.

Her mind filled with images of them naked, doing lewd things, of her in London, Paris, Rome, travelling the world, becoming a sophisticated lady of leisure.

'There's a quaint American expression that I think suits your present temperament,' he said.

She pulled her head back to look up at him.

'Wishy-washy.'

'I'm not wishy-washy.'

'You don't know what you want or how to get it and are too timid to make the attempt to find out.'

'I'm just not sure.'

'Then I'll make the decisions.'

He slipped his arms round her again, this time one of his hands sliding down to cup her groin while the other squeezed one of her breasts.

'Sean!'

'Don't mind me. Just keep stirring.'

'I'm not used to being pawed.'

'But I bet you'd like to get used to it.'

He brought both hands to the catch at the front of her trousers, undid the snap and pushed the zipper down.

Allison felt her heart rate begin to pick up, felt a clash

of embarrassment and excitement inside herself as his hand plunged down inside her trousers, inside her panties.

She swallowed as his fingers eased through the tight, tangled folds of her pubic hair as he sought out then found her cleft.

'What are you doing?' she gulped.

'Seeing if I can make you boil over before that pot.'

'I'm tired,' she groaned.

'That's all right. You don't have to do a thing.'

The tips of his fingers were against the top of her sex, rubbing gently from side to side, then up and down. He licked the fingers of his other hand, then slid that hand down into her trousers while he pulled the first one out.

He again stroked her clitoris as he pulled her hair back and he bent to lick and nibble lightly at the nape of her neck.

'Sean,' she moaned.

She felt the heat kick in quickly, felt the soft, fuzzy excitement rising in her groin, spreading out through her belly, rising to her chest where her nipples rapidly tightened and hardened against her bra.

She felt him pushing himself into her behind, grinding into her. Or thought she did. After a few moments she realised it was she who was moving, she who was grinding back against him.

'Do you like that?' he asked softly.

'Yes,' she whispered.

'Do you know what I'm doing?'

She didn't answer, only groaned softly as she ground herself back.

'I'm masturbating you.'

She felt a shock of shame at the words, mixed with a strange kind of kinky thrill.

'I am, you know. I'm masturbating you. Does the word embarrass you? You were masturbating when I woke, weren't you?'

Still she didn't speak. Her chest rose and fell faster and faster as his expert fingers rolled and rubbed at her clitoris.

He gripped her hair and pulled back sharply, making her gasp as her scalp stung. At the same time his fingers stopped moving against her sex.

'Weren't you?' he demanded.

'Yes,' she gasped, wanting him to resume his stroking.

He did, then eased his grip on her hair.

'I want you to say it,' he ordered.

His fingers stopped and she moaned.

'Say it.'

'I can't!'

'Say it.'

'I was . . . I was . . . masturbating,' she whispered, face red.

'Louder.'

'I was m-masturbating.'

'Louder!'

'I was masturbating!'

'And you want me to continue to masturbate you as I am now, don't you?'

She nodded weakly.

'Say it.'

'Please don't.'

'Why should it embarrass you? Go ahead. Say it.'

'Yes,' she whispered.

'Say the words.'

She groaned, reaching down for his hand, trying to rub it against her.

'Say it.'

'Yes, I want you to masturbate me!' she cried.

His fingers resumed their stroking, more rapidly now, and the heat flowed through her veins as she rolled her head slowly from side to side.

Again he halted.

'Do you like that?'

'Yes,' she whined.
'Beg for it.'
'What?'
'Beg me to masturbate you.'
She gasped, her eyes widening, her body crackling with sexual electricity.
'Please masturbate me,' she begged, breathless.
He turned her round and resumed his careful manipulation. At the same time he seized her hair, easing her head up and back, staring into her eyes, forcing her to look up at him as his fingers sent waves of steaming lust through her body.

She felt her eyes held by his and moaned as she ground herself against his fingers, as her juices oozed between her labia and his fingers pumped inside her.

She felt the pleasure rise up like a towering wave, ever higher, ever wider, ever more powerful. And still he held her eyes as it started to tip. She had an instant's warning, a sudden rise in tension and pleasure, then it collapsed on top of her, swamping her mind and body in a flood of powerful sensations of ecstasy.

She shuddered violently in his grip, jamming herself against his fingers as her head trembled and her eyes rolled back. Her lips quivered and she grunted weakly, senselessly.

Her head rolled back and growling like an animal he closed his mouth on her throat.

Her rubbery legs gave way, and he followed her downwards to the floor, still licking and sucking on her throat, his fingers stroking furiously against her burning sex as she shook and moaned and whined in dazed pleasure.

Then he held her and hugged her and stroked her hair as she caught her breath, smiling in delight, rather than superiority.

'I'm going to make you into a live person,' he whispered.

Five

While she still sat there, weak and languorous in the aftermath of orgasm he stripped off her blouse and bra, then yanked her trousers down and off along with her thong, which he smiled at.

He insisted she remain naked, even while he got his clothes from her dryer and put them on.

'I'm going to teach you not to be embarrassed by things,' he said benignly.

And despite a feeling of mutinous resentment she had agreed, not so much because she thought it would do any good, but because she found she was still aroused, and being naked around him felt deliciously sluttish and loose.

He behaved like a perfect gentleman over dinner, and even helped her wash up afterwards.

Then they went back into the living room, she still naked, still aroused.

'Sit there,' he ordered, pointing to the recliner.

She sat, wondering what he intended.

'Not like that.'

'Like what?' she asked in confusion.

'Slump down more.'

'Why?'

'Because master Sean says so, and you must do as master Sean orders.'

'Master,' she snorted.

'Or I'll spank your bare bottom.'

She snorted again, but slumped down, amused as well as aroused.

'Now I want you to drape your legs across the arms of the chair.'

She stared at him, open-mouthed.

'Come on. It's in a good cause.'

'But I . . .'

'I want to see you.'

'You've already seen me.' She blushed.

'Then you've nothing to be ashamed of.'

'I just can't, well, I mean, I can't sit like that! Not with you right there.'

'Are you ashamed of your pussy? I think it's a nice pussy.'

'I'm not ashamed,' she said in annoyance.

'Then stop trying to act ladylike. You're the same girl I woke up to find masturbating on the floor in front of me.'

She glared at him in embarrassment and resentment.

'It's in a good cause. Come on. Do it.'

Embarrassed, she slowly raised her legs, then spread them and draped them over the two padded arms of the chair.

'Wider. So your knees slip over the arms.'

She obeyed, feeling incredibly vulnerable, even crude, as she exposed herself to him. Her breathing picked up and she felt a hot flush moving through her body.

'How do you feel?'

'Like a slut.'

'Good start. Now how would you feel if a dozen men were here watching?'

She made a face.

'How would you feel if you were on the beach in Rio naked with people walking back and forth around you?'

'I couldn't do that!'

'Why not? You've a lovely body.'

'But I can't just go naked.'

'I repeat: why? They do. And your body is better than most I've seen.'

'It just wasn't the way I was raised.'

'Were you raised to sit like that?'

She shook her head.

'See how we can adjust to new things?'

'It's embarrassing, though.'

'After a while it won't be.'

She supposed that was true.

'Now I want you to put your hands on your tummy, my dear.'

'Why?'

'Because I say so.'

She placed her hands on her stomach, watching him, anxious but excited.

'Slide them up and put them over your breasts.'

She stared at him, then obeyed slowly, starting to understand where he was going, her insides burning up with the thought as she wondered how far she would follow.

'Now squeeze softly.'

She swallowed, licked her lips, then slowly squeezed her fingers in against her breasts, feeling the soft flesh give beneath the pressure.

'Again,' he said softly. 'Squeeze.'

She squeezed her breasts as he watched, her chest rising and falling faster.

'Now I want you to take your nipples between your thumbs and forefingers and pinch them.'

'Why?'

'Because I told you to.'

Again she obeyed, sliding her fingers up to her rigid nipples and pinching them.

'Twist them.'

She twisted them, letting out a small gasp.

'You have quite exquisite nipples. Do you know that? They're quite thin, yet they stick out so that one can slip one's lips or fingertips full around them without touching your breasts. I love hard little nipples like those. Pull on them. Tug them out.'

She obeyed, starting to become light-headed, and wondering if her arousal would lead her to places she ought not to go.

'Now place your hands against the sides of your breasts and push them in together.'

Breathless now, she obeyed, squeezing her breasts in together, feeling the heat as the soft flesh ground together.

The tendons in her thighs strained, and she was exquisitely aware of how open her sex was, of how visible it was to his hungry eyes. Again a mental picture of how she must look flashed through her mind, and she felt a rush of heat.

'Now I want you to slide your right hand down between your legs and cover your pussy with it.'

The words seemed simple, even modest.

She slid her hand down, covering herself.

'Now squeeze softly.'

Again she obeyed, whimpering slightly. Her body felt charged up, as if sparks might fly off her.

'Now move it up and down slowly, rub your hand against yourself. Slowly.'

She stared at him, frozen, realising the trap he had led her into yet unsure she wanted to escape it. The idea of touching herself sexually as he watched was intensely arousing yet unbearably wicked.

'Obey your master, slutty girl.'

She rubbed her hand softly across her groin, up and down.

'Now I want you to spread your fingers apart. Wider. Good girl. Now make sure the middle one is lined up along your soft little cleft, and rub.'

Allison stroked her finger along her cleft as he watched, her body enveloped in a charged cloud of sexual electricity. Again, as before, she wished she could view herself, for she knew that would be even more exciting.

'Faster.'

She rubbed faster, helplessly grinding her hips upwards now, pushing her sex against her stroking finger.

'Stop.'

His voice had become hypnotic, and she obeyed at once.

'Slide your middle finger into your body. Push it inside you all the way to the knuckle.'

Gasping again at what she was doing she turned her finger inward, easily slipped it between her moist lips, and drove it upwards through the soft folds of her sex.

'Now ease it out slowly. Now back in. Now add a second finger.'

She pushed a second finger into her pussy, pumping them slowly in and out as he watched her.

'Squeeze your breast with your other hand.'

She moaned, her behind rising and falling, the muscles in her legs working to drive her upwards against her fingers.

'Now faster, and press your thumb down against your clitoris. Rub it against your fingers as you pump them inside yourself.'

And she did, groaning softly now, panting for breath, exposing herself to him as she pumped her fingers inside her sheath and stroked her thumb across her burning little clitoris.

'That's it, Allison,' he said softly. 'Masturbate for me. Masturbate for master Sean. That's what you're doing. You're masturbating. Show me how hot you are. Show me what you do when you're alone. Come for me, baby. Come while I watch. Come on your fingers.'

She cried out, flinging her head back as she came, thrusting into herself again and again.

She felt his eyes searing her, felt them following her

every motion. She was aware yet uncaring, free, her mind flying, soaring as the waves of pleasure continued to wash over her.

Six

'Bastard,' she groaned, gulping in air as she lay sprawled back against the chair.

'People have called me worse,' he said mildly.

She groaned then sat up slowly, pulling her legs off the arms of the chair and glowering at him from under the loose, tangled fringe that had fallen across her forehead.

'If you do something often enough it doesn't embarrass you any more,' he said, unrepentant.

'I don't intend to masturbate in front of people very often,' she snapped.

'Perhaps not, but an hour ago you could hardly say the word, much less admit you did it.'

She continued to glare at him, annoyed at his smugness, even more annoyed that he was right.

'I bet you're not nearly as ashamed about admitting you masturbate now.'

'All right. All right,' she said. 'I don't like the idea of being trained like a dog or something.'

'The simplest training is the most effective. In your case I'm merely attempting to break down this preposterous embarrassment and self-consciousness you have about your sexuality.'

'You think there are many women out there who want to discuss masturbation with men, much less do it?'

'Most likely not,' he admitted.

He stood and went to the corner, looking at her stereo unit, then flipping through the CDs there.

'Quite an eclectic mix,' he said. 'Bach and Chopin together with Pink Floyd and Genesis and, who's this, blech, new age music.'

He selected a CD and slipped it into the player, then turned it on and came over to her, holding out his hand.

Allison looked up warily.

'Come. Dance with me.'

She frowned in confusion, but took his hand and stood, letting him lead her closer to the open area near the wall.

'Why do you want to dance?'

'I want to see if you can.'

'I can dance,' she said defensively.

'Just not very well,' he commented.

'You don't look like any Michael Jackson to me either!'

'I should hope not. Try and swing your legs a bit more, swing your body in time.'

'I didn't ask for dance lessons.'

'You didn't ask for anything. I'm taking it upon myself to improve you.'

'And who improves you?'

'Perfection cannot be improved upon.'

She made a rude noise.

'As in sex, your dancing shows how hesitant you are. You're too shy to express yourself.'

'God! I just masturbated in front of you! Do you really think I can't dance in front of you?'

'Very well then.'

He pulled back and sat down on a chair facing her. 'Dance,' he said.

'What? Alone?'

He nodded.

'Why should I?'

'Because I said to.'

'I'm not your slave!'

'Ah, but you want to be,' he said slyly. 'Imagine being my slave girl, clad only in chains, helpless and nude, to be used by me for my every pleasure, kneeling at my feet, given to my friends and acquaintances ...'

'Don't be silly,' she said, her chest a little tight.

'Dance. I want you to dance slowly, seductively. Dance as if you're a stripper in a club, grind your hips at me, show me what you've got.'

'I'd feel silly,' she murmured.

'That's your whole problem. You always worry about feeling silly. Just do it.'

Allison began to grind her hips slowly, nervously. She *did* feel silly with him watching.

'Don't tell me you never danced naked in front of your mirror, dancing sexily, seeing how hot you could look. All girls do.'

She had, in fact, but doing it in front of someone else was entirely different.

She rolled her hips, then her head, sliding her hands up her body, over her breasts and her rigid nipples, then up through her tangled hair and up further, thrusting her breasts out as she moved in time to the music.

'Very good,' he said in surprise, 'but move around a bit more.'

Not something she usually did since she had to stay close to the mirror, but easy enough. She felt a wave of pleasure at his obvious surprise, and moved to the side, sliding her tongue along the inside of her cheek, then along her lower lip, giving him the sexy look she had practised before her mirror since adolescence.

She turned her back to him and bent forward slightly, feeling a slight breathlessness at such daring, grinding and rolling her behind.

She turned again.

'No. Turn back, the way you were, but bend over fully. Slide your hands right down your legs to your ankles, and spread your legs wide.'

She hesitated, thinking of how crude that was, but then given what he had already seen she supposed it was no worse, and already she could once again feel the soft thrumming of pleasure in her loins as she rolled her shoulders and twisted her legs.

She bent over slowly, letting her legs come apart, sliding her hands down them, feeling somewhat mortified as her fingers crossed her knees, then continued lower.

'Very nice,' he said. 'Perhaps I'll put you to work in a strip club.'

She slid back up, turned to glare at him, then started dancing faster, her arms going behind her head as her breasts jiggled and shook.

He stood up, his eyes moving up and down her body, and her eyes challenged him saucily. He moved back then, across the room.

'Come to me,' he said.

Say please, she thought, not moving, dancing seductively.

'Now,' he ordered.

She smirked and started dancing forward.

'Not like that.'

She frowned in confusion.

'On your knees. Crawl to me.'

Her mouth opened indignantly, yet with her indignation came a wave of heat and the memory of his earlier words, of her being his slave girl. Flashes of fantasies – of her hands being bound, of a man crudely using her – flittered through her mind, and added heat to her loins.

'On your knees, girl.'

For an instant longer she ignored him, then she dropped to her knees, feeling a soft thrum in her lower belly.

'Crawl to me on all fours.'

She fell on to her hands, then crawled forward, cat-like.

He watched with narrow eyes as she halted in front of him.

'Heel,' he said, turning and walking further across the room.

She followed, feeling deliciously wanton, a raw, carnal heat gripping her now, tightening around her chest and mind as she crawled into her studio after him.

'These are actually quite good,' he said, looking round at her paintings. 'I'm not surprised they're in demand.'

'Thank you,' she said automatically.

'I didn't give you permission to speak, dog.'

Dog? She looked up at him, piqued, but then the heat and excitement took over and she took a deep, shuddering breath.

'Yes. Dog. A hot, randy little bitch on heat,' he said, reaching down to pat her head, then run his hand along her back, along her spine, down to her buttocks.

'Follow, little dog,' he said over his shoulder as he moved into the room, opening cupboard doors and drawers, exploring as if he owned the room.

What the hell am I doing crawling after him, she thought. Yet her chest was tight with sexual tension, her breathing becoming ragged.

He let out a crow of triumph and pulled a long, white, bundled-up rope from the back of a cupboard. She gasped and felt her insides turn liquid. Her breathing became harsher and she felt the air chill on her moist sex as her legs shifted apart.

He moved behind her, then gripped her hair, pulling up and back slowly but gently, forcing her to sit back on her heels. Without being asked or told she drew her arms back behind her back and crossed her wrists breathlessly.

She knew what he intended, and a dark thrill of shocked desire made her tremble.

She felt the rope going round her wrists, felt them

criss-crossing, binding tight, layer after careful layer, until half a dozen loops bound them immovably.

Then he gripped her by the hair and pushed her forward, dropping her on to her belly on the rug.

He walked back to where he had stood before and looked at her.

'Now crawl like the hot, sexy little tramp you are,' he growled.

She swallowed repeatedly, pulling at the ropes, then awkwardly began to crawl forward, wriggling from side to side as she pushed herself across the floor. The floor was hard on her breasts, which she continually rolled and ground down below her as she wriggled forward. She winced and moaned as she slipped on to the rug of the next room and her sensitive breasts and nipples ground against the fibre. Her breathing became more harsh as her thighs rubbed together.

She felt the wall rising again, that wall that had surrounded her before, the wall that shut the world out and focused everything on her pleasure, on the lewd wickedness of what she was doing. She gasped with effort as she worked her way across the rug towards him to lay at his feet.

'My boots got quite dirty today,' he said idly, lifting one foot on its heel. 'I think they want cleaning, my girl.'

Allison didn't understand the remark and looked up, blinking her eyes in confusion.

'Your tongue, girl, clean my boot with your tongue.'

'No way,' she said in sudden indignation.

But it was a sudden instinctive response, and a moment later she felt a wanton thrill at the thought of her, Allison Miller, lying bound naked on her belly licking a man's boots. It was so degrading, so provocatively outrageous!

'Perhaps you want a spanking.'

She looked at his boots, eyes wide.

'Lick your master's boots, slave,' he ordered.

She looked at his boots. They actually seemed quite clean. She licked her lips then leant forward and brought her mouth against the top of his boot, letting her tongue slide out slowly. A hot, bubbling stew seemed to boil within her lower belly as she lapped slowly across the side of his boot.

'That's it, slave. Nasty little trollop. Lick your master's boots clean,' he said in a low growl.

His words made her chest ache, and she let her tongue slide across his boots, looking up at him, her eyes near-glassy now as she trembled with the desire inside her body. She licked downward along the boot and then shuddered as he raised it and presented the bottom.

She raised her head, committed now, thinking briefly that there was nothing she would not do at this point. Then her tongue lapped across the bottom of the boot.

'Vile little girl,' he purred. 'I should march an army between your thighs and let them ride you one by one.'

He reached down and gripped her by the hair, more roughly than before, so she cried out. He lifted her upwards and back on to her knees, then up further, to her feet, holding her hair so tightly she was forced on to her toes and her head pulled back.

His hand shot between her legs and she cried out again as he squeezed her mound hard. Her back arched and she shuddered violently, wrists constantly pulling behind her.

His thumb jammed in against her clitoris and a ball of fire tore into her lungs as she climaxed. She rode his hand in feverish, mindless sexual release as her nervous system exploded with fireworks.

She jerked and shook, grunting and moaning as he continued to grind his thumb up into her. It ached, but the ache was beyond pleasure, in a realm of its own. And then she sagged against him, gulping in air, almost falling but for his arms quickly taking hold of her.

'Hot little sex kitten,' he said with a delighted leer. 'Are you learning what pleasures your body can give you? Are you learning how much enjoyment one can get by abandoning pride and fear?'

He stroked her head as she moaned softly into his chest, then turned her round, letting her bend forward across a table. His knee spread her thighs as he unzipped his trousers.

'Wait!' she gasped.

'Why?'

'I – I want to see me.'

'What?'

'I – a mirror in my bedroom,' she panted.

'Ah, of course.'

He lifted her upright, then marched her into her bedroom and stood her before the mirror. She stared at herself with wide eyes, turning to present her rear and her neatly bound wrists. But something was wrong. The effect was spoiled by several feet of rope dangling down to the floor.

'You should have cut the rope,' she complained.

He smacked her behind and she gasped.

'Don't criticise your betters, dog. You want a more economical use of the rope?'

He picked up the loose rope, then untied her wrists. She rubbed them briefly, frowning into the mirror as he tied two loops into one end of the rope.

'What are you doing?'

Again he smacked her behind, so she yelped.

'Don't question your betters, slave girl.'

She glowered but kept silent as he finished with the loops.

'Bend over, dog, far over.'

She obeyed and he moved behind her, sliding the rope beneath her, then catching it with his other hand. As she watched he brought the two loops around her breasts, sliding them up until they were firm against her ribs, then he began to slowly pull on the two sides of the rope, tightening the loops.

She gasped as the pressure grew on her breasts.

'Not too hard,' she panted.

She winced slightly as the two loops shrank, squeezing in against the sides of her breasts. Then he pulled the rope behind her as he ordered her to stand erect.

She stood, gazing at herself in the mirror, gasping at the sight of her breasts pushed out so tautly.

Sean tied the rope behind her chest, then to her surprise he looped it around her arms just above her elbows and began to tighten it.

'What are you doing?' she gasped.

He ignored her, tightening the loop slowly, forcing her arms back and together, making her shoulders ache and the joints strain until she almost demanded he stop. When her elbows were pressed together he looped the rope around her arms twice more, binding them firmly together, then led the rope down to her wrists, where again he threaded it around them, pressing them tightly together.

With rope to spare he slipped a loop around her waist, then fed the rope down between her buttocks, reached between her thighs and pulled it up between them. She looked down to see it push up against her moist sex, then cleave the soft lips, riding up between them as he led it upwards across her abdomen to the loop that circled her waist. He fed it through, then dropped it back down again, pulled it back between her legs and then up behind her to tie off at the small of her back.

Then he stood away and let her examine herself, watched as she stared wide-eyed at the image in her bedroom mirror, the image of erotic helplessness; of herself bound tightly, her shoulders jerked back to force her breasts up and out, those breasts wickedly bound, the nipples aching, the rope digging up into her soft mound.

'Perhaps I should sell you to an Arab or something,' he said. 'I think you might even like that.'

She didn't answer, only stared at herself, entranced.

He pushed her down on to her knees, and still she stared at her image in the mirror, her breathing coming in sharp, short little puffs and pants.

He pulled back and stripped, then stood before her, gripping her hair and turning her to face him, positioning her so her side was to the mirror and she could continue to watch herself out of the corner of her eyes.

'Close your mouth and form a kiss.'

She obeyed and watched him push his erection against her lips.

'Now keep them tight, but let them slowly open, as if my cock was forcing them apart.'

She pushed her head forward, and let her lips come only slowly apart as his cock moved into her mouth. She started to lick at the head as he pumped slowly in her mouth, her eyes turning to watch herself, and the image making her squeeze her thighs together.

She moaned around his flesh as she licked and suckled softly. He pulled her head back then, taking his cock and rubbing the wet head all over her face as he held her helpless.

'The ultimate requirement for every slave girl is to take a man into her throat,' he said. 'It's something you'll have to learn, and I expect now is as good a time as any to start.'

Into her throat? The idea would have panicked her were she not intoxicated on her own sexuality and the eroticism of what was happening. As it was she felt only a brief anxiety combined with another wave of excitement.

He paused for a moment as if to reconsider. 'Actually, I forgot how new to this sort of thing you are. You don't have to do this if you don't want. I'll not force you to do anything. You do know that, I hope?'

She nodded impatiently. She did know that and he was spoiling the fantasy. She trusted him not to hurt her. She wasn't sure why but she had almost from the first.

He cleared his throat then continued.

'There is a very simple trick to this,' he said. 'It's mental control. You have to have the self-discipline to control your gag reflex. You have to convince yourself you are not going to gag, that there is indeed plenty of room in your lovely throat to hold me. Take a deep breath, and when you feel the tip at the back of your mouth swallow it and keep swallowing.'

He pushed himself into her mouth again and pumped slowly in and out, letting her lick and moisten him. Each stroke was deeper, however, and she felt herself begin to gag on several occasions.

The thought of doing it did something inside her. Her whole concept of herself was of a dull, boring, drab woman. But a woman who took part in such games could not be so, and a woman who would take a man down her throat while bound in ropes – what kind of a woman would do that but a hot, nasty tramp? Certainly no dull, boring woman would even attempt it!

She arched her back more, feeling her nipples straining upwards as she pushed her lips down the length of his cock. Yet instincts prevailed and she backed off, frustrated.

He pulled out and then moved behind her. She watched him in the mirror as he pulled her head slowly back so her back was arched even more sharply and her head was facing up towards the roof behind her.

'In this position there is a straight line between your mouth that goes right down your throat,' he said conversationally. 'You might recall that sword swallowers tilt their heads back like this.'

His cock dangled above her, then slipped into her open mouth. She gasped, gulping in air, then he plunged down. Her eyes widened as she felt him slip through into her throat. There was a wild moment of panic as he filled her throat and slid down into it, and she trembled and shook, helpless to pull away.

She felt his thickness inside her as it slipped deeper and deeper. She pulled at her bonds, instinctively trying to free her hands to grab at her throat.

And then her panic subsided and she felt a shimmer of wonder and delight. She could feel his slick flesh caressing the inside walls of her throat with a feather's touch as it slipped down ever deeper. Then his testicles were against her eyes and her lips were wrapped around the base as he held her tightly, her body trembling and shaking.

He reached down and pinched one of her nipples sharply. She would have yelped in pain had she been able to make a sound. The distraction, however, seemed to take away what discomfort remained, and then the heat rushed in as he slowly, slowly pulled back up, stroking along her tonsils in a way she had never felt or imagined.

It was a touch more intimate than she could have believed, and she felt a smouldering heat and sense of deep satisfaction as he pulled his cock free. She gulped in air, flushed with victory and a sense that she had conquered a new frontier.

He gave her a minute, then pushed in again. She made no attempt to resist as the head of his cock drove into her throat this time, and found it was much easier to take him down. It felt, in fact, supremely erotic as she watched inch after inch of glistening cock slip into her lips until his groin blinded her.

Again he reached down to her breasts, running his free hand across them, stroking and caressing them as he held her head back. He pulled up then pushed in again, pulled up, then pushed in. Allison knelt before him submissively, back arched, head back, arms bound tightly behind her, hands against her buttocks.

He pulled back out, wiping himself across her face as she caught her breath and coughed against the ticklish sensation he had left behind.

'OK?'

She pulled her head back further, opening her mouth demandingly.

Again he pushed in, and she took him deep into her throat. This time he started to pump at once, using longer strokes, moving very slowly but continuously, massaging the inside of her bulging throat in a way she had never dreamt could feel so good.

He began to pump faster, and she heard him gasping. She felt a deep sense of conquest and smug delight at having been able to bring him to such heights without, she thought, really doing anything at all.

And then he was softening in her throat, softening and pulling back. He slipped free quite easily now, and then let go of her hair. She groaned and almost fell, but caught her balance and stared at herself dizzily in the mirror.

A trollop was what she saw, a hot, nasty, crude, sluttish woman, a woman of sexual mystery and wickedness.

Seven

Sean kept her bound like that for several hours. Sometimes they watched television. Sometimes they talked. Often he would pull her across his lap, either on her back or her belly, and run his hands over her body: stroking and caressing her breasts, pinching and tugging at her nipples, rubbing at her pussy.

Allison found that by straightening her body and easing her shoulders back, she tightened the pull of the ropes up against her sex. By doing that repeatedly she was able to climax by herself while lying next to him on the sofa.

She wasn't sure why she found the idea of being tightly bound so erotic and exciting. She had often had fantasies of bondage, probably arising out of her shyness: the inability to think of herself willingly engaging in lewd sex with men, letting them see her naked flesh and touch her in the most intimate of places.

But she spent little time or effort contemplating why she was now so sexually aware. It was sufficient that she was. And with her body in a constant state of arousal, with her nipples erect for so long, so sensitive now that even the slight breeze coming in the window and playing across them made her arch her back upwards, she found her shyness, her hesitation, masked. She found herself in possession of an almost entirely different persona, one filled with lust and heat, and caring only for pleasure and sexual gratification.

In fact, it was hard to concentrate on anything else.

Even when Sean wasn't running his hands over her naked body and she wasn't straining against the ropes to tug them up into her cleft her mind was steaming with a plethora of lewd fantasies.

In all of them she was a prisoner of some sort, an innocent victim of men who lusted after her.

Sometimes the persona was so heady it was hard to think of anything else, anything unrelated to sex.

'What do you think about skydiving?' he asked at one point.

'I – I don't think about it,' she said in surprise.

'I think it's marvellous. You'll have to learn how.'

The thought of jumping out of an aeroplane was certainly exciting, but Allison had her doubts she could do it.

'Hang gliding is another interesting sport, though it requires a bit more effort and learning. What about water skiing?'

'What about it?'

'Have you ever done it?'

She shook her head, not really caring much.

'Have you ever even ridden in a motorboat?'

Again she shook her head.

'You live on the edge of the sea, girl,' he said in annoyance. 'Why haven't you bought a boat?'

'Where would I go?'

'Anywhere!'

She shrugged helplessly.

'You've been wasting your life away.'

Allison didn't feel she could really deny that. Nor was she in much of a mood to care. He dragged her across him again and began to stroke and knead her throbbing breasts. She groaned and arched back over his lap, tugging on the ropes, pulling them up into the heat between her legs.

An orgasm rippled through her and she cried out in bliss, wallowing in the pleasure.

* * *

He teasingly threatened to leave her as she was for the night, but relented after she begged him. He pulled the rope out from between her legs, and she groaned in relief. Then he positioned her on her knees, with her face pressed down against the bed, and mounted her roughly and quickly. She climaxed in less than a minute, and he finished casually, slapped her behind, then untied her.

Both of them were exhausted and slept soundly.

Allison woke to his shaking.

'Come on, you. Time to make me breakfast. I have things to do today, and so do you.'

'I'm tired,' she groaned. And her muscles still ached from yesterday's exertion. Her sex was sore from its unaccustomed workout as well.

'On your feet and into the kitchen before I turn you across my knees.'

She sighed and got up, rubbing at her face, then reached for her robe. He snatched it away.

'I can't stay naked for ever,' she complained.

'Certainly not, just for now.'

She considered arguing. On the one hand she wasn't feeling terribly sensual just then, but on the other it was flattering and somewhat exciting that he wanted to see her naked all the time. She shrugged, sighed and got up, then made her way into the kitchen. She made breakfast for him as he wandered the small house and the grounds around it.

'Do you get many visitors up here?' he asked, the screen door slamming behind him.

'No. None, really, unless I call someone to come for some reason.'

He nodded, then sat down at the table as she served his bacon and eggs.

'You'll have to learn to make more interesting food if you're to become a satisfactory slave,' he said.

She slapped the back of his head as she went by, then yelped as his hand smacked against her rear.

She rubbed it and glared at him before sitting down.

'Show more respect to your betters, Allison.'

'You're not better, just bigger.'

'That'll do for now.'

She snorted and he glanced up at her and frowned.

'You'll pay for that, girl.'

She stuck her tongue out at him.

'And that.'

'What is it we're doing today?' she asked.

'I'm going to the nearest town to make arrangements to have the *Wanderer* raised. You're going to decide the absolute minimum you need to pack to take with us.'

'I didn't say I would go with you,' she said softly, looking down at her plate as she idly toyed with her fork.

'Of course you didn't say it,' he sighed. 'That would require making a decision and a commitment. It would require trying something new and moving away from your safe, secure little hideaway and out into the big, nasty world.'

'I do have things I need to do,' she said weakly.

'Such as?'

'Well, my painting for one.'

'You can take paints and canvas with you and paint on the boat.'

'I don't know,' she said worriedly.

'I realise that. That's why I'm giving the orders. Left to yourself I think you'll always choose the safest course, and the safest course in your life is to do nothing. I think you've held to that long enough. Time to risk a little embarrassment and discomfort.'

'I suppose it will take a while to get your ship raised.'

'No, not more than a day or two. They'll spend a couple of days cleaning it and then we'll be off. I thought we'd go to London first, provision there, then head across to Europe.'

'I . . .'

She stared at him in an agony of indecision. Her home was already starting to feel like it was being torn from her. It was so snug and secure here. She was in total control and never encountered difficulties or problems.

Or much of anything else, for that matter.

'You need to get some sun,' he said. 'You're dead pale.'

'Sunlight isn't good for you.'

'Lack of sunlight isn't good for you either. Keys? I won't be long.'

She gave him her car keys, then set about trying to decide what to pack, or even if she should pack. The idea was preposterous.

And yet, after a short time alone she realised how empty the house felt without him, how unimportant everything was. She didn't want to go back to that again.

Before long she was worrying he wouldn't come back, that he would just decide there were better prospects elsewhere. She thought about going on to Europe on her own, but had no idea what she would do there other than wander the streets and shops.

She finally heard the car and felt a wave of relief that surprised her. When he came in she ignored him.

'Miss me?'

'Did you go somewhere?'

'I see you're still naked as I ordered.'

She frowned at the realisation. Now why hadn't she dressed?

He held up a package and she glared at it suspiciously.

'For you. I bought it in town.'

'What is it?'

'Open it.'

She opened the bag and reached in, taking out a small two-piece bathing suit in hot pink.

'This is too small,' she said.

'Try it on.'

'It's too small. I know my size.'

'Try it on,' he said insistently.

She rolled her eyes, then stepped into the bottom and pulled it up as far as she could. She then dropped the string of the top over her head and pulled the cups against her breasts, reaching back behind her to fasten them.

'I told you. The snap won't even reach.'

He turned her and tugged hard on the strap, then snapped it together. Then he reached down and slipped his fingers into the string of the bottoms and yanked up, forcing much of the rear in between her buttocks.

'There now,' he said, turning her, and adjusting the cups over her breasts.

'It's far too small!'

'It's perfect.'

The cups covered the centre of each breast, though with ample cleavage displayed. The pale white sides of her round globes were bare as well because the cups were unable to reach completely around.

'Haven't you ever heard that you should wear a size too small?'

'What is this, two sizes too small?' she demanded, trying to tug the rear of the suit out from between her buttocks.

'Three. Don't worry, though. You look fabulous, very sexy.'

'I'm not going to wear this anywhere,' she said, blushing slightly.

'You know that women often wear less than this. Thongs are quite common on many beaches.'

'Well, maybe so, but I've never worn even a two-piece.'

'And you want to change all that, don't you. You want to be hot and sexy and to do daring things.'

'Well . . . yes, in a way, I – I suppose I do. But I could never walk on a beach like this.'

'Certainly you can. It wouldn't mark you out as unusual.'

'But all the men would look at me . . .'

'And what? And think what a hot, sexy, gorgeous lady you were? Yes, I expect they would. Would that bother you?'

'I – I don't know,' she sighed. 'I mean, in a way I kind of like the idea but, well, it's just all so different from the way I've always been.'

'And we agreed the way you've always been is boring and you're wasting your life.'

'I didn't agree,' she said, lowering her head slightly.

He tilted her chin up with a finger, then kissed her softly.

'You might not have agreed with me but you know it's true.'

He pulled back and winked, then moved away.

'Now come with me. We'll take some things down to the beach and find my sunken boat so I can mark it for the salvage team.'

'What things?' she sighed

She followed him out to the car and found him already at the boot pulling out diving tanks and a deflated rubber raft. They made several trips down to the beach carrying everything, Sean hefting a motor over one shoulder while Allison struggled with air tanks.

It felt strange and erotic being out of doors in the skimpy bathing suit, and her nipples tightened and hardened almost instantly. It wasn't like being naked, and yet – it was. She looked round as they moved back and forth between the car and the beach, worried someone would come by and see her dressed as she was.

And yet she knew Sean was right. There was nothing especially indecent about the bikini. She knew other women wore such suits on crowded public beaches without a trace of embarrassment.

But to her it was far, far too revealing. She kept tugging at the bottom, as if she could somehow manage to cover her buttocks. It felt unnatural the way the suit was pulled up between them. That women willingly and deliberately wore suits that bared their buttocks was a strange concept.

Then Sean stripped to his own bathing suit, a small, tight pair of trunks that had Allison once again admiring his powerful, athletic body, broad shoulders and muscled arms and chest.

The rubber raft inflated itself with a small tank of compressed gas, then the two got in and Sean pushed off and started the motor.

'God, it sure bounces on the waves!' she yelled over the sound of the motor.

'We don't have far to go,' he yelled back.

And they didn't. Allison guided them to the area she remembered spotting the *Wanderer* and Sean anchored the boat to a small rock outcropping. He pulled on the air tanks, winked at her, then jumped over the side.

She looked down into the water, then around her, a trifle nervous. She realised that, unlike her morning walks, she had nothing to cover herself with should someone arrive.

And then, as if in answer to her worries she saw a distant object, barely more than a smudge on the horizon. As she watched anxiously it grew and grew, coming directly towards her. She looked into the sea but there was no sign of Sean, and there was simply nothing in the raft to cover herself with.

It was a large black boat and it continued to come closer as she prayed Sean would show up before it arrived. Then he burst out of the water, climbing into the raft as she tried to hide down at the bottom.

He pulled the mouthpiece out and gazed at the approaching boat.

'Who are they?' she gasped. 'What are they doing here?'

'They're the salvagers. They're why I let that little balloon up a few minutes ago.'

'But I'm hardly wearing anything!' she gasped. 'I'm practically naked!'

'Nonsense. You look wonderful. You've nothing to be embarrassed about.'

Allison's mind cringed at the thought of climbing up on to the boat under their eyes, yet she saw no alternative.

All the time she was being taunted when young the very last thing she had ever wanted was to allow anyone to realise she was embarrassed or hurt. That still held true. She would have to brazen it out like she used to, pretend that nothing at all was bothering her, be aloof.

But it was so hard. She prayed they would go about their business but both men came to the side of the boat as a ladder was lowered. Sean had her climb up first, and both men's eyes moved over her admiringly as one helped her up. She was desperately aware of how small the bra cups were and how much they strained outwards against the push of her breasts.

'Thank you,' she mumbled, quickly turning to present her front to them, even more embarrassed, for some reason, about her nearly bare buttocks than she was about her breasts.

'Well, you made good time, Paul,' Sean said jovially as he climbed aboard.

'Aye, wasn't far to go,' one of the men said.

He was in his mid thirties, about her height and broad-shouldered, with a moustache and a hard face. His hair was shaggy and his hands rough-looking.

The second man was ten years younger, with short straight brown hair. He was an enormous man, perhaps six feet seven or so. But he had an attractive grin on his handsome face.

'This is Jim,' Paul said, 'my diver.'

He and Sean shook hands while Allison slipped the

heavy tank over his shoulders and lowered it to the deck.

The boat was a rough working boat, not a pleasure cruiser like Paul's. Its deck was unpainted and crowded with nets, air tanks, rubber sheeting and machinery for a heavy winch in the back. There were also rolls of plastic piled on top of each other, each the width of the deck.

'How are you going to raise it?' she asked, her curiosity getting the better of her.

'We cover her up, make her airtight, then pump the water out and air in. She'll lift on her own,' Jim said in a deep voice.

He and Sean were soon manhandling the heavy rolls of plastic over the side of the ship and into the sea. Then both donned large double air tanks and slipped into the water.

Allison was left on her own on deck with Paul, squirming a little inside even as she put on a show of indifference to him.

It might be that men pretty much ignored women dressed as she was on crowded beaches, but this was not a crowded beach, and Jim was from a small village in Southampton; he probably didn't go down to those places very often. It was soon evident to her that whenever she wasn't looking directly at him his eyes moved to her body and raced along every inch of it.

There was nowhere to hide on the open deck, and she refused to show her discomfort by trying to hide herself with her arms and hands. She looked round for a place to sit, but there were no chairs and the heaps of equipment strewn about the deck were filthy.

Every few seconds his eyes would flit over to her, skim along her body, then slide away. She pretended not to notice, but felt a warm flush of embarrassment whenever it happened.

The awkwardness was joined by annoyance after a

few minutes, and then the embarrassment began to fade. After all, it wasn't as though she really had anything to feel awkward about. She had known for some time, intellectually, at least, that she was attractive. And her actions with Sean had robbed her of some of her shyness about her body.

If he wanted to get an eyeful there really wasn't any reason he shouldn't. No doubt he was thinking how hot and sexy she looked, and wishing he could see her in even less.

That thought made her embarrassed again. She wondered what he was doing to her in his mind, what thoughts lay behind his eyes. Was he thinking of what he would like to do to her? Was he imagining how soft her skin was and wishing he could slide his hands over it? Was he imagining himself squeezing her breasts through the tiny bra cups, perhaps forcing them out of the cups so he could lick at her nipples?

Her mind was aflutter with these thoughts as she looked out over the water. She saw him, from the corner of her eye, turning his head again, looking at her. She swallowed nervously, feeling a little thrill in her stomach.

He wasn't an unattractive man, though not exactly handsome. He was a rough, unsophisticated, local man. She imagined him going back to town and telling his chums at the bar about this sexy girl he'd had aboard his boat, one with a tiny little bikini that barely covered half her boobs.

Allison was deeply aware of how her breasts strained at the tiny top, of how the small bottoms pulled up so high on the hips and in behind. She felt like an exhibitionist under his eyes.

But she knew he couldn't do anything, not with Sean due to return soon. And she felt an odd little flush of power at the way he was behaving. It was she that was causing him to keep turning his head, her lushly displayed body that was arousing him, putting naughty thoughts into his head.

She turned with a bored sigh and looked out the other way, then leant forward a little to put her hands on the rail, knowing her behind would push out at him.

She felt her insides quivering, felt a little tingling between her legs. She was sure he was looking at her behind, licking his lips and fantasising about bending her over the rail more, maybe tugging her bikini down.

She straightened up, face flushed, and tossed her hair. She felt a small thrill of excitement as she turned round. He was looking away from her, of course. She turned slightly to one side, then reaching up to her hair she slid her fingers through it.

She could feel her breasts push even more tautly against the bikini top as she arched her back, and a sudden fear that it would snap made her quickly pull her arms down and straighten.

'So, you ever been on a boat before?' he asked awkwardly.

She started in surprise, then shook her head dumbly.

'Ah, it's a lovely feeling to be out on the sea, you know.'

'I suppose so,' she said. She paused, searching for something to say. 'Is it hard to, um, steer?'

He grinned widely. 'Naah. She steers like a car. Come here. I'll show you.'

She stepped closer, half reluctant, half excited, and he put his arm round her as he pulled her in against a wooden steering wheel.

'See, just like a car,' he said, moving behind her.

'Ah,' she said, not knowing how else to respond.

'This here is the throttle.' He showed her a silver knob. 'You got your speed indicator, your engine temperature gauge, your revs . . .'

'What's this?'

'Compass.'

'Oh,' she said, feeling silly.

His breath was warm on the back of her neck. And when he reached forward to adjust the compass she felt his body pushing against her, felt his erection against her nearly bare behind.

He pulled back, then coughed and turned away.

Allison resumed her breathing, surprised by the level of arousal she was experiencing. It must be, she thought, being dressed like this, all alone, being practically naked with this strange man.

She wondered what she would do if he tried something. It wasn't as though she had a real relationship with Sean. He wasn't her boyfriend. They hadn't even dated.

He leant in again and his hardness pressed up between her buttocks more firmly as he reached round her to adjust something on the control panel.

Allison felt her insides glow, her breathing becoming more difficult as she felt him start to roll his hips, grinding his hardness into her.

There was a splash of water off the side and he jerked back. Allison moved to the rail and looked out as Sean and Jim popped to the surface and began to swim towards the boat.

They climbed back up and removed their air tanks. Then Jim slipped on a replacement set and jumped back into the water, carrying a long hose in his hand that was attached to an air compressor.

Sean put his arm around her waist and pulled her in against him, kissing her casually on the side of the face.

'Is it all finished?' she asked.

'He's got to force the air out and inflate the two bags we attached to her fore and stern. But that's a one-man job.'

His hand slipped down and squeezed her behind gently.

She widened her eyes and turned to give him an

anxious look, flicking her eyes at Paul to show him what she meant.

He just grinned.

'No place to sit down around here?' he demanded.

'You can clear off some of that crap from the top of the engine cover,' Paul said, pointing at a box-like structure just behind the winch.

Sean lifted off some equipment then sat down, uncaring of the dirt.

'Have a seat,' he offered, patting the spot next to him.

'It's too dirty,' she replied, wrinkling her nose.

He laughed in amusement, then gripped her waist and pulled her up on to his lap, ignoring her feeble protest, his arms sliding round her.

'That better?'

'Only slightly.'

She glanced nervously towards Paul, who hadn't seemed to notice.

Sean's hands were flat along her stomach but she was slightly embarrassed to be sitting on his lap in front of someone. Then she felt his tongue along her shoulder and quickly turned her head, eyes glaring. 'Sean!' she whispered.

'Shy?' he whispered back.

She didn't answer. Again Paul didn't seem to be watching, and now that she thought about it she wondered why she cared if he saw her and Sean kissing or hugging. It was no big deal.

Except that she was sure he had been, and probably still was, mentally undressing her and thinking of all the things he would like to do with her himself. That made her stomach fluttery even without Sean pressed up against her.

She looked down towards his hands and realised her nipples were hard and thrusting out quite visibly against the thin fabric of her bikini. Her face flushed and she swallowed nervously, wondering if Paul had noticed.

His hands rubbed her stomach slowly, and again she looked away from Paul and checked him through the corner of her eye. His head turned slightly and she was sure he was watching.

Sean licked at her shoulder again, then kissed the back of her neck.

'You'll get lots of diving in yourself when we head for Bermuda.'

'Is that where we're going?'

'Eventually.'

She felt the tip of his index finger slip an inch inside her bikini bottom and swallowed nervously, her heart rate taking a quick leap. The fingers stroked her skin from side to side and she looked again to see Paul apparently engrossed on a piece of equipment.

The finger slipped further down inside, stroking from side to side against her soft abdomen. The bikini was so small that even with all the rest of his hand outside the tip of his finger was sliding through her moist pubic hair.

'Sean,' she whispered.

'Cold?' he asked.

'No. I mean, well, a little.'

He wasn't referring to her stiff nipples, was he? God! Was it her fault they were hard? She wasn't the one who wanted to wear this little teeny bathing suit!

He reached down, gripping her thigh and pulling her back a little, adjusting her on his lap. His hand didn't move off afterwards, and stroked the inside of her thigh high up next to her bikini.

He eased his finger out, then patted her stomach idly.

'He'll be up in another twenty minutes or so,' he said. 'Then it'll be quick work.'

His fingers slipped back down and she gulped anxiously, feeling both embarrassment and a deep, piercing heat.

Her eyes darted from side to side as anxiety and

worry joined the excitement filling her mind. She had no idea what Sean was doing, or what he intended to do.

His hand slipped a bit deeper and she gasped and twisted round so she was sitting sideways, in the process pulling his hand free and giving him a wide-eyed, silent admonishment which he cheekily ignored.

'I can hardly wait to get you back home,' he growled. 'That suit is turning me on.'

Again she felt a mixture of embarrassment and heat. That he would so blatantly talk to her like that, leaving no doubt in the mind of this strange man about what he intended to do, was only going to feed Paul's interest.

He chuckled and hugged her, in the process his hands rising up to just under her breasts.

'Don't you think she looks hot in this bikini, Paul?' he asked.

Paul turned his head fully and stared at her, and Allison looked away, blushing.

'Sure does,' he said.

'She's shy.'

'I am not!' Allison protested sternly, eyes still on the deck.

'She's never worn a bikini before.'

'Well, she certainly looks good in one,' Paul said.

'That's what I keep telling her.'

He stroked her thigh, kissing her cheek lightly; his lips then eased up the side of her throat and down over her shoulder.

Allison was fighting to keep her breathing even, to keep her expression aloof. She had ample experience in ignoring teasing, which was what Sean was doing, yet this time it was different. This time he wasn't teasing her to make her feel bad. She was sure of that. And there was a sexual element that had caught hold of her and was making her lower belly throb with need.

Again she felt like an exhibitionist as Paul's eyes roamed her barely clothed body. It excited her to know he was hot for her, that he was thinking of her in that way, but it also embarrassed her.

And Sean was making things worse as he rained little kisses on her. Most were safe, on cheeks, chin, head and shoulders. But then he bent and kissed the soft, round curve of her breast just beside the bra. He chuckled as she squirmed.

'Like that, sexy girl?'

She didn't reply, not trusting her voice.

Then he kissed her on the lips, much harder than before, his tongue sliding into her mouth. She kissed back automatically, feeling herself falling into the kiss, into the passion that rose up around her.

He drew back after long seconds, then licked a trail down her chest and into her cleavage, lapping at the upper curve of her breast.

Allison's eyes shifted aside and she saw Paul watching and licking his lips. She felt a wave of heat and trembled helplessly.

'Do you know what I want to do to you?' Sean asked in a whisper she knew Paul could hear.

She jerked her head from side to side.

'I want to strip you naked, put you down on all fours and ride you until you drop,' he whispered in the same tone.

His hand slipped up and cupped her breast firmly, stroking it softly, then squeezing. She shuddered and felt the sex-heat shimmer inside her, felt her body sizzle with desire.

She felt like a tramp and wondered what Paul thought of her: whether he had an erection, if he was all hot and bothered looking at Sean paw at her.

His fingers slipped into the cup and stroked across her erect nipple, making her gasp, then he tugged it down and slipped his lips over it, sucking gently but firmly.

God!

She felt the excitement howl through, her, trembled at

its impact. She was gulping in air desperately, looking away, out to sea, anywhere but at Paul or Sean.

Her nipple throbbed as he sucked on it, and she felt the pressure of her swelling breasts as they sought release from the restraining cups.

She realised it no longer bothered her what Sean did to her in front of Paul, that each new step he took shot her excitement higher at the knowledge Paul was watching.

It was the wickedness of it, the wantonness, of letting a man paw at her, grope her, while another man watched. It was simply not something one did, not unless one was a slut and a tramp.

For someone who had always been extraordinarily careful of her behaviour and dress in public lest she draw attention to herself it was a dizzying experience.

She felt the pressure of the straps abruptly let go as he unsnapped the catch. She gasped and started to raise her arms, instinctively seeking to cover herself as her bra fell away, but he laughed and held her arms gently but firmly.

Then he bent and sucked on her nipple again, this time harder, his tongue whipping across it as she squirmed and gasped and tried to keep from seeing Paul.

He released her arms and they fell numbly to her sides as he brought his hand up to cup and lift her breast, squeezing it as his teeth nibbled around the nipple.

'You have lovely breasts, you know. You shouldn't wear a top at all.'

She only gulped in reply.

'Don't you think she has lovely breasts, Paul?'

He bumped her round so her back was to him, then as she tried to cover her breasts, seeing Paul's eyes on them, he lifted her arms up above her head. He pinned her elbows together with one hand as he gently pushed against her back, forcing her chest out.

'Gorgeous,' Paul said.

'There aren't many sets as perfect as this,' Sean bragged.

'Nope. They're pretty damned nice,' Paul agreed, licking his lips.

Allison met his eyes, hers wide and dazed, her body now gripped by a crackling sexual electricity that was making her twitch and jerk.

Sean squeezed one of her breasts, then slid his hand down her heaving chest and over her bikini panties, cupping her crotch through them. His fingers tugged at the knot to one side and it came free. She made no attempt to move as he pulled the material away from her and dropped it to the deck.

Naked now, she stared up at Paul, almost unable to breathe for the tightness in her chest; a flush spread over her face and breasts as Sean tugged at her thigh to open her legs.

She spread them slowly, then suddenly pulled them wide with a gasp, on the edge of climax without a touch.

'She's a hot little minx, Paul,' Sean said. 'I don't know when I've ever had better than her wrapped around my cock.'

The words cut into Allison's mind like a razor and she felt a deep, intoxicating lust taking hold.

Sean continued to hold her arms together above her head at the elbows. When his other hand slipped between her thighs and squeezed her pussy she cried out, arching her back sharply as she came.

Her head jerked back quickly and repeatedly in a serious of fast, muscular spasms, her back arching as she ground herself against Sean's hand.

Paul's eyes burned into her as Sean's fingers quickly found her cleft and began to rapidly roll and stroke her burning clitoris. She cried out again, her head jerking from side to side, her body roiling and crackling with pleasure and lust.

She felt his finger pierce her and slide in deep as another rush of ecstasy poured over her raw, ragged mind. She felt it slipping upwards through the soft, hot, wet folds of her pussy, burrowing deeper as Paul watched intently.

She collapsed weakly, her head hanging low until Sean pulled her arms back to arch her back. Her glassy eyes looked at Paul as he stared hungrily, and she felt Sean's finger pumping slowly in and out of her, rubbing across her exquisitely sensitive clitoris.

She could feel Sean's erection beneath her as she tried to gain control of her breathing.

Then he stood, forcing her up as well, pulling his hand away from her crotch. He held her arms aloft as Paul moved closer, then cupped her behind before sliding his hand up her back to push her chest out.

Allison was breathing in rapid little pants and puffs as Paul looked down at her, his crotch bulging.

He reached up then hesitated. His eyes met hers and found the hunger there matched his own.

Allison gasped as his hands cupped her breasts, squeezing them upwards. His fingers dug into the malleable flesh, forcing her nipples out harder. She thought her head would explode from the pressure inside it.

A leer appeared on his face, then his right hand slipped down her body and drove in between her thighs. She gasped as he palmed her mound, then squeezed roughly. Her left leg lifted and her foot shook in mid-air as his fat, dirty thumb jammed roughly up against her clitoris and ground against it.

Her body shook, her leg jerking as he continued to grind his thumb against her clitoris. His fingers sank into the softness of her and she impaled herself on them with breathless, wanton desire, aching from the thickness, almost sobbing.

'Do you think she wants it?' Sean asked.

'I think so,' Paul growled.

Sean bent her head back further.

'Do you want it, Allison? Do you?' he whispered, sliding his hand up to cup her breast.

She couldn't speak, could only gurgle helplessly.

Paul gripped her leg and lifted it, pulling it high. She remembered the exercises she did each morning, the old ballet one she still did, and was almost doing now.

Sean pulled his hand free of her sex at last and she let out a long, wavering gasp of breath.

'Tell him you want it,' Sean whispered, 'otherwise he won't touch you.'

'I – I – I – w-wan-want it,' she said in a choked sob.

She gasped anew as he jammed her leg higher still, up and back, her thigh feeling tight and taut as her leg was forced straight up and back against her shoulder.

She didn't even see Paul's cock as Sean held her head back, but she felt it as it rubbed up and down against her sensitive mons, as it traced the line of her cleft, as it pushed in, splitting her lips. He thrust in sharply as pleasure and heat rolled through her, burying the length of his erection inside her hot, tight sheath.

'Jesus, she's hot,' Paul gasped.

Her knee was pressed against her right shoulder, her leg straight, toes pointed up at the sun high above her. She was on her toes, shaking, trembling, sobbing as the pleasure and excitement set spasms rippling through her body.

Paul slipped back and she felt his long staff sliding down her tunnel, then he thrust in again – hard, and she gasped, the breath driven from her as he impaled her. Again he slipped slowly out then once more thrust in hard, burying himself deep in her squirming, heaving belly.

'Tight,' Paul gasped.

'She hasn't been well used yet,' Sean said.

'Oh God!' she sobbed as another orgasm ripped through her.

She bucked helplessly between them, her body shaking as the pleasure boiled uncontrollably.

Paul began to thrust into her then with hard, deep, powerful strokes, not hesitating as before but pumping with unstoppable motion, his thick organ sliding back and forth between her swollen pubic lips and pushing upwards, putting pressure against her aching clitoris. The climax redoubled its strength and drove the breath from her. Her eyes widened and then rolled back.

Paul gripped her hip and thrust in deeply, then shuddered as he spent himself inside her. He clutched her tight, his fingers digging into her flesh as he emptied himself in her quaking body, then, finally, he let go, stumbling back.

Sean grabbed her leg as it started to fall, then let it down slowly, but even so she groaned as the strain on her thigh tendons eased.

He picked her up in his powerful arms, then sat back on the engine, chuckling as she trembled and gasped softly.

Eight

'That was rotten,' she said with a glare.

He grinned at her as he set the air tanks down beside the car.

'That's not what you were saying an hour ago.'

'You practically gave me to that man! A stranger!'

'You can only give what you own. I don't own you, my sweet. You were perfectly free to say no.'

'But you, you ...' She stamped her foot, at a loss for words. 'You manipulated me to the point where I wasn't thinking straight.'

'Manipulated?' He chuckled as he opened the boot. 'Let me see; I squeezed and licked at your breasts a little and slipped a hand down into your panties to finger you. Is that all it takes to get complete control of you?'

She opened her mouth indignantly.

'It seems to me you were pretty damned hot before I even touched you. Your nipples were hard as soon as you stepped outside and stayed hard right through to when old Paul was giving you his all.'

'That doesn't mean anything! It was cold!'

'Ha! It was cool in the water, not cool at all above it. Face it, my sweet, you were hot as a spitfire when I climbed out of the water. If I hadn't showed up when I did you two would have been doing it on the deck anyway.'

'We would not!'

She was far from certain about that, of course. If they

had been left alone for a longer period . . . well, but they hadn't.

'You shouldn't just grope me and strip me in front of a man like that!'

'Face it, Allison, what you've got is the guilts. You got royally screwed by a complete stranger and loved it, but that doesn't fit in with your quaint old English image of yourself. So you're trying to blame someone else for it.'

She glared at him indignantly, not at all calmed by knowing he was absolutely right.

If she had been bound, she thought, she would have felt better about it. Of course Sean had been holding her arms, so in a sense she was helpless to stop the man's brutal rutting.

But inside she knew it was her own decision. She had become aroused by being in the too-small bikini, even more aroused around Paul. She had been posing and teasing him even before Sean had come back from underwater, and her horniness had been rising steadily.

But she didn't like to think of herself as a nymphomaniac play toy of some crude man.

Why not was a question she shied away from.

'In any case, as I manfully restrained myself there I think I deserve an appropriate reward.'

'R-restrained yourself?!' she sputtered.

'Yes. I considered putting you down on all fours and taking care of my own sexual tension, but Jim was due up any time and he's something of a religious prude. However, the sight of you being ravished by Paul certainly did nothing to calm my own ardour. As such –' he grabbed her and lifted her in his arms '– I require you to submit to me now.'

She stared at him, open-mouthed, then scowled. 'Forget it.'

He set her down again and stepped back, then quickly stripped. He posed for her, shifting and turning his body, curling his arms in and making muscles. She couldn't help smiling.

'What are you doing, you great loon?'

'I'm showing you my marvellous body.'

'Why?'

'So you'll become desperately aroused.'

She laughed even as her eyes roamed his muscular physique and followed the lines of his pectoral muscles and washboard stomach. He turned and she eyed his buttocks, stifling a desire to reach forward and slap them.

'It won't work,' she said.

'Of course it will work. Women can't resist the sight of me.'

He *was* beautiful. His body was simply fabulous. She hadn't painted many nudes but she told herself that now she simply must.

'I must paint you,' she said.

'One day, my precious. In the meantime . . .'

He turned and placed his hands on his hips. 'In the meantime I would like to take you to your bed, tie you spreadeagled, and torture you for a while before mounting you like a wild beast.'

She widened her eyes.

'Would you mind terribly?'

Allison stared at him in astonishment. Never having met anyone like him she found his impudence astonishing.

'T-tie me to the bed?'

'Yes. It's not that I fear you running off, of course. It's just that you might climax so explosively you'd hurt yourself otherwise.'

'Well, of course,' she said.

He smiled and took her hand, then led her after him into her bedroom. He quickly removed the too-tight bathing suit, lifted her up and set her in the centre of the bed.

She lay there as he moved to her dresser, wondering if she were mad. Her groin was still a little sore from the force of her earlier sex on the boat and she was amazed that after so short a time she was feeling ready for another rutting. She stared up at the ceiling, wondering what manner of woman she had turned into.

'These are useless for anything else anyway,' he said, producing several of her silk scarves.

'Those are my scarves,' she protested.

'Dull and boring. You can afford better.'

He wrapped two around her wrists, two more around her ankles, then tied her to the four posts of the bed. She lay there looking up at him, feeling herself becoming mildly aroused as she pulled against the scarves.

'Now what should I do with you?' he said. 'You're completely helpless, of course. Perhaps I should invite half a dozen or so sailors in here to ravish you. Hmm, let me go and see if any are about. Oh, but first . . .'

He produced another scarf and despite her objections tied it over her eyes, blindfolding her.

'Sean!' she said accusingly as he left the room.

She listened for the sound of the floor creaking that would tell her he was back, wondering what he was actually doing. The thought of him bringing back a dozen men like Paul was exciting, in a fantasy sort of way, but she knew he wouldn't do that.

She heard the floor creak, then heard his voice.

'Come on, Fred, Jack, John, Mike, Adam. She's in here waiting for you! You've each got your five pounds I hope.'

She raised her head involuntarily, but refused to be baited, though her heart did beat somewhat quicker.

'Take your seats and have a look. I'll show you all how to drive a woman mad.'

'I know there's no one there,' she said.

She felt his weight on the bed and lay her head back, anxiously waiting for the feel of him against her.

'Now some men prefer to gag their women,' Sean said, 'but I rather enjoy hearing their cries of pleasure.'

Allison yawned enormously.

'Sometimes they get cheeky, of course, but I can take care of that,' he said.

She felt a slight touch, feathery soft across her upper chest. She strained her senses, trying to identify it. She felt it again, this time over her nipple, then down her breast. She gasped as she realised it actually *was* a feather of some kind.

She felt it trace along the curve of her breast and dust back and forth over her nipple before sliding down along her ribs.

She gasped as it tickled, pulling and straining at the scarves.

'Ah, that's a lovely sight,' he said softly, 'your back arched, your lovely breasts thrust out, the muscles moving beneath your skin.'

The feather slipped over her stomach and up along her ribs on the other side, then into her armpit briefly before sliding along her throat.

'Sean!' she groaned in complaint.

It gently caressed her cheeks, then moved down to tease her nipple, flicking lightly across it so that she wanted . . . more.

The feather slid down further; down along her stomach and tracing its way over her hip, crossing to stroke her inner thigh and dance along her tight mons.

She felt his fingers opening her sex, blushed at the knowledge he was so close to her down there, then gasped as the feather brushed against the clitoris.

'Oh!'

It brushed again and again, and she ground her hips lewdly, feeling the pleasure well up inside her, the heat igniting within her stomach. Blinded, it was as if all her other senses had grown. There was nothing to hear, however, so her mind focused entirely on the feel, on the touch against her skin.

'Sean!' she cried, the feel of the feather growing too much to bear, her clitoris throbbing and burning.

It moved off, then stroked her right nipple, then her left. The feel was tantalising, for it wasn't enough. Even while it made her body twitch and shake it wasn't ... enough.

'Sean,' she groaned.

'You see, lads? It doesn't take much to turn any woman into a randy little bitch on heat,' Sean said cheerfully.

'Bastard!'

She felt his finger against her, felt it slide inside her body, and helplessly drove herself up against it.

Then she felt something else, something that made her eyes widen beneath the scarf, made her go quite still even as her insides seemed to fairly melt with a hot, steaming upwash of pleasure and bliss.

His tongue slipped into her.

It curled and twisted, then eased up along her pink cleft and she felt it lap at her clitoris. It was incredibly soft and warm and wet, and her body ached with the wonder of it.

She groaned aloud, bucking up against him helplessly, only to have him withdraw.

'Hmm, do you like that, Miss Miller?'

'Yes! Oh yes!'

'Haven't you had that done to you before?'

'No,' she groaned.

'I see. Well, I'm not surprised. I should have thought of it before, in fact. Would you like me to continue?'

'Yes!'

'Very well. All you have to do is beg me.'

'You bastard,' she moaned. 'Please!'

'Please what?'

'P-please lick me!'

'Lick what? Your pussy? Would you like me to eat your pussy for you, love?'

'Yes! Please!'

'You know what to say.'

'Please eat my pussy, Sean,' she gasped as his feather taunted her again.

'What a trollop, begging to have her pussy eaten. Don't you think so, lads?'

The feather continued to stroke over her clitoris and she writhed helplessly.

'Sean! Please!'

His thumbs spread her open and she felt his tongue licking along the insides, then stroking upwards. She groaned in bliss, grinding herself upwards as her insides revelled in the glorious feel of his tongue against her clitoris.

'Oh God!'

'You see, lads? Get your mouth against them and they're helpless.'

'Don't stop! Oh, don't stop!'

'Ah well, I'm in no hurry.'

His hands moved over her body, his fingers squeezing her nipples, then his hands pushing in against the sides of her breasts, crushing them together.

He moved back briefly and she heard him strike a match. Moments later she cried out as she felt the sting of heat against her nipple. She felt another, then another, gasping and yelping each time. She smelt the scent of the burning wax then, and realised he had lit a candle and was tormenting her with the hot wax.

'Sean!' she cried.

'Not too eager, my sweet,' he said.

She gasped again and again as the hot little droplets of wax rained down on her nipples and breasts. She jerked from side to side but could not escape the scarves' tight bondage.

He chuckled and she felt him breaking the hardened wax away.

'Too hot, my sweet? I wouldn't want you to be uncomfortable.'

She cried out again, this time as something cold and

hard pressed against her upper chest, then slid along her body, up over her breast, slowly circling the nipple before riding over it.

It was easy to identify it as an ice cube.

'Sean! Don't!' she gasped.

He chuckled evilly, the ice cube sliding down off her breast, then up along her ribs, making her squeal and squirm as it left a cold, wet trail behind.

She writhed helplessly, squealing and crying out as the ice cube moved over her body, now over her nipple, now sliding down her belly, now along her thigh and up her ribs.

Then abruptly he abandoned it and she felt his tongue plunge into her sex. He licked hungrily, his fingers driving into her as she began to grind then buck herself up against him, gasping and moaning as her heat and arousal quickened, her mind swimming in bliss.

'Oh! Oh yes!'

It was like nothing she had ever felt in her life. It was as though his tongue were made for her, as though her sex had been waiting for something so delicious against it for ever. Her entire body thrummed with sexual energy as his tongue worked at her throbbing, burning little clitoris.

He chuckled throatily. 'How are we, my sweet? Too hot? Perhaps this will cool you off a tad.'

This time he held two pieces and slid them up both sides of her body, up and down against her ribs, then in along her armpits and over her arms.

He rolled them over her breasts, circling each nipple, then eased them down her belly and abruptly popped one inside her.

'Oh! Don't! Take it out!' she gasped.

She felt his lips against her as he sucked the cube back out. But then he pushed it back in again, sliding it in deep with his thumb. She felt its chill go through her as she squirmed and rolled her hips. Again he sucked it back out, sliding it up her body and along the nape of her neck.

She strained against the scarves, gasping and yelping with each new touch. He slid it down along her cleft once again, rolling it back and forth until abruptly pulling it free and replacing it with his mouth.

The difference was a jarring clash, from icy discomfort to soft, gentle warmth, then quickly to heat. He caught her clitoris against his lips and sucked steadily, then blew a stream of air over it before lapping energetically.

Her insides began to throb and pulse and the blood raced through her veins as pleasure overwhelmed her. She felt an orgasm rising up around her ready to crash down and opened herself to embrace it.

Abruptly he pulled back and she felt ice against her sex. She squealed in disappointment and shock as the ice slid up and down her body, cooling her down rapidly. Her curses brought only chuckles in response. Yet soon the ice was gone and again his tongue was sucking on her nipples, licking and chewing until they both strained with desire, so hard and sensitive a breeze made them flicker and sparkle.

Then his mouth moved down between her legs again and she moaned as he began to lap at her clitoris. His finger plunged into her aching tunnel, pumping in and out as his tongue rolled over her clitoris. Allison felt her body floating on a sea of pleasure, felt the waters rushing faster and faster.

Then he drew back once more, and ice jarringly took his place. She almost cried with disappointment and cursed him roundly.

Again his tongue worked her up to the edge of the abyss, only to have ice draw her back, then again, then a final time.

She thought she was being driven mad by the constant stimulation, by the way her nervous system was led racing up to the edge of climax only to be yanked back. She ached with the need to come, yet could do nothing to satisfy the craving within her.

Again his expert tongue worked her up towards the heavens, turned her body into a thing of throbbing, feverish need. She prayed silently, desperately, for release, for him to let her come. She felt him pull back and almost screamed, yet instants later he thrust his erection deep inside her.

She felt his manhood drive deep, then tear back, stroking powerfully in and out even as his fingers stroked across her clitoris. She felt the orgasm break over her and opened her mouth to scream but couldn't breathe. Her body shuddered violently, her mind exploding. Her body was racked by convulsions as a blinding torrent of heat swamped her in ecstasy.

She thought she would die, but didn't care. She rode the stormwave to the point of delirium, the longest, most powerful orgasm of her life, then collapsed breathless as it slowly, finally subsided.

The next several days passed in relative calm. They talked, ate, slept, made love, swam and watched television. Allison remained nude or wore some of her sexy lingerie. Sean often tied her wrists behind her back, and sometimes bound her elbows back as well.

Allison found herself tremendously excited when he did, though she never asked for it. Something prevented her from admitting so openly how intrigued and aroused she was by such helplessness.

The hole in his boat was quickly repaired, though it had to be thoroughly washed out because of the salt water which had got inside, and everything damaged by the water, including the mattress on the bed, needed to be replaced. Sean elected to sail for the nearest harbour, Braceridge, where he knew he could find replacements.

She packed boxes and suitcases but shortly after the

boat had set off she found that most had been left behind in the car.

'You won't need them. We'll get you a new wardrobe with more interesting clothes,' he said when she confronted him.

'I like my clothes!' she exclaimed.

'They're boring and drab. You need brighter things, tighter things, shorter skirts and higher heels.'

'You want me to wear high heels on your boat?' she asked sarcastically.

'No. That's why I kept the tennis shoes. Don't worry, we'll find you plenty to wear in Braceridge.'

'And who's going to pay for it?'

'Well, me if you like.'

'Really?'

'Why not?' He shrugged magnanimously.

'Well, they'd better be nice is all I'm saying. And I get to pick them.'

'Oh no,' he laughed, 'we're not putting you in nun's clothes. I'll pick them.'

'I'm not going to dress like a slut,' she warned.

'Why? I thought you wanted to *be* a slut.'

She had no answer to that.

She wandered along the deck, looking down into the water. She was wearing the pink bikini, and very much aware of how tight it was against her breasts and buttocks.

The wind ruffled her hair and she constantly brushed it aside as she sat in the bow of the boat, cross-legged, and stared at the sea ahead.

She was filled with a profound sense of uneasiness. She wasn't used to uncertainty of any kind. Her life had been nothing if not secure, with her always knowing what awaited her on the morrow.

Now she had no idea. She didn't even know where she would sleep tonight. She had her credit cards with her and that provided some sense of security. She could always find a hotel room somewhere and check herself in; rent a quiet, comfortable box in which to hide.

She had no idea what Sean planned for her. The scuba diving sounded interesting, especially somewhere like the Caribbean, but she was far from sure she wanted to experiment in skydiving and the like.

Already she was missing her cosy little house.

She wandered back, hand on the rail, then dropped into the rear deck, slipping past him to go below. He reached out and slipped a finger into the rear of her bikini bottom, pulling her up short.

'We're away from the shore. You can get rid of that now.'

She thought about arguing, but didn't. It was tight and pushed in uncomfortably against her mound, as well as her breasts. She unfastened it and slipped it off, feeling a familiar little rush of heat as she stripped naked before him.

He nodded and returned his attention to the wheel as she padded down the stairs and into the main cabin.

She really ought to take the opportunity to get a bit of sun, she thought. Unfortunately, she had not thought to bring any suntan lotion. Sunbathing wasn't a normal activity for her.

She got a book, anyway, as well as a portable radio, brought them up on deck, walked past him and up to the bow of the boat, then sat back and turned on the radio.

She lay back on her side and began to read, thinking as she did how odd it was to be lying naked on this strange man's boat. If someone had suggested she would be doing that a week or so ago she'd have thought them mad.

She looked up half an hour later to find him standing over her, holding two thick leather straps.

'What are those?' she asked idly.

'I had a sailmaker sew these up for me,' he said, showing them to her.

'What are they for?'

'I'll show you.'

He squatted beside her and took her wrist, then wrapped one of the straps round her wrist, buckling it tightly. She licked her lips as she gazed at it, noting the heavy ring set into the leather.

'How does that feel?'

'OK,' she said with a gulp.

He held her other hand out and slipped the other strap around it, and buckled it tightly. The leather was tough but soft and thick, and she gazed up at him in anticipation as he grinned lewdly.

'We'll get much more professional stuff at Braceridge, of course.'

'If I let you,' she said.

He snorted and lifted her to her feet, then led her back by the hand until they were next to the main mast. He untied a rope anchored to a ring, then slipped it through the rings on both of the leather straps. She watched her wrists snap together and felt a rush of adrenalin and heat.

He stepped back a pace, then turned to a heavy crank and began turning it. Allison gasped as she felt the slack tighten and her wrists pulled upwards. She cocked her head back and saw the rope running up the length of the mast.

Then she was pulled up sharply against the mast and turned quickly, her back to it, her hands high above her head.

He turned the crank again and she gasped as the rope pulled up tighter, forcing her to her toes.

'Well now, fair damsel,' he purred, cupping her breast, then sliding his hand up and down her tautly stretched body. 'Now that we're at sea I can do anything I want to you. I can reveal to you my job as a white slaver.'

He chuckled evilly, his hand slipping between her legs, fingers stroking against her soft cleft.

'Ah yes, you'll fetch a pretty penny in the Middle East,' he said, sliding his fingers along her cleft. 'Arab sheiks are always looking for pretty young things for their harems.'

'Maybe they'll buy you then,' she retorted.

'Snotty talk like that is not acceptable, wench,' he growled in what she presumed was his best attempt at a pirate accent.

He slid his hand into her hair, then tugged it back, twisting it until she yelped. 'Apologise to your master.'

'I – I apologise,' she gasped.

'You apologise to your master. Call me master.'

She felt her heart skip a beat as she stared up at him. Her muscles spasmed and she felt the heat burning hotter as his finger continued to stroke against her sex.

'Master,' she groaned.

'Filthy little slave,' he said. 'What are you? Hmmm? Say it. Tell me what you are, slave.'

'I – I'm a filthy little slave, master,' she gasped.

'Again.'

'I'm a filthy little slave, master. I'm a nasty, slutty little tramp!'

The words burned in her mind.

'And what can I do with you, slave?'

'A-anything you want, master,' she panted.

He chuckled cruelly, then reached down and gripped her right leg, lifting it, raising it as Paul had a few days earlier.

Allison groaned as the leg rose.

He pressed the knee straight back against her shoulder, then straightened the leg, forcing the back of her foot all the way back to the mast. He reached up then and tangled the ropes around it, holding it in place.

Then he stepped back to admire his handiwork as Allison groaned and panted for breath, looking up, then down at herself, then back at him, excitement rushing through her as she contemplated her predicament.

'Perhaps a day or two in that position and you'll never close your legs again,' he said with a smirk.

His hand stroked back and forth along her lewdly displayed sex, then he dropped to his knees, and Allison let out an explosive gasp of pleasure as his tongue slipped across her clitoris.

His fingers eased her open and his tongue began to leisurely explore her pink flesh, teasing her with its light touch as it caressed her clit, then stroking along the inside of her lips before pushing up into her soft, moist centre.

She started to grind herself against him, the pleasure catching hold and enveloping her mind in a warm, sensuous mist.

Her body jerked awkwardly against the mast as she gasped and groaned in pleasure.

Then he pulled back with a grin. He reached up and undid her ankle, then lowered her leg slowly to the deck.

'What . . .'

He returned to the crank and started turning it, and with a gasp she was lifted off her feet. The thick leather dug into her wrists as she hung there gasping, legs jerking feebly.

He stroked her sex again, then gave it a kiss before going back behind her to the wheelhouse. She moaned helplessly, trying to look behind her, determined not to beg him for relief.

Her shoulders soon began to ache, as did her arms and wrists, but she paid that little heed.

She was wrapped up in a fantasy of herself as a helpless prisoner of pirates, hung naked from the mast, later to be ravished by dozens of evil thugs.

She squeezed her thighs together, gasping as she jerked lightly on the end of the rope. The gentle motions of the waves made her sway slowly, her buttocks grinding lightly against the wooden mast each time the ship hit a wave.

She was backed into a corner, staring at them all with wide eyes. They laughed as they grabbed her, one particular blond pirate tearing at her dress until she was naked. He spun her about, lifting her arms up high above her and pinning them together at the elbows with one huge hand as he presented her to the crew.

'Now what shall we do with this little lovely, my lads?' he asked the gathered ruffians.

Their reply was a long growl of hunger as dozens of pairs of eyes stared lustfully at her naked body, their eyes sliding over every soft curve, their crotches bulging with excitement.

She groaned, bouncing even more against the mast as her legs writhed and flailed. She twisted around and found herself pressed face-first into the mast. Her legs wrapped around it and she gasped as her soft mons jammed in against another rope.

She began to grind herself against the rope, her legs grinding her pelvis up and down as heady sexual bliss filled her mind with fantasies and pleasure.

Her legs tightened around the mast, sliding her body up and down in quick, desperate motions, her breasts sliding along the hard wood, her nipples on fire.

Then the rope holding her wrists slackened and she gasped as she slid downwards. Sean had arrived without her even noticing, and had lowered her so her feet were again touching the deck.

'I didn't say you could masturbate with my mast,' he said dryly. 'Slaves don't get to jerk off without their master's permission.'

'You bastard!' she gasped.

'Oh, naughty, naughty.'

He turned her to face the mast again, then smacked her behind with sharp, hard spanks as she yelped and cried out in pain.

He turned her round again, grinning as he spread her legs.

She stared at him, gasping for breath, waiting for him to touch her.

He slipped to his knees in front of her and pursed his lips as he reached for her sex. His fingers deftly spread her open, then he blew a stream of air up and down her sex before turning away.

He quickly tied a soft rope around her right ankle, then fed the rope round behind the mast, wrapping it round her other ankle and then pulling both ankles back so they were pulled far apart and back alongside the mast.

He tied the rope, then raised it, sliding it round her right leg just above the knee. As with her ankles he fed it behind the mast and round her other leg, forcing it back hard. Again he lifted the rope, this time forcing it up, though not without some effort, between her right thigh and the mast.

He encircled her thigh a bare inch or two from her mound, then tugged the rope back behind the mast and round her other thigh. He bound the ropes together behind her and pulled it up, sliding it over a hook.

He still had plenty of rope to spare. He wrapped it round her hips, then her waist, then her lower chest, binding her firmly. He criss-crossed her chest, cinching the rope in tight, then circled her just under the arms.

Finally he reached up and unbound her wrists, only to pull them back behind the mast and tie them there, pulling up hard and tight.

He stepped back to examine her appreciatively, then dropped to his knees again and began to lap against her cleft, his tongue light and gentle as she quivered and groaned and tried unsuccessfully to grind herself against him.

She could not move an inch, however. And his tongue moved infuriatingly slowly and lightly across her glistening flesh.

'Faster!' she gasped.

'Slaves don't give orders,' he said. 'Slaves beg their masters if they want things.'

'Please! Please, master!'

'Please what?'

'P-please! Lick me! Please lick me, master!'

'Lick what?'

'My . . . you know! Please!'

He rose, sliding his hands slowly over her body, tweaking her straining nipples, lightly caressing the underside of each breast.

'Beg me, slave.'

'Please! Please lick me, master!'

'Why? Because you're a sex-crazed little tramp?'

'Y-yes!'

'Because you're a nasty, craven little tramp?'

'Yes! Please!'

'Tell me what a slut you are. Tell me how badly you want my tongue up your soft, hot little hole.'

'Bastard!' she gasped.

'Perhaps I'll leave you like this and go and watch a movie.'

'No! Please! I'm a slut! I'm a cheap, sex-hungry little tramp! Please, master!'

He slid his hand over her head and face, pushing his fingers against her open mouth, then into it.

'First my tongue, and now you want my manhood inside you? Maybe you'd like my fingers, as well, hmm, slave girl? Would you like that? Would you like me to shove my fingers up into your hot little sex?'

She moaned and licked at his fingers, sucking on them appealingly as she begged him with her eyes. He pumped his fingers in and out of her mouth, twisting them around inside, probing at the inside of her cheeks, twisting her head from side to side.

He leant closer, his mouth against her ear.

'Do you want me to masturbate you?'

'Y-yess!'

'Say it then.'

'Please, please masturbate me,' she begged. 'Please masturbate me, master!'

He smirked and slipped his fingers against her swollen opening, rubbing the tips of his spit-wet fingers up and down against her clitoris as she gasped and moaned and strained against the ropes.

'Faster! Oh, please, master!'

He rubbed harder and faster and her head jerked against the mast, rolling and twitching, eyes rolling back as her body strained rhythmically against the ropes.

'Oh God yes!' she gasped as he rubbed and stroked against her moist sex.

He paused. 'What was it you wanted me to do again?' he asked idly.

'Masturbate me! Masturbate me! Please! Please masturbate me!'

She gasped as he started to rub again. Her jaw slackened, her words slurred. Her head began to tremble as it pulled slowly backwards, her eyes closing. A low gurgling moan came from her as he rubbed harder and faster, her body quivering, straining desperately against the ropes, her groin desperately trying to push out against his fingers.

Then she made an incoherent cry of pleasure, her chest thrusting out, her breasts grinding against the ropes as she gnashed her teeth and hurled herself from side to side in uncontrollable passion.

He continued rubbing until with a final heave she collapsed against the ropes, groaning breathlessly. Then with a grin he turned away, going below.

Nine

Braceridge was not large as towns went. But as a coastal town it was well equipped with all manner of gear for outfitting boats and ships. Sean had little difficulty purchasing equipment to replace what was damaged and destroyed when the *Wanderer* went down.

They also shopped for clothing for her, things that Sean said would be more attractive and fashionable on their journey south.

While Allison reluctantly agreed her own clothes were not exactly stylish and was trying to force herself to experiment a bit more, her opinion and his were radically different when it came to judging what was and wasn't acceptable.

She tended towards loose trousers, sweaters and blazers, while Sean kept buying skin-tight miniskirts, tops and dresses.

They compromised. She bought the loose, comfortable clothes she wanted, and let him buy the sexy things he wanted.

She hoped she would eventually work up the courage to wear the things, though she didn't know when. But thinking of the way Paul looked at her in that too-tight bikini made her loins ache and her mind swirl with sexual imagery.

Wearing a new brown sports jacket, white slacks, a green blouse and brown shoes – which to her mind all looked quite smart – they went to a hairstylist and

Allison sat anxiously as Sean and the woman behind her discussed what kind of cut would look best on her.

Allison had never really had time to have her hair styled before. Or the inclination, for that matter. She kept it straight and mostly long, and didn't do much with it beyond blow-drying it after every wash.

She vetoed most of the things the two offered up, and finally settled for a trim, but with a little wave, and some work on the front so her hair would sweep across her forehead in a more dramatic fashion.

She was feeling a little contrite as she and Sean got back into the rented car and drove away.

'I'm sorry,' she said. 'I suppose I'm just not ready for too big a change at once.'

'Not ready? You've gone from masturbating by yourself at night to spending hours naked and bound, from being a near virgin to letting strange men do you without so much as buying you a drink first. And you're not ready for a new haircut or clothes?'

He snorted, then reached across, shoving his fingers between her thighs and cupping her mound. He squeezed repeatedly as she swallowed and looked out of the window, worried about being observed.

Then he lifted his hand briefly, undid the front of her loose trousers and plunged his hand down inside.

'Sean!'

'Not ready for a sudden change?'

His fingers slipped up and down her cleft as she gasped and wriggled worriedly. Then they pushed slowly inside her, stroking across her clitoris. He pressed his thumb down on her little button as his fingers plunged in and out of her warm little opening, and she felt a wave of heat and desire rising up from her groin as she spread her legs and slumped lower in her seat.

'Do you want to be a hot little slut or not?' he demanded.

'I – I do,' she gulped.

'Say it!'

'I want to be a slut!' she groaned. 'I want to be a hot, randy slut!'

'Then start dressing like one. Stop pretending!'

He drew his hand back, leaving her sighing softly. Her hands slipped to her groin and she squeezed it as she closed her legs.

'Now then,' he said, 'let's get some clothes for a hot little tramp like you.'

The dress they bought was not quite as bad as the sluttish clothes he had purchased elsewhere. It was a soft brown fabric, not nearly as tight across the chest, and the skirt wasn't quite as short. However, the skirt was both shorter and tighter than anything she had ever worn before and she fought to keep from blushing as she walked out of the shop in it, displaying what she thought of as a shocking amount of leg.

Again, once in the car Sean slipped his hand between her legs and into the thong she was wearing, pumping two fingers up and down inside her as his thumb manipulated her clitoris. She groaned unhappily when he slipped them out and pulled to the kerb.

'Just another minute,' she begged.

'No chance. Come on.'

She pouted and folded her arms over her chest, not getting out until he went round the car and opened her door.

'What now?' she sighed as he took her hand and led her into another shop.

This one was different right from the start, however: grotty and dark and small. One shelf ran the length of the narrow shop, and the first thing she came face to face with was row upon row of rubber penises.

She giggled at first, but then as Sean gave her a significant look blushed, looking round her even as her heart began to pound with both anxiety and excitement.

'Which do you think would be your size?' he asked.

'You're not going to buy one, are you?' she whispered.

'Damned right I am, probably two or three.'

'But . . .'

'Hmmm, maybe this one,' he said, lifting up a long, thick pink rubber dildo.

He looked at her, then handed it to her. 'Hold this,' he ordered.

'Bugger you!'

She tossed it back to him and he glared at her. She scowled back.

He led her further down the aisle, plucking another big dildo from the shelf, then a long vibrator with batteries, then another that plugged into the wall.

'People will think we're perverts!' she hissed, her head turning from side to side.

'I am a pervert, and you're a slut, remember?'

Edible oils and lotions were next, then a selection of bondage equipment, including metal handcuffs and studded leather wrist restraints.

'Ahh, old-fashioned stuff,' he said with a grin, plucking down heavy metal shackles and chains.

A man passed near them, looking at the shackles, then at Allison. Her face burnt at what he must have thought.

'That man . . .'

'Thinks you're going to get chained up and screwed. You are. So? He's probably thinking how lucky I am and wishing he could have you naked and in chains.'

Her mouth opened and closed and she glared at him.

But she looked nervously back and felt a rush of heat at the realisation he was almost certainly right. That man would love to tie her up and use her, she thought, even though he didn't know her at all. Maybe he would even think about her the next time he masturbated, and imagine he had her at his mercy.

Every time one of the men in the shop saw her his

eyes discreetly moved across her body, and she felt another little flush of heat.

They moved to the end of the aisle, where there was a collection of whips and crops and canes which Sean examined closely.

'Forget it,' she said.

'Bad girls need a little discipline now and then.'

'Not me.'

'No one asked your opinion, slave.'

He piled the things he had picked up already on a glass counter, then took down a thin crop and swung it from side to side. It cut through the air with a soft hiss. He bent it to test its flexibility, then nodded slowly.

'This looks just about right. Do you think that would sting, slave?' he asked in a normal tone of voice.

A man in the next aisle looked up and she blushed and turned her face away.

'Do you?'

'Yes,' she whispered.

'Maybe it's too lightweight. You're a very bad girl sometimes.'

Once again he spoke in a normal tone of voice, and the man in the next aisle peeked over the top at her.

Sean's hand slipped down to cup her behind measuringly, and Allison caught her breath, her eyes flicking from side to side even as the heat rushed upwards into her chest.

Then Sean's hand was pressing against her back between her shoulders, bending her over against the glass case.

'S-Sean!' she whispered.

'Are you going to be a bad girl?' he asked.

She drew in a deep breath.

'No,' she whispered.

She bent over more, then her eyes widened and she shuddered as she felt his fingertips sliding up and down her thighs. She felt the back of her skirt lifting slowly, slipping up and over the soft flesh of her taut bare buttocks.

She cringed inwardly, knowing the man in the next aisle was viewing her shamelessly bare behind, but the heat inside her was a live thing, devouring all fears and concerns, pumping up her desire to a scalding need.

The skirt slipped up higher, baring her behind completely, save for the small cover the thong afforded, then she felt the thin crop stroke along her skin.

She braced herself as she heard a short hiss, then gasped as it struck her behind. It stung, and she clenched her fingers into tight fists beneath her chest.

'Hmmm. That is light. Maybe a heavier model. Or maybe I should just use more force.'

She heard the hiss again, a little longer, and let out a muffled groan as the stinging bit into her behind.

'Can I help you?' she heard.

She turned her head slightly and saw another man, the man who had been behind the cash register.

'I was just testing this to see if it was heavy enough,' Sean said airily.

She turned her red face away, closing her eyes.

'And is it?'

'I think it might be.'

She felt her skirt sliding back down. Then a moment later he pulled lightly on her hair and she straightened, still trying to look away from the man standing behind them.

'Tell me, do you have any nipple clamps?'

'As a matter of fact we do.'

Sean took her arm and followed the man. She was aware that at least two men were watching them and her insides swirled with turmoil as arousal fought shame.

'Ah, these look nice,' Sean said.

Allison looked up, her mind so flustered she had no idea what he was even doing. Something to do with nipples? There were chains hanging from little hooks, small, fine gold and silver chains, most about a foot or so long.

Sean took one down and examined it.

'Do you like this, slave?' he asked.

She flushed again as the shop assistant leered at her. She nodded abruptly, looking away.

'We should try them on,' he said.

He reached behind her neck and unsnapped the dress.

Allison stiffened in shock, her arms starting to rise to prevent the top of her dress from going down, but then she halted her arms in place, overcome by a tremendous wave of sexual need as Sean, pausing only a moment to see her reaction, lowered the front of her dress.

She had no bra beneath, and her nipples ached as the cool air struck them.

She was almost shaking with excitement and felt a sudden terrible fear that she was so hot, so wet, her juices would seep out and trickle down her thigh.

She watched, eyes wide, as Sean took one end of the gold chain and pressed it against her right nipple. She saw that there was a small loop in the end, and as she watched Sean slipped it over her straining nipple. He then twisted a tiny screw and the little loop closed tightly.

She gasped, her nipple throbbing, then aching, then burning as he tightened it further.

'Ow!' she finally gasped.

He slipped his fingers along the length of the chain and placed the other end against her left nipple, sliding the loop over her rigid pink bud, then closing it until she again gasped.

He let go of the chain, which dangled loosely down, hanging between her nipples.

'Looks very nice,' Sean said.

Allison could barely talk. Her nipples burned like fire and her fingernails were digging into the palms of her hands even as she squeezed her thighs together.

'It will certainly help to keep her on her toes,' the man said lasciviously.

'Oh yes,' Sean said, chuckling.

He gripped the loose chain, then lifted it, tugging on her nipples and forcing her on to her toes, forcing her to arch her back to raise her breasts higher.

He let the chain drop with a grin, then lifted her dress and fastened it behind her neck.

'We'll take that one.'

They moved on to a collection of rubber and plastic clothing, many with studs and heavy straps and buckles.

There the man took her size, then he and Sean had her try on a pair of thigh-high, glistening plastic boots that had the highest stiletto heels she had ever seen in her life. She could barely walk in them. He purchased them and a similar pair of shoes, then a kind of plastic bustier that merely cupped her breasts without covering an inch of them, a heavy studded collar, like a dog collar, gloves that matched the boots and which came up well past her elbows, and a padded blindfold.

'These are every man's dream, of course,' the man said as he indicated a series of gags.

'Oh yes. We must get a few of those,' Sean said, nodding.

They finally moved back to the goods he had already collected, and piled most of it into her arms. That made the breath hiss out of her since it pushed against her throbbing nipples.

'I can get you a bag,' the man offered.

'No need. We have everything except . . .'

He held up one of the plastic dildos. 'This.'

He looked at Allison, who cast her eyes down.

He chuckled, then slipped his hand beneath her skirt.

She moaned softly, but made no effort to resist him. She shifted her feet further apart as he tugged the crotch of her thong aside, then pressed the rounded nose of the rubber phallus against her entrance.

She felt her lips straining as they were pushed in and back, forced apart by the thickness of the dildo. Then it was sliding up inside her, over and through the tight silken folds of her dripping sex until Sean's fingers pressed against her.

Then the palm of his hand was pushed against the base of the dildo and he jammed it up.

She let out a soft cry, stiffening in both pain and pleasure.

He took her arm and led her up to the front of the shop, where the man slowly – she thought it took an eternity – tallied up the amount they owed.

Allison didn't even know what it was. Her insides were twisting and bubbling, her mind spinning. She was sweating heavily and trying to control her trembling body as the sex heat roared in hungry desire. Every inch of her body seemed raw and sensitive, and she knew that almost anything would drive her over the edge into a tremendous orgasm.

There were now half a dozen men in the store apart from the sales assistant, and the thought of having a violent climax which would draw the attention of every one of them was both terrifying and darkly arousing.

Then Sean was putting a large bag into her arms and lifting two others as he led her out of the shop. She stumbled and almost fell, but his strong grip on her arm supported her to the car and opened the boot.

He took her bag and put it in the back with the others, then opened her door and helped her inside. She sat down slowly, gasping and hissing as the seat pushed up against the small section of the dildo which still protruded from between her vaginal lips.

He got in his side and turned, grinning at her.

'Bored?' he asked.

She didn't answer.

He chuckled and reached behind her neck, undid her dress and tugged it down to bare her breasts.

She saw the man from the shop looking out at her but didn't care. The pressure was too high, too intense. She jerked her legs apart and grabbed at the base of the dildo, pushing up as her fingers sought her clitoris and rubbed it furiously.

Sean tugged repeatedly at the chain, making her nipples explode. She knew, deep inside her, that the shop assistant was watching, but that only added to the intensity of the firestorm that swept through her mind and body. Her head slammed back against the headrest repeatedly as her legs and feet jerked and twisted violently on the floor and a high-pitched, warbling cry of sheer ecstasy was torn from her tight throat.

The car started and pulled away from the kerb, but she didn't notice. She lay slumped in the seat, jerking and twitching, eyes closed and mouth wide.

'Now you're a slut,' Sean said, smiling.

Ten

Sean checked them into a hotel for the evening. By then she had her scattered wits back together – mostly. She was aware enough to blush as the receptionist eyed her. Wearing the little minidress and high heels was uncomfortable enough. But the chain was still attached to her nipples, still biting into them; and they were swollen and fat, pushing out obviously against the tight top of her dress.

And despite the intensity of the orgasm that had threatened to tear her apart earlier, the hot, consuming sexual desire had hardly faded at all from her overheated body.

They went up to their room and were no sooner inside then Sean peeled her dress up and over her head. He tugged her thong down and off, leaving her wearing nothing but the chain dangling between her swollen nipples.

'Well, my sweet, what should I do with you?' he asked, sliding his hand down to her mound and pushing up against the dildo there.

'Anything you want!' she gasped.

'Well, now *that* sounds interesting.'

He opened the box which contained the long black boots and winked at her. She grabbed them and drew them on, zipping them high up along her legs and then standing there unsteadily on the stiletto heels.

Sean upended one of the bags on the bed, then fished among the contents and drew out a short, thick black strap. He winked at her, then turned her back to him. She pulled her arms behind her and shuddered with excitement as she felt the strap slide around her upper arms, ease down to just above her elbows, then slowly close, forcing her arms back sharply.

She gasped in discomfort as her shoulders ached and her elbows were forced together, but her insides throbbed and pulsed with wicked delight.

Sean buckled the strap in place, then slipped another around her wrists, binding them flat against each other.

He led her over to a very narrow table, a telephone table no more than eight or ten inches wide that sat against the wall. Above it was a small picture and he lifted the picture off to bare the hook behind it.

Then he gripped the centre of the chain pinching on her nipples and tugged it up and out.

'Ow!' she gasped as he forced her to bend forward over the table.

He slipped the chain over the hook, then slid his hand over her bare behind, stroking and squeezing it.

He returned to the bed, bringing back two pairs of handcuffs. He snapped one around each of her ankles, then forced her legs wide apart and snapped the handcuffs to the two legs of the table.

'How do you feel, slave?' he whispered, pulling the hair back from her ear. 'A prisoner to my desires, helpless against my lewd, perverted wishes?'

His hand slipped around her waist and down between her legs, a single finger sliding along her cleft.

'Do you want me inside you?'

She whimpered and nodded jerkily.

'Slave. Nasty little tramp. I bet you don't even care whose it is either. If I invited Paul here you'd be just as glad to get him up your hot little pussy, wouldn't you?'

'Yes! Oh yes!' she gasped weakly.

His hand pulled back around and caressed the crease between her buttocks before sliding slowly down between her thighs. He gripped the tip of the dildo with his fingers, then drew it downwards. He pulled it halfway free, then thrust it back deep, making her quiver and moan.

'Hot sexy tramp,' he whispered, slapping her behind.

He pulled the dildo back down, then thrust it up again – hard, forcing her up on to her toes as she trembled and moaned.

He began to pump the dildo slowly inside her and she ground herself lewdly back, helpless to resist the fiery lust that had hold of her mind. She found herself wishing he had done this in the shop, right in front of all those men, wishing . . .

Sean drove the thing up deep, burying it inside her, then pulled his hand away. He caressed her backside for a few seconds, then turned away, moving to the bed and transferring many of the packages of clothes and sex toys into dresser drawers.

'Sean!' she groaned.

'Yes, my sweet?'

'C-come back!'

'I'm busy at the moment. Amuse yourself, will you?'

'You bastard!'

'Naughty, naughty.'

Allison groaned in frustration. She was bent awkwardly forward at the waist, yet even so, with her legs spread as they were, the chain was pulling uncomfortably at her nipples, distorting the roundness of her breasts as her nipples were stretched.

The thick dildo felt delicious inside her. She loved the sensation of fullness. Yet it wasn't moving, and in her present position there was nothing she could do to stimulate herself, not even rub against something.

She knew he was taunting her, and her pride wanted her to resist, to stand as she was and ignore him, to see how long he himself could stay away from her, to ignore what must be quite an erotic sight to him.

But she realised almost at once that she could only lose such a battle. Sean had apparently had a great deal of experience in such things, and so was probably not nearly as aroused as she was.

Her nipples burned, her shoulders ached, and her back was uncomfortable from maintaining her half bent over position. But most of her discomfort was coming from the throbbing heat between her trembling legs.

'Come back here and do something!' she demanded, turning her head.

'Do what, my sweet?'

'You know what! Fuck me!'

'Such crude words for a sensitive artist to use. Surely you can put your case in a more literate manner.'

Allison groaned, twisting from side to side, her legs pulling feebly against the handcuffs.

Sean moved over behind her and grinned, his fingers easing the hair back from her ear as he leant in and licked at the nape of her neck.

She turned her head sharply, pressing her lips against his and he cupped and squeezed one of her breasts, making her wince as it tugged harder against the chain.

His right hand coasted slowly down her spine, fingers caressing her satiny flesh until he was fondling her out-thrust buttocks, squeezing and massaging them. His other hand eased down her stomach then and in-between her trembling thighs.

He cupped her mound, palming it. The dildo was now almost fully inside her, the base only an inch outside her straining pubic lips. Sean's fingers circled her sex, then began to rub softly against her moist, sensitive button.

She gasped and threw her head back, grinding against his hand as the heat roared up inside her.

Then his hand abandoned her behind only to slap down sharply across it.

'Ow!' she gasped.

'Naughty little tramp,' he whispered, his finger continuing to stroke back and forth against her clitoris.

Again his right hand cracked down on her buttocks, then again, slowly, measuringly, squeezing the soft flesh between slaps as he whispered abuse in her ear, abuse that sounded wrenchingly exciting.

'Hot little sex slave. Bound and chained for the whip, are you? Would you like me to whip your round bottom? Do you think I should bring up a row of sailors to line up behind you and use you? You'd like that, wouldn't you? Tramp. Slut. Whore.'

His hand slapped repeatedly down against her behind, but the sharp little stinging pains could not fight back the thrumming pleasure that filled her body. Instead she found the little shocks blending with the heat inside her, like petrol on flames it burned only hotter as she gulped in air and laid her head well back, eyes closed.

His left hand suddenly palmed her mound again as his right slipped down beneath her buttocks. He linked fingers and then heaved up.

Allison's eyes shot open and she gurgled in a mixture of pain and shocked pleasure, the pressure of his hands jamming the dildo fully into her soft, weeping sex; forcing it the last inch, somehow burying it entirely inside her trembling body as an orgasm bloomed like a starburst inside her.

She sobbed in dazed pleasure, her head bouncing helplessly, her legs spasming as Sean jerked up repeatedly against her crotch, lifting her right off the floor only to let her drop back again. Then his fingers came apart and his right hand began slapping furiously against her behind as two fingers of his left found her clitoris and mashed against it with blurring speed.

Her mind overloaded and her vision swam, then she sagged weakly, uncaring of the pain as she pulled heavily on the chain.

Sean held her up, then slipped the chain over the hook before letting her lean against the wall. He bent and removed the handcuffs from her ankles, then carried her back on to the bed and took off the high boots.

He unstrapped her arms and wrists, then massaged her shoulders and upper arms before kissing her lightly on the head and cheek.

'I think you need to be cleaned up a little,' he said.

He picked her up and carried her into the bathroom, then set her down on the edge of the counter, letting her slump back against the wall as he pulled soap and washbag from under the cabinet.

He hummed softly to himself as he grinned at her, then ran the water. He gripped her thighs and pulled her away from the wall, letting her slump down even more, then spread her legs wide, lifting her feet and setting them on the edge of the counter.

He rubbed water into her groin, soaking it, then soaped it. His soapy fingers glided easily over her soft flesh, and she sighed softly.

Then she felt a tight little tug at her pubic hair. She opened her eyes and looked between her breasts to see a razor in his hands.

As she watched he slowly and carefully shaved along the top of her mound, slicing through her soft thatch of pubic hair.

'Wha-what are you doing?' she asked weakly.

'Shaving you.'

She thought about that for a long moment, trying to understand it.

'Why?' she sighed.

'Why not?'

She couldn't think of a reason. If he wanted to trim her pubic hair he was welcome to it. It wasn't something she enjoyed doing herself, and the only reason she had was that the sexy lingerie she liked to wear was too high cut not to.

He shaved carefully, the razor sliding along her thigh and buttocks, up and down alongside her cleft as his fingers probed at her to tighten the skin. It didn't occur to her at first that he was trimming far closer than she ever had, and then suddenly she realised that he wasn't trimming but removing everything.

Oddly, the realisation neither shocked nor embarrassed her. She wondered briefly if she ought to stop him, but then decided there was little point by then.

It was as if she were slightly intoxicated, caring little for the consequences, only for immediate pleasure. She was languorous in the aftermath of her climax and in the soft bliss that clung to her at her exciting sexual escapades.

Even as she half lay, half sat there, legs spread, she felt little flushes of heat at being so lewdly exposed to him. Her flesh was warm, her nipples still tightly clamped with the chain hanging across her chest between them. She still had the dildo buried inside her, and it ached, but ached pleasantly.

Now Sean's fingers were moving deftly over the soapy slick entrance to her sex, stroking and pressing as the shaver cut away her hair.

She wondered what it would look like, if it would be as lewd as she imagined.

And then he was splashing water over her groin, washing away the soap and stubble. She felt a little thrill of heat as he ran his hand over her, amazed at how different the sensation was without any pubic hair between her flesh and his.

He grinned at her, then his body began to sink below the edge of the sink, easing down until only his head was visible to her. She watched, eyes blinking rapidly as his hands moved back and forth over her buttocks, thighs and sex.

Then she felt his tongue sliding up and down her narrow cleft, using little pressure at first, then easing in between her damp pussy lips, sliding up and down her furrow and probing deeper into her small hole.

Her juices started to flow anew and she groaned in weary pleasure as she spread her legs wider.

But he stood up then, and much to her chagrin lifted her off the counter and set her down in the bath, pushing her on to all fours and then running his hand slowly over her body.

She stared down at the white enamel beneath her, her hair falling down around her face and blinding her to all else as the water was turned on.

She raised her head momentarily to see him take a hand shower from the corner of the bath. Then the water poured down around her and she stared downwards again.

Her head and shoulders and back were quickly soaked. The pressure of the hand shower moved up and down her body, in between her legs, then under to spray against her breasts. Water poured down from her hair as the shower was turned off.

A moment later soap was applied to her back, and his big hands began to move over her shoulders and back. She groaned as his hands reached under to knead and rub her swollen breasts, soaping them up heavily in the process.

He soaped her legs above the knee, then pulled her left foot up and back. His hands kneaded and massaged it as he rubbed soap into it. Then they slid upwards along her ankle and lower leg to the knee, his hands gliding over a layer of slick, slippery soap.

He released her foot, letting her knee come down again, then pulled the other foot back and soaped that, squeezing and rubbing her toes, rolling her foot on her ankle as his thumbs pressed into her heel and insole.

He let that go as well. A moment later she felt something cool and liquid poured on her head, and seconds after that his fingers began washing her hair, scrubbing and rubbing at her scalp as they worked the soap into a lather in her hair.

She felt like an animal, a pet of his as she knelt there on all fours. It was certainly the oddest bath she had ever received, and, she decided, strangely comforting. She found she liked feeling like a pet, liked giving all control to him, even in this. She merely had to kneel there as he did all the work.

After several minutes of scrubbing she felt his hands slide down her body and over her buttocks, this time one of them easing in between her legs and rubbing back and forth over her bare mound.

She started to feel a soft thrumming from down there again and weakly marvelled that she could become aroused so quickly after the two powerful orgasms she'd already had that morning.

The dildo was still buried deep within her sheath, and she could feel her insides squeezing down on it repeatedly as Sean's fingers stroked against her clitoris. She began to grind herself back against him, gasping softly as the sexual tension built up within her.

He halted, his hands sliding up her sides, then cupping her breasts and squeezing deeply, fingers digging into the soft warm flesh, pushing them together, then pulling them apart so the chain tugged on her nipples and made them sting.

She heard the shower go on again, and water began to pour over her head, moving in a slow motion from side to side as his fingers slipped through her hair. The shower went off, and he pulled her hair back away from her face, twisting and squeezing it together behind her as she turned to look up at him.

He smiled, then peeled his shirt up and off. He stood up and she watched as he undid his belt and unzipped his trousers. He shoved them and his underwear down and off, then slipped off his shoes and socks.

He knelt beside the bath, his hand going to her hair,

turning her face to him and rubbing his erection against her forehead, cheeks and nose.

She opened her mouth and his manhood found it and slipped inside, sliding over her tongue as she began to suck gently. He held her hair tightly, pumping slowly in and out of her mouth. His other hand moved down her back and in between her breasts, then down beneath to cup and stroke her bare mound.

Then up again, and she felt his finger pushing against her wrinkled anal opening. Her eyes widened and she flicked her gaze from his sliding penis to his face, looking up at him enquiringly, even anxiously.

His wink reassured her, but she shuddered anyway as she felt his soapy finger ease down into her rectum and probe slowly around inside.

He began to pump the finger in and out gently even as his erection slipped back and forth between her lips. She moaned, pushing back as his finger pushed deeper, blinking her eyes at the odd feeling of it twisting around inside her.

He pulled back, then stood and climbed into the bath in front of her. He gripped her hair, urging her upwards, and she gasped and rose on shaky legs until she was facing him. This time his mouth met hers as he pulled her soapy wet flesh in against his.

His hands moved up and down her back, down on to her buttocks, his fingers dipping inside her rectum again, pushing and probing as his tongue swirled against her own.

He turned her and pushed her against the wall. She felt her excitement and anxiety mount as his hands moved over her back, then took her wrists and raised them up high, placing them against the tiled wall.

She felt the head of his cock against her anus and closed her eyes, moaning as she shifted her feet further apart. It pushed in again and again in short little thrusts that battered away at her sphincter. There was no pain as it slowly eased inside her, then drove slowly upwards.

Each time her sphincter clamped down his hands would move beneath her to tug on the chain dangling from her nipples and the sharp little sting would distract her body long enough for him to send his thick erection driving another inch or two upwards.

She was surprised at how easy it was, at how deep he went before she began to feel cramps.

Her insides felt absolutely stuffed, with the dildo high in her belly and now Sean's cock up deep in her rectum. She turned her head round, meeting his lips with hers, her tongue shooting out even as she gasped from a sudden cramp.

He pushed up even higher, until she felt his testicles against her soapy behind, until his hips were pushing in hard against hers, grinding her against the wall in front of her.

His hands moved up and down her body as he began to grind his pelvis, twisting his thick manhood around inside her.

She groaned, letting her hips move with his, then in the opposite direction. She reached down between her legs with one hand, slender fingers stroking at her clitoris as she wallowed in the heat and pleasure.

But Sean jerked her hand up and slapped it against the wall, holding both hands there as he began to pump inside her.

Having never been sodomised Allison had little to compare it with, but though it was not the greatest experience of her life it was certainly pleasurable. Her insides were slowly turning to mush as her body filled once again with sexual need. As his movements ground her breasts against the wall she felt hot little flickering bursts of pain and pleasure from her aching nipples.

Sean's hands slipped around her hips and over her belly, then gripped her thighs, pulling them apart, then lifted her right off her toes as he jammed himself deep, burying his erection high inside her as she trembled and moaned.

He eased her down, then thrust up again, her legs yanked up and apart as he thrust himself inside her rectum.

Again he set her back down, though her legs were shaky, and now began to pump steadily, gradually building up speed as her anal muscles adjusted to his presence.

Soon he was thrusting in hard and fast, his hips slapping wetly against her soapy behind, his breath hot on the back of her neck.

He cupped her sex with one hand, his thumb stroking against her clitoris as his fingers pushed up against the base of the dildo. His other hand tugged repeatedly on the chain, making her yelp and moan as it bit into her nipples.

The heat rose to dizzying levels, and her head lolled weakly as she gave herself fully to the feast of sensory delight.

Then he suddenly halted his motions. He reached up to her breasts and his fingers began to roll against the sides of her nipples. She felt the chain fall away, then a moment later the sudden blast of pain from her relieved nipples.

She trembled and groaned as he held his loins jammed in against her bottom, his hands gently stroking her breasts and nipples.

He once again began to drive himself forcefully against her, his hands gripping hers and slapping them up high against the tiles, his heavy body jamming her against the wall as he repeatedly impaled her on his eager erection. Allison's aching nipples, just released and filling with a quivering overload of relief were roughly slapped and ground against the wall as she cried out again and again.

The orgasm hit her and her mind collapsed under the pressure, flung into a world of pleasure and bliss.

Her head rolled back dazedly as her body continued

to jerk in time to his hard thrusting and his cock pumped steadily inside her numbed rectum.

His hand moved down between her legs and squeezed hard, his thumb pushing her clitoris down against the base of the dildo even as his body continued to slap hers against the wall.

She heard him curse, his voice coming from a far distance, then his arms shot up, pulling her own arms up and back, forcing her back to arch violently as his hands slid behind her head and his arms locked around hers.

He threw his hips into her with a series of furious thrusts, filling her repeatedly with his hot male flesh.

Then he finally halted, spent, and they both sagged weakly to the bottom of the bath, gasping for breath.

Eleven

The music pounded heavily in the darkened room. Allison looked round nervously, glad of the darkness and still embarrassed at wearing such a short skirt.

The disco was nothing like the sophisticated ones in London or Paris, Sean said, but it was certainly exciting to her, for she'd only been to one, and that had been five years earlier.

She was wearing a black dress which consisted of a single narrow band across her breasts and puffy sleeves from the wrists to a few inches below the shoulders. Her shoulders and belly were bare, with two narrow bands of material going down her sides to the tight, short skirt.

Her hair shone like gold, for Sean had spent a great deal of time styling, drying and brushing at it while she sat before the mirror in the bathroom, wrists bound behind her.

She was not wearing the ludicrously tall stiletto-heeled boots or shoes, but the heels she did have on were still fairly high. She wore a small gold and sapphire choker round her neck and a matching bracelet round one wrist.

She was almost as nervous about her dancing ability as she was at her appearance, and looked round self-consciously at the other women as Sean led her directly on to the dance floor.

She had never tried to dance in such a tight short skirt, and that added to her anxiety. However many times she had looked at herself in the mirror it was still very easy to believe that something was showing other than her legs.

But Sean grinned encouragingly, and despite herself she found she was enjoying the dancing.

She did her best to imitate the movements of the other women round her, and when she decided she was more or less succeeding her worry began to fade somewhat.

An hour later she was in a wonderful mood, filled with happiness as she and Sean sat at their table and tried to talk above the pounding music.

When a stranger walked over and bent over the table to say something to Sean she wasn't able to hear. She watched Sean smile and nod, then the man beckoned someone and sat down, sliding his drink on to the table. A moment later a woman appeared and joined him.

'I'm Jeff Rose,' the man said loudly. 'This is Brenda McKnight.'

Rose was a handsome young man, though not in Sean's class, she thought idly. He had short brown hair, grey-blue eyes, a strong chin and a slender but athletic-looking body. Brenda was a buxom, but otherwise slim, short young woman with long chestnut hair and bright brown eyes.

Brenda, Allison thought a little less than charitably, barely looked old enough to be drinking, while Jeff was probably in his mid twenties.

'Haven't seen you around here before,' Jeff said.

'We're just in town for the day,' Sean replied.

Jeff nodded and pointed at Brenda. 'We go to Haverdale College. I'm in my last year and Brenda's just started.'

'We don't do anything,' Sean replied. 'We're the idle rich.'

Jeff laughed while Brenda's interest quickened.

'Oh?' she said. 'What did you do to get rich?'

'Was born right,' Sean said with a charming smile.

She giggled, and Allison glared at her. From the grand and mature age of twenty-eight she thought the girl unbearably childish.

'Allison, on the other hand, is a renowned artist,' Sean said. Jeff looked at her appreciatively but Brenda ignored her, fixing her gaze on Sean.

'So if you're rich what are you doing in Braceridge?' she asked.

'Just stopped here temporarily to get a few things for my yacht,' Sean said airily.

Allison glared at him, noticing that his Scottish accent had noticeably thickened. She wondered if he could possibly be flirting with the little tart or was just trying to annoy her.

'You have a yacht? I've always wanted to go sailing around the world,' Brenda sighed, blinking her big eyes at him sadly.

'It's a delight,' Sean said, winking.

'So like, where are you going next?'

'Probably to London, then across to France.'

'Oh, wow. That would be so cool, going to France on a yacht,' Brenda said.

She was leaning forward across the table, her arms almost cupping her breasts, squeezing them together from the sides and up from below. Allison glared at her, noting how thin and low-cut the girl's top was and how her breasts thrust out against the tacky fabric.

'Would you like to dance?' Sean asked.

'Oh yeah!'

He never looked at Allison as he took Brenda's hand, brought it up to his mouth to kiss the back of it, then led her out on to the dance floor.

'He really own a yacht?' Jeff asked.

'Well, he owns a boat, a sail boat. I don't know that you'd call it a yacht.'

'How big is it?'

'About sixty feet,' she said, watching the two dance

together, frowning at the way Sean's hands moved on the girl's shoulder and side.

'Smashing. You get some great fishing further out if you have the right equipment. You ever do any deep-sea fishing?'

She shook her head idly.

Sean and Brenda were pressing in close together, and she saw him bend to whisper something in her ear. The girl giggled and turned her back to him, and Sean's arm slipped around her waist as he dirty-danced with her, grinding his pelvis into her behind.

She felt a tight dagger of anger and jealousy as she watched them, ignoring Jeff until he tapped her shoulder.

'What?'

'I said do you want to dance?'

'No. Yes.'

She stood up and he jumped up after her, grinning as his eyes moved appreciatively up and down her body before turning to walk with her to the dance floor.

Allison tried to manoeuvre them close to Sean and Brenda but there was too much of a crowd. She watched as the girl let out a laugh at something Sean said, then she reached up and kissed him full on the lips.

Sean kissed her back, his hands briefly squeezing her behind before he slid them back up to safe territory and started to swing her from side to side.

He looked over her at Allison, met her eyes and winked.

She glared back, then turned her attention to Jeff, dancing closer to him, letting her breasts push in against his chest and sliding her hands over his back.

She told herself she was being silly, that Sean was only teasing her. After all, though the girl was undeniably pretty she was still nothing more than a child. She was short, her hair wasn't as pretty as Allison's, and though she had a big chest she had a cheap taste in clothing, she thought, ignoring the fact that Sean had selected her own outfit.

She felt one of Jeff's hands creeping down towards her behind and looked across at Sean again. He and the girl were dancing tightly together now, his leg between hers, their bodies grinding as the girl slid her tongue along her lower lip and gave him a look that as far as Allison was concerned said 'Do anything you want to me'.

She glowered at the girl, irritated and angry, thinking what a slut she was – and not in the exciting, seductive way she considered herself either. She saw Sean turn to look at her and jerked her head away, then deliberately licked at the side of Jeff's neck, nibbling lightly as his hand cupped her behind firmly.

A few minutes later they all returned to their table. Allison scowled at Sean, who ignored it blissfully as he and Brenda continued to flirt with each other. In response, Allison smiled and flirted with Jeff.

She suspected Sean was behaving this way to get a reaction from her, but the lack of self-confidence she had always experienced around men shone through and made her deeply suspicious and worried. Maybe he wanted this younger girl. No doubt she would be easier to manipulate, and God knew she seemed eager enough.

The thought of being left behind, of going back to her dull little life in her dull little house was unthinkable.

It was Brenda who suggested they go to another bar, one with more 'action'. Sean quickly agreed and the two of them rose, followed quickly by Allison and Jeff. Allison tried to get close to Sean, to get between him and Brenda, in order to speak to him but she failed.

When they reached the car Sean ushered Brenda into the front passenger seat while Allison and Jeff slipped into the back. She glared daggers at the back of his head as they pulled away, Brenda giggling about how tough this other bar was and how loud the music.

Jeff meanwhile was sliding his hands up and down Allison's shoulders and arms, leaning in to nibble at the side of her throat. She gasped as his hand slipped under her skirt and groped at her sex. She shoved it back and glared at him silently.

But being openly rude or causing a scene simply wasn't in her, so she said nothing to either him or Sean as the car moved quickly through the streets, then pulled over to the kerb in a rough section of town.

Once again Brenda skipped out alongside Sean, leaving Allison walking behind them with Jeff, who squeezed her behind familiarly.

The club was small and ugly, filled with cigarette smoke, the floors sticky with spilled beer. She looked around worriedly, wishing she could get closer to Sean as they walked through the crowded, noisy bar.

Someone groped her behind, and when she turned to glare at Jeff found him on the other side of her with his hands in his pockets. She flushed and looked quickly forward, not wanting to meet the eyes of whoever had touched her.

They found an empty table and sat down, hardly able to talk because of the noise of the crowd and the music. Brenda spent a lot of time with her lips at Sean's ear, saying Allison knew not what.

'Your girlfriend has lovely breasts!' Sean said at one point to Jeff.

Rather than being offended the younger man grinned and winked. 'You ought to feel them!' he called back over the noise.

He turned and looked at Allison then, before turning back to Sean. 'Your girlfriend has nice breasts too!' he called.

'She's not my girlfriend!' Sean replied. 'She's my slave!'

Allison blushed but Jeff only laughed, not taking it seriously.

'I've won contests, you know!' Brenda called.

'Really?' Sean replied.

'Bikini contests and wet T-shirt contests. I won two wet T-shirt contests here last month!'

Allison looked at her in distaste. She had no doubt she was the kind of bimbo that would enter a contest like that.

'Well, congratulations!' Sean replied. 'I don't doubt it at all. I ought to enter Allison in one!'

Allison looked at him and her mouth opened indignantly, but his eyes caught hers, and her anger vanished, replaced by sudden anxiety and a quivering in her stomach.

'Well, she can try it tonight!' Brenda replied.

Sean grinned at Allison and she knew this was exactly what he had planned, why he had agreed to come to this cheap bar; she had seen the 'Wet T-shirt contest' sign at the entrance. Her chest ached as she looked round at the rough men and women in the bar and imagined herself up front on the stage.

The idea was appalling but undeniably arousing as well. To have all these men looking at her breasts, hooting and calling, wishing they could get their hands on her, was a deliciously sluttish idea.

And yet to make a public spectacle of herself was terrifying, let alone doing it half naked.

Her mind flicked back to the sex shop, to the men watching her, eyeing her bare breasts, her bare buttocks. She felt a thrill of pleasure mixed with a stomach-wrenching fear, remembering how she had fantasied about Sean doing her right there in front of them all.

She hardly heard what Brenda said, and a few moments later the girl jumped up and went to the bar. Sean moved next to Allison and whispered into her ear, 'She's going to enter the two of you in the contest.'

'I can't!' she gasped.

'Of course you can. Remember how hot you got this

afternoon with those men watching you? You'll be lucky if you don't come on stage.'

'I – I Sean! I can't! I – I haven't the clothes! I don't have a T-shirt!'

'They supply it.'

'I can't wear a T-shirt with this dress!'

'Quite right. You'll have to remove it.'

'But then I'll be in my thong!' she gasped.

He grinned and waggled his eyebrows at her.

'I'd love to see you in your thong,' Jeff growled, his face a leer.

She turned and gaped at him, then snapped her mouth shut and whipped her head round to stare at Sean again. She looked up at the little stage, then back at Sean again. He laughed and threw an arm around her shoulders, pulling her against him and hugging her tightly.

'Oh, come on, love! You'll get a big kick out of it!'

'I can't!' she moaned.

'It's all done!' Brenda squealed, sliding into the chair Sean had vacated.

She gazed across at Allison and gave her a smug look. 'Unless you want to back out,' she said.

Allison glared at the girl. Brenda obviously had a lot of confidence in her own body, and justifiably so. Yet Allison thought she was only a cheap little tart. She knew her own body was lush and full enough to please any man, and considered herself far more beautiful, intelligent and erotic than Brenda.

She was, she suddenly thought, with considerable surprise, now a hot, sensuous woman, a woman who had engaged in bondage, who was able to deep-throat a man, who had undergone sodomy and many other exciting, wicked acts. She felt resentment and contempt that a young, ignorant girl like Brenda should feel herself superior.

Still, she had never been much for competition, for it

was too embarrassing to lose, to be upstaged, rejected; and she looked round the bar nervously, wondering which other women would be in the 'contest', and she was filled with a sudden fear it would be just her and Brenda.

The music stopped and a voice spoke into a microphone. 'Those ladies competing in the wet T-shirt contest please come up on stage.'

Allison felt her insides clench and twist, and clung to her chair as Brenda stood up with a wide grin. Sean winked at her as he patted Brenda's behind, and she stood up hesitantly, then followed Brenda through the crowd, her heart in her throat as the men eyed the two.

Other women were coming forward as well, almost a dozen of them. She felt a wave of relief as they all climbed on to the stage, then slipped to the back behind a cheap curtain.

Several men were waiting there and they looked over the assembled women with wide smiles on their faces.

'OK, here's your T-shirts,' they said, tossing them to each of the girls. 'One size kinda fits all. Put 'em on and when we announce it you all come out on stage together and stand in a line. We'll go down the line pouring water on your chests and then one by one you walk forward, stroll up and down the length of the stage, and then go back to your place.'

Allison was staring at the 'T-shirt' in alarm. It wasn't a T-shirt, in fact, but a tank top, incredibly thin and obviously too small. Several of the women were already slipping their own tops up and off. Only one other, besides herself and Brenda, was in a dress, and she had already taken it off.

The men went up front, leaving them alone, and Allison began to undo her dress, her heart beating faster with every second.

What in God's name am I doing, she asked herself.

Then the top of her dress came down, baring her

breasts. She unzipped the skirt part and let it slide down her legs as Brenda was doing. She saw the girl's heavy breasts dangling below her like udders, and licked her lips worriedly.

The girl straightened, and Allison felt a little better. Her breasts were very large, but because of that they sagged somewhat, and weren't nearly as perfectly round and firm as her own. Still, in a tank top that might not be so obvious.

Brenda was wearing only a G-string, and Allison swallowed as the girl lifted her arms over her head and pulled the tank top down over her breasts. She had to yank hard to get it to fit over, and then it was tight enough to support the heavy orbs almost like a bra.

Allison quickly pulled her own tank top over her head, sliding it down with only a little difficulty. The thought of going out on stage dressed as she was made her tremble, but she was determined to compete with Brenda.

Though she hated to admit it, if it weren't for her fears the idea of parading around like she was would have had her bubbling over with heat by now. Even so she felt a distinct tingle of anticipation between her thighs.

Nobody knows you here, she thought to herself, and no one will ever see you again anyway. It doesn't matter what they think of you or what they say.

She heard the microphone making whining noises, then a voice shouted into it, 'Shut up out there!'

The crowd noises softened and the voice continued.

'All right. It's time for our nightly wet T-shirt contest. We got a lot of cute women here, some of them old hands at this, some of them virgins . . .'

There was a howl of laughter and obscene comments that interrupted him briefly.

'I want you all to give a nice round of applause to these generous young ladies who are taking part in our contest.'

Allison felt movement ahead of her, and her heart pounded as she followed Brenda and the rest out from behind the curtain amid howls, whistles and applause.

She felt a moment of terror as she stepped out on to the stage, cringing under the many eyes and the laughter and shouts. She looked down at her feet at first, unable to meet the eyes.

The line of women halted and faced the crowd, who leered and yelled appreciatively.

Allison slowly raised her eyes, heart in mouth, starting to feel the fear ease and the excitement picking up. She felt a little bit of safety in numbers and in the laughing and preening of the other women with her, few of whom seemed the least bit embarrassed.

Beside her Brenda was leering at the crowd, yelling back at them and sliding her fingers through her hair, pushing her hefty chest out at them as they hooted in appreciation.

Allison could start to make out some of the individual yells now, and to her shock, embarrassment and excitement, a number of them seemed to be directed at her specifically.

Allison, Brenda and another woman, a black woman, were the only women not in pants or shorts, and so they were receiving even more interest from the crowd than the rest. Brenda basked in it, and Allison was starting to feel the excitement of so much flattering male attention herself.

I'm taking part in a wet T-shirt contest, she thought, in dazed amazement.

The men came down the line of women carrying large jugs of water, pouring them on each girl's chest as she arched her back and pushed her breasts out. Several gasped, and her heart pounded faster as the men got closer.

They soaked the top of the girl on her left, and Allison felt her pulse race as she saw how utterly transparent the shirt became, as if it were hardly there at all.

Then the man was grinning at her as he held the jug over her chest.

'Stick your boobies out, darlin',' he said.

She blinked her eyes in shock, then obeyed, gasping as the water – cold, cold water – poured over her chest in a small stream.

Her nipples were instantly erect, of course, as the shirt went sheer.

Then they moved on to Brenda, who arched her back eagerly.

Allison was still gasping from the cold as the men yelled their approval, and she fought the urge to cover herself as the shirt clung to her rounded breasts.

She saw a man near the front of the stage staring at her in delight, and jerked her eyes away. A few feet over another man whistled and made a face as he looked at her. Again she looked away, inhaling deeply, startled at the applause.

Then the woman at the head of the line stepped forward to the edge of the little stage and paced its length slowly, smiling a little but looking almost bored. The next woman pranced excitedly; young like Brenda, with frizzy bleached-blonde hair, she made faces at the crowd as she sashayed along.

The next woman took her walk, moving slowly, seductively, grinning, no, leering at the crowd. She paused near the centre and slipped the tight, clinging wet shirt up and over her breasts, baring them completely to howls of approval.

Allison swallowed and looked around her for someone to order the girl to pull the top back down, but none of the other women seemed surprised, and the men on stage just grinned and laughed.

The next girl did her little walk, then the next, who also slipped her top up over her breasts, then halted to do a quick bump and grind at the men before laughing in delight and scurrying the rest of the way back to her place.

Brenda stepped out then, and the applause was deafening. She basked in it, sauntering along the stage, pausing to turn to the audience several times. The first time she slid her hands up behind her head and arched her back sharply. The second time she pulled her arms in against the sides of her breasts, pushing them out even more tautly as she cupped them from underneath.

Then she did a little shake that had her big breasts bouncing up and down to whistles and cheers.

In a way Allison couldn't help admiring her. She was also, she realised, jealous. Brenda was the girl Allison wanted to be, sexy, uninhibited, wild and not self-conscious about a single thing.

Of course she was also crude. She saw herself as being more sleekly, seductively sexual as opposed to the cheap tart Brenda was.

But her uninhibited sexuality was obvious and the crowd could see it too. Allison's mind spun as she realised Brenda would almost certainly win the contest, for the men were responding as much to her own delight and excitement as to her looks.

Then Brenda returned and it was her turn. She froze for a moment, then stepped forward slowly. Her pace quickened as the crowd shouted its approval. Her excitement mounted as she moved to the edge of the stage and then, her hands moving almost without thought, she slipped the sheer, wet shirt up over her breasts, letting it cling to her chest there as she bared her breasts completely.

The crowd yelled as she opened her mouth and excitedly ran her tongue along her lower lip. She ground her hips slowly as she moved her hands up her wet belly to cup her breasts, as if offering them to the crowd.

Her embarrassment faded at their cheers, replaced by

a wild excitement as she shifted to one side, then, hands caressing her breasts, strolled along the edge of the stage.

She turned – the wrong way – letting them see her bare behind, and pushed it out a little as she waggled it from side to side, just like she had for Sean when he had made her dance for him.

Breathlessly she turned, rolling her head slowly as she pushed her arms against the sides of her breasts, groaning a little as she bent forward.

Then she turned and sauntered back along the stage, her fingers coming through her hair as she let her tongue waggle at the audience.

She paused and turned to them again, shifting her legs apart, her pussy throbbing now. She arched her back further and further, then swung her head from side to side so her long hair brushed against her behind and her breasts thrust out taut and firm at the audience.

Then she backed up into her place, beaming, heart pounding and breathless.

'I didn't think you had it in you!' Brenda yelled over the noise.

Neither did she, Allison thought in amazement. She giggled helplessly as the next girl moved forward, then slowly tugged the shirt back over her breasts.

One of the men moved to the microphones and called out for Allison, Brenda and a girl named Susan to step forward. Then he moved in front of them and got the audience to applaud for each girl.

Allison won – just.

She felt elated and stupidly happy. She forgot her anger at Brenda as the girl hugged her good-naturedly, then they all moved backstage to dress again. Towels were provided, they wiped off their fronts and got back into their tops and dresses.

She blushed as she emerged with Brenda, moving among the crowd towards their table. Many eyes were on her and she felt a tight sexual tension inside herself, a hot, self-assured sensuousness she had never felt in public before.

Sean kissed her and hugged her, his hand going round her and slapping down on her behind, squeezing it tightly as he congratulated her.

She blushed hotly, knowing how many eyes were on them, but felt a surge of sexual heat and pride at the same time.

'You were great!' he shouted over the noise.

'Thanks!'

'Come on, let's get back to the hotel.'

She was all for that and followed him and Brenda out, pausing only to collect her prize, a T-shirt, a real one this time, which said in big letters across the front 'Winner! – Maxwell's Wet T-Shirt Contest'.

Something to show to my granddaughter, she mused as she followed the others out of the door and back to the car.

Twelve

Allison was in a much better mood now, feeling eager to get Sean alone and speculating on how she could possibly blow *his* mind for a change. She didn't even mind Jeff's pawing and suggestive words and looks, playing up to him, teasing him back with the confidence her win had given her.

She got a little giddy every time she thought about having actually taken her dress off and taking part in a wet T-shirt contest.

And winning!

She was both delighted and scandalised by her behaviour. It was certainly a far cry from her shy moping during college: the way she had walked around the halls and grounds with her head down to avoid being talked to, avoid being noticed.

Brenda didn't seem to have taken her loss badly and was still teasing and flirting with Sean up front, but Allison no longer minded that much. *She* had won the contest, after all. The big-busted chit of a girl had nothing to teach her.

She was annoyed when Sean invited the two of them upstairs, but did her best to hide it. She neither wanted to appear rude nor like some sexually starved nympho.

She quickly interposed herself between Sean and Brenda, however, when they got out of the car and slipped his arm around herself as they headed through the lobby, then up in the lift.

Sean kept the lights low as they talked about places he'd been in the *Wanderer* and places they were going.

Brenda didn't think much of Bermuda.

'You should go to Cancun, Mexico,' she said. 'It's really wicked there.'

'Well, maybe I will later. I want to show Bermuda to my slave here, though,' he said, sliding his hand behind Allison's neck and squeezing.

Allison blushed a little as the other two laughed. Sean had called her his slave a couple of times but she was sure the other two just took it as a joke.

'This is my slave here,' Jeff said, grabbing Brenda and pulling her against him.

His lips crushed hers and they both moved together in a hot, fast, passionate kiss.

'You wish,' Brenda said when they pulled back. 'If anything you're *my* slave, chum.'

Again they kissed tightly, with Brenda giggling as they wrestled on the sofa. Sean pulled Allison in against him and she kissed him, glad the other two were distracted, still mildly embarrassed about public displays of affection.

That embarrassment faded almost completely within seconds, however, and she realised her threshold of shyness had been pushed back some considerable distance by what she had done over the past couple of days.

Even when his hand came up and cupped her breast she felt almost no shame, her tongue pushing into his mouth as her hands slipped over his shoulders and kneaded the muscles there. He leant his weight in against her, easing her back on the sofa while across from them Brenda and Jeff went at it in like manner.

Her breathing was becoming more ragged, and she groaned as his hand slipped into her top and stroked her rigid nipple. Then he undid the top of the dress, tugging down the front as his lips moved over her swollen breast.

She looked aside nervously and her eyes went wide as she saw Brenda, her top pulled down, bending over Jeff as he sat back on the sofa. His trousers were open and Brenda had pulled his erection out. It was stiff and Brenda's tongue slipped up and down its length, making it shine wetly.

Jeff grinned at her and she pulled her eyes away, feeling both embarrassed and aroused as Sean's teeth gnawed on her nipples.

She looked back to see Brenda's head bobbing up and down over Jeff, his hands alternately sliding through her raven hair and pawing at her heavy, hanging breasts.

Then Allison groaned as Sean's hand eased up under her skirt and began to stroke her throbbing sex. In seconds he had her thong tugged aside and his fingers were rubbing deliciously along her soft, moistening cleft.

She rolled her head back, sighing in pleasure as the sexual electricity crackled through her. Her hands squeezed Sean's biceps and slipped through his hair as he opened her skirt and tugged it away.

Then she heard Brenda groan long and low. She turned her head and gasped at the sight of the young woman. Brenda was still wearing her dress, though it was half down. She was straddling Jeff, however, facing him, and her skirt was tugged up above her bare behind as she rode up and down on Jeff's upthrust manhood.

The girl showed no shame as she squealed and moaned and gasped in pleasure, bouncing wildly on top of him.

Allison stared in fascination as Jeff's cock appeared then disappeared into the girl's body, only to reappear again. Brenda's behind jiggled and she yelped and moaned loudly each time she slapped herself down against him.

The sight was crude but exciting, and she found herself urging her on even as Sean slipped the remnants of her own clothing off and began to move downwards between her legs.

His tongue slid along her cleft and she groaned, gripping his head and grinding herself up against him, the pleasure rising ever higher, her body beginning to thrum with the sexual passion which had swept through her so often since she had met the man.

Only a week ago, she thought, wonderingly.

Brenda was yelping even louder now, as Sean lifted Allison's legs over his shoulders and pressed his mouth in against her. His tongue whipped up and down against her clitoris as his lips and teeth nibbled and sucked at her pink flesh.

Then he pulled back, grinning at her as she moaned and looked up beseechingly. He peeled his shirt up and off, then stood up. He kicked off his shoes and socks and slowly undid his zipper.

Allison licked her lips as she watched, her eyes following the movements of his hands as he pushed the zipper lower, then let his trousers down.

'Oh! Oh! In me! Yes!' Brenda cried, bouncing even harder and higher on top of Jeff.

Allison watched her, sliding her hands up her own body and squeezing her breasts, pinching her nipples as she waited for Sean.

Suddenly he grabbed her wrist and pulled her into a sitting position. A moment later he pulled her upright and lifted her over his shoulder.

He turned, and she giggled hotly, thinking he was taking her into the bedroom. But instead he brought her over to the table and sat her down on the edge.

He slid the box with her boots in it out from under the table, then opened it and took out one of the boots. He took her ankle, then slipped the boot on, sliding it up all the way, then zipping it in place.

The second boot followed.

'Oh, cool boots,' Brenda groaned.

Allison looked over at them and saw the two were lying on their sides on the sofa now, both naked, Brenda spooned in against Jeff as he casually cupped one of her breasts.

'Walk around for the lady, Allison,' Sean ordered. 'Show her how nice you look in your boots.'

A little embarrassed now that she was the centre of attention, Allison nonetheless obeyed, walking slowly back and forth in the high-heeled boots, feeling a liquid heaviness in her loins as three sets of eyes watched her.

'I should shave my pussy like that,' Brenda remarked.

'Yeah, do it,' Jeff agreed. 'I bet it's easier on the tongue.'

'Well, if it would inspire you,' Brenda cooed, turning her head and sliding her lips against his.

'Come here, Allison,' Sean ordered.

She walked back to him, trying to control her breathing.

'Take the leather restraints and buckle them on your ankles,' he ordered.

She bit her lip and turned to look anxiously at Jeff and Brenda.

'Never mind them. They already know what a tramp you are.'

She gasped and trembled, her face flushing. She felt a wave of anger towards him, but it was overridden by the rush of fiery sensual lust inside her.

She picked up one of the restraints, examined it briefly, then started to raise her leg, intending to put her foot on the edge of the table. Sean halted her, gripping her hair loosely.

'No,' he said. 'Keep your legs straight and bend over to do it.'

He turned her slightly so the other two were directly behind her, and Allison swallowed repeatedly, taking several deep breaths before slowly bending at the waist.

She slipped the restraint around her ankle, buckling it in place, then straightened, hair tumbled around her face. She picked up another restraint, gave him a reproachful look, then bent over again, once more showing two virtual strangers her bare cleft in the most revealing of positions.

She straightened once more as Sean pulled out a chair and sat down.

'Now your wrists,' he ordered.

She slipped a restraint around her left wrist and buckled it, then did the same to her right.

'The collar, slave.'

Again she gasped lightly, heat sizzling along her spine. She picked up the studded collar and obediently slipped it around her slender throat, buckling it behind her head.

'Brenda, my dear? Would you give Allison a hand, please?' Sean asked sweetly.

Allison jerked her eyes up to him anxiously as Brenda giggled and slipped off the sofa.

She padded over to stand beside Allison. 'What do you want me to do?'

'Bind her wrists back behind her.'

Allison pulled her arms back, trembling weakly. She felt Brenda's hands seize her wrists, then felt her fumbling with the clip that locked the two leather restraints together.

'Now help her with that belt, my dear.'

Brenda examined the mass of toys and leather goods and then squealed in delight as she pulled a belt up.

An oddly shaped belt, Allison saw, a belt that had two buckles and was shaped like a T. She felt the blood rush to her face as she saw the thick, bulging leather protrusion on the lower part of the belt.

Brenda giggled as she fitted the upper part of the 'T' round Allison's slim waist, then buckled it together in front. The lower part hung down at the back between her thighs.

She reached between Allison's legs and carefully drew it through, then took the protrusion – a leather dildo – and pushed it against her hungry opening.

Allison fought to hold still, unable to look at the younger woman as she felt the thing being pushed up inside her body. She wanted to curse her away, but shuddered as she felt the thing sliding up into her, groaning softly as it filled her aching sex.

Brenda drew the end of the belt up into the buckle in front of her and tugged so the thing squeezed up sharply against her.

'Harder, my dear,' Sean ordered.

Brenda grinned at Allison, then yanked up harder, making the blonde woman's legs shake as it jammed in against her mons. She then buckled it in place and stepped back.

'Now the bra.'

The 'bra' was really nothing but a leather support device. It thrust her breasts up from underneath without covering them at all. And that left her aching nipples free for the nipple clamps, which Brenda eagerly tightened around her nipples, giggling as Allison yelped in pain.

'You can thank Brenda for her help now, slave girl.'

'Thank you,' Allison whispered, head down.

'Louder.'

'Thank you,' she said more loudly.

'Thank you, *mistress*,' Sean said.

Allison drew in a deep breath that made her nipples burn inside the clamps. 'Th-thank you, m-mistress,' she said.

'No problem, slavey,' Brenda said with a laugh.

Sean removed his pants then, and sat back in the chair, legs spread.

'Come here, slave, and bend over,' he ordered.

She obeyed, and he shifted her so she again had her back to the other two.

'Spread your legs wider.'

She obeyed, light-headed now as she panted for breath.

'Now bend over.'

Standing, legs straight but spread, she bent over at the waist, far over, until she could slip her lips over the head of his cock.

She began to slide her lips up and down, moaning every time he reached up and tugged on the chain locked to her nipples.

Behind her Brenda and Jeff watched intently. With her legs spread they could see the chain dangling between her breasts, could see how her nipples stretched as Sean tugged on it, and could witness her lips sliding up and down his cock.

'All the way, slave,' Sean said, his hands in her hair.

She groaned and bent over further as she took him into her throat.

It was uncomfortable, but she heard Jeff exclaim in shock and excitement behind her, and felt a deep satisfaction that she had upstaged Brenda.

Her lips slid slowly up and down on his glistening staff, her back hurting more than her throat did as he rubbed along her tonsils.

As she moved she squeezed down rhythmically against the thick leather toy inside her, moaning in pleasure, wanting it to move, wanting it or something to pump into her. She ached, and felt herself becoming wetter and wetter as she stood in the unnatural position fellating Sean.

His fingers moved roughly through her tangled hair as he lay back, his eyes closed, groaning softly as her lips rode up and down along his shaft. She lapped against the head of his cock each time she backed up and it popped out of her mouth, and his fingers tightened in her hair when she did.

He started thrusting up into her then, jamming her head downwards as he grunted in excitement and pleasure.

Then he let out a long, low groan as he came, his seed

spilling down her throat as he held himself lodged deep inside her.

He released her with a groan and she eased her head up, then tried to stand. Her back was too weak and her head too dazed, and she awkwardly fell to her knees, gasping and gulping in air.

He heaved a sigh, then slid his hands up behind his head and glanced across at the other two.

Brenda's hand was pumping slowly up and down on Jeff's cock as the two watched Allison.

'Jeff, my lad, would you like a little taste of that?'
'What? Yeah, sure!'
'Allison, crawl over there and take care of Jeff.'

Allison felt a wave of dismay, not because she was upset at doing it but because she was so hot and frustrated herself and wanted immediate relief.

But she obeyed, turning and shuffling across the rug on her knees until she was kneeling in front of him. She glanced up at Brenda, but saw no sign of jealousy or concern on the younger woman's face as she looked back.

'Yeah! Suck this, baby!' Jeff commanded as Brenda slipped her hand off his shaft.

Allison obediently leant forward, taking him into her mouth, slurping on him as she bobbed up and down with longer and longer strokes. Then, with his erection wet with her saliva, she took a deep breath and slipped down all the way, taking him down her throat.

'Jesus! You gotta learn this, Brenda,' Jeff groaned.
'There must be a trick to it,' Brenda said dubiously.

Allison wrapped her lips around the base of Jeff's shaft, her nose pressed in firmly against his groin. She suddenly recalled that Brenda had been sliding her pussy up and down on Jeff's fleshy tool only minutes earlier and her eyes widened as she instinctively jerked her head back up.

Or tried to. Jeff was groaning and thrusting up into her throat as his hands pushed down on her head. For endless seconds there was nothing she could do but kneel there as he made use of her mouth and throat. By the time she slipped her lips up and off to gulp in air it seemed pointless to try to resist further contact.

She swallowed repeatedly, making a face, then bent to take him into her mouth again.

Jeff sighed again as she slid down to the base of his cock, his fingers sliding through her hair. She gasped as she felt him tugging at the chain. Her nipples ached and burned, little needles of pain digging into her sensitive flesh as she heard Brenda giggle.

She pulled her lips up and realised it was Brenda who was tugging on the chain. The girl drew her hand back with a smirk, and Allison glared at her for a moment before Sean pulled her over backwards on to the floor.

'Roll over,' he ordered.

She obeyed, gasping as her nipples were ground down below her.

'Now raise your bottom. I think Jeff wants to thank you. Don't you, Jeff?'

'Yeah, sure.'

Allison eagerly pushed herself up on to her knees, the side of her face pressing into the rug as she watched Jeff slip off the sofa and move behind her.

'Ow!' she yelped as a hand smacked against her rear.

'Raise that bottom higher!' Sean ordered, 'and spread those legs of yours.'

She obeyed, groaning as she felt Jeff's hand squeeze her through the belt.

He undid the buckles then pulled the belt down. She hissed as he drew the glistening black dildo out of her moist sex, then tossed the belt aside.

'Now doesn't that look ready and eager?' Sean said.

'Sure does, mate,' Jeff grinned, his hands moving over her upthrust buttocks.

'Brenda, why don't you take your boyfriend's erection and put it into Allison,' Sean suggested.

Allison wanted to say no but her need was too great. Her pussy felt vacant and hungry as she knelt there submissively. She groaned as the other girl knelt behind her, feeling a wave of shame as Brenda giggled then took Jeff's cock and placed the moist head against her cleft.

Jeff slipped into her easily, driving through the tight, silken flesh as he buried himself in her heat.

She groaned aloud, and the others laughed, Jeff slapping her behind, Brenda giggling and calling her a slave, and Sean reaching beneath her to squeeze one of her breasts.

Jeff began to pump almost immediately, his hips slapping against her behind as his fingers dug into her hips. He had little finesse, simply thrusting in straight, hard and fast.

But just then Allison wasn't looking for anything but what she was getting, and she grunted in pleasure with each stroke, her mind slipping deeper and deeper into a sexual haze as she felt the pleasure roar up inside her.

She turned her head aside and opened her eyes to see Brenda still kneeling behind her, looking down at her behind excitedly as Jeff threw himself against her.

Allison gasped and felt a hot flashing excitement at displaying herself in so intimate, lewd and carnal a way to these people she didn't even know. She mewled in helpless sexual pleasure, her behind starting to grind back in wanton lust as she revelled in the glory of the hard riding she was being given.

A firestorm of pleasure tore through her body as she climaxed, and she cried out, at first heedless of the witnesses to her ecstasy, and then basking in their eyes and ears upon her.

'Yes! Oh!'

She gasped and grunted repeatedly, thrusting her shapely rear back against Jeff's hips, which slammed into them and rocked her forward again with each stroke.

'Yeah. Give it to her, Jeff!' Brenda squealed. 'Look at her come!'

Allison gasped as a hand slapped against her behind.

'Dirty little slave!' Brenda said. 'Coming on my boyfriend's cock like that!'

Allison moaned, the orgasm shaking her mind and body. Yet she was not spent, though the air puffed out of her in desperate gasps. Her body was still aflame with lust and desire, and she moaned in bliss as Jeff's hardness continued to thrust into her with deep, powerful strokes.

A hand slipped beneath her belly, Brenda's hand, and though her mind tried to shrink away from it she let out a soft cry of overheated pleasure as Brenda's fingers found her clitoris and pushed it back against Jeff's cock.

Another orgasm rocketed upwards into her swirling mind, starbursts of heat and joy going off all over her body as she sobbed in dazed delight.

And then Jeff spent himself, cursing violently as he thrust into her with special fury. He began to slow, yet Brenda's fingers began rubbing violently against her clitoris as the orgasm continued to burn through Allison's mind.

Only when Jeff pulled out and she fell on her side with a groan did Brenda halt with a smirk. 'Nasty old slave,' she said.

Thirteen

Allison was glad to see Jeff and Brenda go. It wasn't Jeff, actually, that bothered her, it was Brenda. Being seen like that by Brenda, having Brenda slap and paw at her made her very uncomfortable. Many of her fantasies were submissive ones where strong men treated her badly and used her for their pleasure, sometimes more than one man at a time. But having a woman there sneering at her felt degrading.

And it particularly irked her that Brenda had called her an 'old' slave. She was only twenty-eight, after all. Surely only a very stupid girl would think that was old.

Being bound and submissive, being used and treated like a whore in front of someone whom Allison considered in every way her inferior was just too much to take.

It was particularly galling when the girl slapped her bare behind, rubbed her pussy and called her names in a sneering tone of voice.

After they left she took a long bubble bath while Sean watched television, then they munched on snacks room service brought up before going to bed.

She didn't complain about either Brenda or Jeff. She spent a lot of time thinking about the events of the day, however. She quickly realised that she was moving further and further from the shy recluse she had become, and wondered just how far she was capable of going, just what lewd activity she and Sean had not yet taken part in.

* * *

They set sail for London the next morning.

Much to her annoyance and frustration, however, before the boat could leave the marina Jeff and Brenda showed up with a mass of luggage. Allison was shocked at their presumption at first, but when Sean greeted them without surprise she knew he had either invited them or at least consented to them coming along.

She scowled at the back of his head but he ignored her as he helped Jeff haul the suitcases aboard.

Brenda, like Allison, was wearing a tank top and shorts, though hers were considerably tighter and the tank top was cut off to bare her belly.

Had Allison been alone she would have protested, even angrily, but her reluctance to cause a scene, especially one where outright rudeness was called for, kept her mouth tightly closed even as the men cast off the lines.

She had no idea where they were going to put them, however. There was only the one double bed, and though it was fairly big it wasn't large enough for the four of them. She said as much to Sean when he came below.

'It'll hold three: me, Jeff and Brenda.'

'What about me?' she demanded, stung.

His lips quirked upwards and he grinned at her, ruffling her hair until she shook his hand off. 'Oh, I've got plans for you, dear slave, don't you worry.'

That did not, of course, stop her worrying. She was still uncomfortable about being around the two younger people after the previous night. And she was certain Sean would further embarrass and degrade her in front of them on the trip.

Yet a part of her she tried to deny found the thought of that not entirely unpleasant.

Her first acts with Sean, especially where he bound her and forced her to crawl before him had done something inside her, twisted her mind into a shocked state that had exposed her to stunning pleasure. And though she still found it exciting to give herself to him, to allow him to use and degrade her as though she were his possession, his mindless sex toy, she had started to become accustomed to it.

The thought of exposing that side of her in front of others was still shocking and embarrassing. While she didn't think there was anything Sean could make her do with him alone that would embarrass her, the same was not true of strangers.

Particularly Brenda.

She continued to be indignant that Sean would treat the little trollop as though she were somehow the equal of himself and Jeff and the superior of his little 'slave' Allison.

Despite her lack of self-confidence and shyness Allison knew herself to be intelligent, knowledgeable and talented. And she was reasonably certain, after spending a few hours around Brenda, that the girl was none of those things.

At nineteen that wasn't surprising, of course, but the girl seemed to consider herself smugly superior and when Sean went along with it Allison found herself glowering at the two of them.

Not long after they left port, for example, Sean ordered her to go below and put Brenda's things away in the dresser and closet.

'There's no room,' she protested.

'Make room. Take your things out.'

'And put them where?' she demanded.

'You can throw them over the rail for all I care, all except the things I bought you.'

'I will not.'

'Don't use that tone with me, girl.'

She glared at him and folded her arms over her chest.

Suddenly she yelped as he turned her round, bent her across the rail and delivered a series of hard smacks to her bottom that made her yowl in pain.

Then while her mind was still gasping he yanked her upright and hugged her tightly against him, chewing and licking at her face and throat before turning her so her back was to him. His hands quickly slipped up under her tank top, and then down the front of her loose shorts.

She was all too aware that the other two were sitting a few feet away and watching, Brenda with that smirk on her face. She flushed unhappily, but Sean's fingers stroking up and down her bare little cleft were sending flickering flames of lust up through her body, and the punishment, the dominance he was showing her, made her mind leap at the outrage.

'Are you my slave or not?' he demanded, his fingers rubbing expertly at her clitoris, sawing up and down her soft cleft.

'I – I . . .'

'Say it. Say it.'

'I'm your slave,' she stuttered, fighting to keep herself from grinding her loins against his fingers.

He yanked her top up and off and threw it into the water, then undid her bra, sending it after the top. He turned her roughly and shoved her against the rail, bending her over as he yanked down her shorts and panties, then pulled them off and tossed them overboard.

He slapped his hand against her bare behind again and again as she cried out in a mixture of outrage and excitement, the heat like a bonfire now as she was so lewdly, so outrageously abused in front of Jeff and Brenda.

His hand drove between her squirming thighs and she groaned as he squeezed her. His finger probed against her, then squirmed into her soft, moist tunnel, thrusting and twisting around inside her as his other hand continued to spank her bare behind.

'Jeff. Go below and get the chains for this little slave,'

Sean growled, not pausing as his hand continued to crack down across her burning red bottom.

Jeff hurried back up with the box of sex toys and restraints Sean had packed and Sean fished the heavy shackles from it. With Jeff helping he quickly fastened them around her wrists and ankles. They were joined together by chains linked to a wide metal belt around her waist and a heavy metal collar around her throat.

Her wrists were chained together in front of her, but also chained to the front of her collar so that she could not move them below her waist. She would not be able to touch herself between the legs.

The tingling heat between her thighs was not to be relieved. Indeed, Sean obviously wanted her in a high state of arousal as he gave her orders.

Soon she was scrubbing down the deck on her hands and knees as the other three sat back in the padded seats drinking and chatting. Whenever one wanted a drink they would call out to her. 'Slave,' they would yell, and then rudely order her to fetch them a drink or food, or whatever else they wanted.

It was especially galling to have Brenda giving her orders as she lay back slumped in her seat, wearing a tiny bikini and sunglasses.

She made lunch, and called them down, and the three of them sat at the tiny table off the galley eating. But when she tried to sit next to Sean he rudely shoved her away.

'On the floor, girl,' he ordered.

She hesitated, then lowered herself to her knees as the three looked at her. She lowered her eyes, embarrassed and uncertain. Again she felt a surge of defiance, yet there was something deeply exciting about this submissive game, about playing the tramp, the helpless slave to Sean's will.

She watched him pick up her plate of food and put it on the floor.

'Eat,' he ordered.

She bent and reached for it then cried out as he gripped her hair and yanked up.

'No, slave, don't use your hands. Use your mouth. Eat like a dog.'

She felt her chest tightening and she moaned as he released her hair, then slowly lowered herself, bending her legs beneath her as she eased her lips down to chew at the food and lick it off the plate.

'You'll eat on the floor from now on and thank me for letting you,' Sean said airily.

She wasn't sure she liked that idea, but decided to go along with it for now.

After finishing the dishes she scrubbed the floor in the little galley, though it seemed clean to her, and waited on the three upstairs. She rubbed tanning lotion on Sean, Jeff, and even Brenda, hating the girl's little knowing smirk.

She was allowed on deck to watch the sunset, which she found quite beautiful.

With full dark on them the others went below to watch videos. Sean positioned Allison behind the wheel and chained her in place, ordering her to keep an eye on their heading. She knew that was a pointless exercise since she had heard him telling Jeff earlier about the automated steering system the boat had, and how it would steer itself by satellite.

An hour later Brenda came up from below and looked her up and down with a smirk.

'What a stupid cow,' she said with a sneer.

Allison flushed and glared at her, but said nothing.

She brought her hand out from behind her back and showed Allison the vibrator she clutched.

'I brought you something, dear,' she taunted, moving closer.

Allison eyed her distrustfully as the girl clicked the small toy on and pointed it towards her.

'Get away from me!' she snapped, scowling and twisting aside.

'She doesn't want to,' Brenda called down.

Sean emerged a moment later and Allison dropped her eyes as he took the vibrator from Brenda and came over to her. She gasped as he slowly pulled her head back by the hair, then began sliding the buzzing tip of the vibrator over her nose and face.

'Now you aren't going to disobey your master, are you?'

'But, Sean, I ...'

He slapped her behind and she yelped.

'My name is master. Say it.'

'M-master,' she whispered.

'Louder.'

She flicked her eyes at the smirking young brunette, then lowered them.

'Master.'

'And yours is?'

'Slave,' she whispered, her skin tingling.

'And do slaves obey their masters?'

Her stomach pulsed and her pussy throbbed.

'Yes.'

'Yes what?' he demanded, tugging on her hair again.

'I – I ... yes ... master,' she gasped.

'What your master wants is for you to be so bloody hot for it that if you sat down you'd burn a hole in the chair. Now you're going to do what your master wants, aren't you?'

'Yes, master,' she said slowly, feeling her chest tightening and her stomach clenching at the words.

He slid the vibrator down on to one of her nipples and she gasped as it quivered in response.

'Are you going to give me a hard time about it?' he demanded.

'No, master,' she groaned as the vibrator slipped between her legs and began to rub back and forth.

Sean turned her to the wheel again, and this time chained her ankles in place so she couldn't move aside. He motioned Brenda forward and Allison turned her eyes away as she felt the vibrator rub faster.

She quivered in shame, knowing it was Brenda holding it. But the feeling of heat was undeniable, and she moaned in pleasure as Brenda forced it through her taut pussy lips and up into her body.

The girl pumped it slowly in and out and before long Allison was helplessly grinding herself back against it.

Brenda laughed then and drew it out of her, gave her a slap on the behind and went downstairs, where, Allison noted dazedly, Sean had already disappeared.

She cursed them both but a short time later Jeff came up holding the vibrator. He grinned at her as he let the side saw along her sex while his free hand groped at her breasts.

'Too bad your boyfriend has so much money,' he whispered, 'otherwise I'd be tempted to buy you from him. You're one hot little slave, and kinky too.'

He squeezed her breast tightly and she winced.

'That hurt? But then again who cares if it hurts?' he said in a low drawl. 'It isn't like you got a choice. You're a walking, talking sex toy. I can do anything I want to you, right?'

She grunted as he stopped sawing the rounded tube along her moist cleft, angled it upwards and thrust deep, forcing her up on to her toes.

He chuckled as he chewed on the nape of her neck and pumped the vibrator inside her. He eased it out of her and gave her breast a final squeeze before turning and going back downstairs.

She was allowed to calm down, but then Sean came up with a smirk.

'How are you enjoying the vibrator?' he asked. 'I've been saving them but I knew they'd have a great effect on a nasty little girl like you.'

'I . . . Sean, I feel so . . .'

'Hot? Sexy?'

'Embarrassed,' she hissed.

'Of course you do. But you'll get used to it. Soon you won't be embarrassed at all and you'll be the perfect slave. You want to be a sex slave, don't you?'

'I – I suppose so,' she gulped.

'No supposing, love. Either you want to have a try at slavery or you don't. Do you?'

'Yes,' she whispered.

'Yes master,' he said, slapping her bottom.

'Y-yes, m-master,' she gasped.

He put his arm around her and pressed into her from behind. His right hand cupped and squeezed her right breast as his left eased down to her cleft, his fingers stroking softly up and down its length.

He licked and nibbled on the side of her throat, his teeth nipping lightly as he sucked with growing pressure. Meanwhile his fingers squeezed, pinched and rubbed at her nipples and clitoris as she began to push herself back against him.

She felt his erection against her behind and groaned. She felt the vibrator click on then and felt it against her hot, now aching little opening. She spread her legs, trying to push herself back against it but he refused to penetrate her, content to stroke it lightly along her clitoris and pussy before turning it off and going back downstairs.

Brenda came up next, and Allison cursed mentally. She looked at the vibrator the girl carried hopefully as Brenda snickered.

'Want this, slave? I bet you do now, and I bet you don't care who jams it in either.'

She walked up beside her and looked her up and down, then held up the vibrator.

'You want this inside you, slave? Hm?'

Allison hesitated, then nodded shamefaced.

Brenda snickered and Allison lowered her eyes.

'You gotta say it.'

'I – I want it,' Allison whispered.

'What do you want, slave girl?'

'Th-the vibrator,' she said, her voice quivering.

'Where?'

'In-inside me. Please?'

'So, you want me to use this on your pussy. Is that right?'

She nodded, face red.

'Say it then.'

'I – I want you to use the vibrator on my p-pussy,' she whispered.

'Call me mistress,' Brenda purred, slipping her hand between Allison's thighs and cupping her bare, shaved mound.

'Please,' she groaned.

'Please, mistress,' Brenda chided.

'P-please, m-m-mistress!'

Brenda laughed. 'You really get off on this kinky slave shit, huh? You must be a real nympho. I bet you've done just about every guy you ever met.'

'Please,' Allison groaned, 'please, Brenda!'

'Call me mistress.'

'Please, mistress!'

'Too bad you're all chained up. I bet I could get you to crawl around and beg for it on your knees.'

She touched the nose of the vibrator lightly against Allison's clitoris then yanked it back as she groaned and arched her back.

'Turn around then, stupid, and bend over.'

Allison bent her head, then, embarrassed beyond measure but excited even beyond that, she leant forward, still chained by the wrists to the wheel.

'Further, you cow,' Brenda snapped.

Again she hesitated. I can't do this, she thought in an agony of indecision.

But then she bent further, spreading her legs as far as the chain would allow. She winced, then half sobbed as Brenda thrust the vibrator up inside her, pumping it furiously up and down as she slapped her behind.

'Oww! Oh my God!' Allison gasped.

'Yeah! I bet you like that,' Brenda sneared, 'don't you, slave girl!'

She smacked Allison's behind and Allison whimpered in shame and anger. Yet the heat outweighed it and she desperately pushed herself back against the vibrator as the teenager thrust it up into her with hard movements.

Brenda clutched it in her fist tightly, and the side of her hand punched against Allison's mound with each thrust, sending a wave of blistering heat up into her swirling mind. Still she pushed herself back, cringing mentally at the way she was degrading herself, humiliating herself in front of Brenda.

She felt the climax approaching, felt it rolling up around her, surrounding her and mounting higher and higher as it got ready to swamp her mind.

Then Brenda yanked the vibrator free and stood back.

Allison whimpered, grinding herself back for long seconds before turning beseeching eyes on the smirking girl.

'Well, ta ta,' Brenda said.

'No! Oh please! Please come back! Please, mistress!' she sobbed.

Brenda turned and skipped back to the stairs, then disappeared, leaving Allison in the grasp of a deep, terrible need. She tried grinding her thighs together, but after the excruciating vibrations coming from the little sex toy that seemed almost irrelevant. So desperate was she for relief she looked around for something to push herself against, a sharp corner or edge. But nothing was within reach.

Sean came up next, and to her relief he unchained her

and took her back below deck. Allison blinked her eyes in the light, looking around at the other two sitting back comfortably on the small sofa set against the wall.

Sean unlocked and removed her shackles, including her collar, then holding her by the arm, swung her around and sat her in a low chair that faced the sofa. He lifted her legs up and tugged so she slumped down, then spread them wide and draped them over the arms of the chair.

Allison looked up at him anxiously, knowing what he wanted. A wave of embarrassment and lust rolled over her as one, and she turned slowly to see the others watching her with interest.

'You know what we want to see, slave,' he said.

Her hands started to move to her body, then halted. Again her eyes moved over them as her mind rolled and spun.

'I – I – I can't,' she moaned.

'Do it, slave,' Sean ordered.

'Yeah, slave girl,' Brenda sneered. 'Sean says you diddle yourself in front of people. We want to see it.'

Allison hated her, yet even as her shame rose she felt her excitement deepening. The humiliation, the degradation, touched something inside her, something long hidden, and her shame in front of a woman was far greater than in front of Sean or any other man.

'Whenever you're ready, slave,' Sean said.

Her hands moved almost of their own volition, and the moment her fingers felt the warmth of her sex she forgot anything but her own pleasure. The fires banked within her sprung up full-blown as her fingers sank into her wet centre, and she began to stroke rapidly against her clitoris even as the other three watched from only feet away.

She squeezed her breast, gasping in pleasure, the sexual fever taking hold and burning her up as she began to buck against her own fingers, panting for breath as her muscles began to tighten and release, tighten and release.

'Look at that,' Jeff said with a laugh of delight.

'God, what a whore!' Brenda exclaimed.

Allison rolled her head back, then forward, and her eyes fixed on Brenda, staring helplessly at the girl's giggling, smirking face as the orgasm tore into her.

Her head shot back against the back of the chair and she cried out, jerking and grinding against her fingers as the climax sent scalding pleasure pouring through her mind.

The climax peaked, then peaked again before slowly settling to a soft, languorous, blissful calm that left her slumped in the seat with her eyes closed.

The applause made her moan and cringe inside, yet oddly it also roused her pride, catching hold of that part of her that had always wanted to be thought of as a sexy, seductive tramp.

She was pulled out of the chair soon after, her body limp, and half carried, half dragged into the small bedroom between Jeff and Sean.

Aided by Brenda they slipped the leather restraints around her wrists and ankles, then brought her to the foot of the bed. A thick round horizontal post ran between the two high corner posts of the four-poster bed, and she was lifted up on to it, her ankle restraint bolted down to one of the corner posts. Then, as she groaned and gasped at the tight ache in her thigh, her other leg was slowly forced back until it too was lying straight along the footboard in the other direction. Then it too was bolted to the post, and she was doing the splits along it.

Her arms were lifted up and apart, chains binding them to strong rings bolted higher into the corner posts. Finally, straps were wrapped around her legs at thigh and knee to force both legs flat against the narrow footpost.

Helpless now, she looked at the three as they grinned at her, and felt her stomach flutter as she wondered what would come next. Positioned as she was on top of the lower bedpost facing the bed she had no idea what they had in mind.

Jeff fetched a heavy gag and handed it to Sean. The gag was a thick leather belt that fitted completely around her head. There was a round leather ball attached to it which he pushed into her open mouth. Then the belt was strapped and buckled behind her.

Unable to move or make a sound she watched helplessly, eyes blinking, as Jeff, Sean and Brenda disrobed, then they all climbed into bed, the men sliding their hands over Brenda's lush young body.

Already aroused once more by her tight bondage, Allison felt her body heating up as she was forced to watch the carnal play on the bed before her.

Jeff and Sean suckled and chewed on Brenda's heavy breasts together as the girl moaned and reached down to grasp their erections with her hands.

Brenda grinned up at her smugly as she pumped her small fists up and down against them. The men slowly drew back, then rolled her on to her stomach and pulled her up on all fours.

Allison watched her pert lips slide over the head of Jeff's cock, then began bobbing back and forth, slipping lower and lower even as Sean moved up behind her and ran his hands over her shapely rear.

Allison felt a stab of jealousy as she watched Sean slide his erection back and forth along the girl's cleft, then push his cock into her. She watched inch after inch slip between the girl's pussy lips and disappear into her body as Sean's hands moved over her back and buttocks.

Brenda squealed in delight, pulling her lips off Jeff's cock.

'Yeah! Yeah! Do me, Sean! You know you're tired of

that ugly old slag! Do me good, Sean! I'll give you better than she ever could!'

Allison glared daggers at her as she watched Sean pump in slowly, changing angles and directions as his hands moved under her slender chest to cup her big breasts.

She watched his fingers digging into the soft flesh as he pumped harder and harder against her from behind, his hips slapping against her upturned buttocks as the girl returned her lips to Jeff's quivering erection.

Long minutes passed as the three on the bed positioned and repositioned themselves. Brenda lay on her back as Sean straddled her and cupped her breasts around his cock, then began pumping into her cleavage. Meanwhile she tilted her head back and tried to take Jeff down her throat.

Allison felt hot little stabs of victory each time she gagged and failed, but then a vast disappointment as she saw Jeff's cock bulge in her throat and slide deep down inside her.

Her lips suckled at the base of his shaft as he cheered her on, then she eased her own lips back down and off, laughing as she coughed before gulping in air and trying again.

On and on it went, and despite her jealousy and anger Allison got more and more aroused watching the carnal trio. Although bound tightly she was able to grind her mound ever so slightly against the round wood below her. It was enough to help raise her to feverish heat, but not enough to push her over the edge and into orgasm.

Brenda was totally uninhibited in bed, crying out her pleasure, cursing for more, grinding and thrusting against the men as they used her repeatedly. And even then, as both men lay back tiredly, spent, she was still filled with a hot seductive lust. She taunted and teased them, trying to provoke them to more, and when that failed to work she turned and eyed the blonde woman bound so helplessly at the foot of the bed.

'How long do you think it would take me to make her come?' she asked.

'The way she looks? About two seconds,' Sean said, yawning.

Brenda giggled and shuffled forward on her knees, grinning impudently at the older woman. She tweaked her nipples and twisted them from side to side, then slid a small hand slowly down her sweating belly, down over her abdomen and between her legs.

Her middle finger reached for Allison's clitoris and stroked it with a feathery touch, then drew back as she giggled again.

She combed her fingers through Allison's hair, reached behind her and undid the heavy strap around her mouth and jaw, then slowly worked the thick ball out of her mouth. Allison coughed and gulped in air through her mouth as Brenda grinned at her.

They were at almost the same level now, for though the footboard was higher than the mattress Brenda's kneeling position raised her up to equal it. She ran her hands slowly down Allison's body as she watched the woman's eyes focus once again on her and watched her tense.

'Do you want it, Allison?' she whispered. 'Do you?'

'I – I . . .'

Brenda leant forward, her face closer and closer to Allison's until their stiff nipples touched. Allison jerked her head back, eyes getting wider, then flicking from side to side.

'Do you want me, slave girl? Do you? I can make you come. Want me to?'

She kneaded Allison's shoulders, then let her hands slide down her sides and on to her hips before moving back and forth along the outside of her tightly bound thighs.

'You want it, slave girl?'

Allison moaned weakly. She knew something like this

would arise, knew it was Sean's intention to make her have sex with a woman.

And yet he wasn't making her do anything, hadn't even suggested it. He was lying back smugly watching her. It was the girl, the little slut Brenda, who was pushing it, and Allison found herself strangely drawn to her even though she had never really thought about sex with women before.

Watching Brenda work on the two men for the past hour had made her see the girl as a sexual creature, the kind of sexual creature she longed to be herself, and now as the girl knelt in front of her, her body still coated in sweat from the men's hot use, her own body responded with a lust that was uncontrollable, unstoppable.

'I . . .'

But she couldn't bring herself to admit it. She wished the girl would just do it, just grab her and ravish her the way Sean did. She was loath to admit her desires for her.

'Kiss me,' Brenda ordered. 'Kiss me, slavey, kiss me hard, on the lips. Come on.'

Allison eased her face slowly forward, trembling with the heat and lust inside her, her mind throbbing dizzily as the girl grinned at her. Then their breasts pressed together again. She drew back, then hesitantly eased forward once more, feeling a hot rush of sexual daring as her breasts pushed firmly into Brenda's big orbs.

Their lips met ever so gently, and Brenda's hands slid around her head, fingers sliding through her tangled blonde hair as she pushed forward far more firmly, her tongue pushing into Allison's mouth as she ground her body against the other woman.

Allison moaned at the sensation. The feel of another woman's breasts rubbing heavily against her own was like nothing she had ever imagined, and her heart and lust soared as her breasts began to pulse with shocked delight.

Brenda's hands slipped down her back, stroking up and down, then down further on to her buttocks as she kissed savagely, her tongue stabbing deep into Allison's mouth.

Her hand moved around to the front and her fingers sought the top of Allison's sex where it pressed against the wood, stroking roughly, painfully, furiously. Allison cried out, then again, then her body was struck by a blast of sexual energy. A climactic shockwave blasted through her and she stiffened then trembled violently as a breathless groan of wonder escaped her gaping mouth.

It was so powerful it hurt. Her abdomen began to cramp up as her mind reeled from the force of the pleasure tearing through her nervous system.

Fourteen

She half hung there as she gulped in air, dazed, drained by the power of the climax that had rocked her. When she nervously raised her eyes she saw the three of them grinning at her triumphantly, and felt a wash of embarrassment mixed with a strange kind of quirky delight at her own deviate behaviour.

Why she found her own humiliation so sexually arousing was beyond her, but that seemed to be the case. Perhaps, she thought, it appealed to some masochistic side she hadn't known she possessed.

'Was that nice, slavey girl?' Brenda asked, smirking.

Allison refused to answer, and gasped as the girl slid her arms around her once again, pulling her body in tight. The feel of her large, soft breasts against Allison's own was undeniably pleasant and sensual, and her insides seemed to have settled only slightly from the powerful orgasm Brenda had given her.

The brunette slid her hands up and down her back, then leant in, kissing the side of her cheek and then sliding her tongue slowly up under her ear, then down along the nape of her neck.

Allison squirmed mentally, being subjected to lesbian advances she'd always been taught were wrong, yet bound up in the sexual heat and pleasure possessing her body. She gasped as Brenda suddenly yanked her head back and bit down on the nape of her neck, then on the exposed front of her throat.

The pirates eased aside and another one walked up to her, a female pirate who looked her up and down with a sneer. The woman opened her shirt to expose large, perfectly round breasts and rolled her tongue lewdly along her lower lip as the men looked on in delight.

'I'm going to teach you how to make love with a woman, you dainty little virgin,' she said with a sneer.

'Ohhh!' Allison gasped as Brenda's mouth dropped to engulf one of her rigid pink nipples. Brenda cupped both breasts, lifting them up and squeezing softly and rhythmically as she sucked and licked at her nipple, then she let her tongue trail lazily down the blonde woman's taut belly, circling her bellybutton as she bent lower.

Allison pulled weakly against the straps as Brenda's tongue caressed her abdomen then eased lower, her lips brushing the bare skin alongside her exposed cleft, licking at it where it pressed down against the rounded wood of the bedboard.

'D-don't,' she gasped.

Brenda's tongue lapped out, incredibly soft and wet and warm as it nudged the top of her cleft. She felt her insides squirm as Brenda's tongue dipped in and around the hood protecting her clitoris, then she arched her back violently as Brenda placed her lips against it and sucked.

She bucked helplessly, gasping for breath as Brenda eased the power of her suction and licked instead, then she straightened, smiling wickedly.

'I think you like this whether you'll admit it or not, slavey,' she said.

'Try this on her,' Sean said, leaning forward and handing her one of the vibrators.

Allison gasped with both anticipation and anxiety as Brenda clicked the thing on. It nudged her pussy where it met the board and her body began to shake almost at once, starting at her mons and then spreading up and out through her body.

'Let me untie her a little,' Brenda said. 'I can't get at her pussy properly.'

She ran her hands up and down Allison's bound thighs, then paused and began to unstrap her legs.

Allison groaned as her legs were released and she bent them ever so slowly.

She bent then, and raised Allison's legs up on to her shoulders. Allison bit her lip but made no attempt to discourage the girl, in spite of her continued efforts to pretend she wanted no part of her.

She shuddered as the girl's soft tongue licked up and down across her mound, then closed her eyes as it slipped between the moist lips of her sex and twirled inside her. She felt tremors within her lower belly as Brenda's tongue caressed the insides of her pink sex.

Her tongue eased out and up, and again made the most delicious contact with her clitoris. Allison drove herself up instinctively, grinding her sex into the girl's mouth as Brenda licked harder and faster. Her legs started to jerk and bounce and her breathing became more and more ragged.

'She seems to appreciate your tongue, Brenda,' Sean said in a droll voice.

'Maybe she'd appreciate this too,' Jeff said, tossing something to the bed next to her.

Brenda let her legs slide down off her shoulders as she straightened, then let out a whoop of delight as she snatched up the strap-on dildo Jeff had tossed her.

She quickly donned it, and Allison blinked warily at the thick, slightly curved plastic phallus jutting up from between the teenager's legs.

'I get to fuck you right proper now, slavey,' Brenda said with a laugh.

She lifted Allison's legs up again, sliding them over her shoulders, balancing her precariously on the narrow wooden beam as she worked the thick dildo into her body.

Allison closed her eyes slowly, shuddering under this

new humiliation. Bad enough that the girl should lick her down there, but now it was as if she were a man; as if she were, like the other two, lording her stiff cock over Allison and using her for her own pleasure.

Yet it felt so good! She had almost wept at the emptiness inside her pussy as she had watched the three cavort in front of her, and it felt so delicious having the thick dildo sliding up high into her belly.

Brenda buried it inside her, and rolled her hips from side to side, then let her lips slide across Allison's as she began to pump. She gripped her behind where it rested on the foot board, forcing her legs up high and back as she leant her own torso in against her.

Allison's pussy squeezed down against the dildo, and she cast aside her pride and fears, using her legs to ride herself back up on to that hard wand, gasping with effort and pleasure as she felt it sliding in and out of her.

Then Jeff and Sean were there, gripping her ankles, which still had the restraints on them, lifting them up and apart then chaining them to the corner posts with her wrists.

Never had she felt so open, so vulnerable and bare. Her back and thighs ached, yet she was intoxicated on the sexual heat, and paid them no mind, fighting to drive herself back against the hard dildo as it pumped within her.

'I'm doing you now, baby,' Brenda groaned, chewing on the side of her throat. 'Doing you proper!'

She pumped faster and faster, easing her upper body back to look down and stare, as Allison did, at the sight of the glistening plastic phallus as it hissed in and out between Allison's tautly gripping pussy lips.

Her soft belly and hips struck Allison's buttocks, then her hands slid down her back to grip her and swing her in against the dildo. Allison hung freely then, swinging in time to Brenda's strokes, gasping in pleasure and heat as the thrill of sexual abandon crept over her again.

She clenched her teeth, then threw her head back, basking in the joy that filled her, in the loss of inhibitions and the pleasure and heat of her flesh.

And then the dildo was pulling back, and Brenda was smiling at her as she slipped it off. Sean moved behind her and began to undo the straps, releasing first her ankles, then her wrists, letting her slide down on to the bed as Brenda straightened and took her into her arms.

The two women fell back, arms entangled, breasts rubbing and squeezing together, legs scissoring as Brenda crushed her lips against Allison's.

Sean and Jeff sat back and watched with interest as their bodies writhed slowly together, Brenda's hands squeezing and kneading Allison's perfect round buttocks.

The brunette jerked away suddenly, then switched around on the bed, straddling Allison's head as she bent, dropped her body down and began to lap at Allison's pussy once again.

Allison gazed up into the girl's own softly furred mound only inches over her face. She ran her hands over her behind, then licked her lips and, as she felt Brenda's mouth against her slit, pushed her own tongue up and out, sliding it along the brunette's tightly closed pussy.

She did her best to imitate what Brenda was doing, her excitement driving her enthusiasm on as Brenda's tongue lapped at her clit. Then she groaned as she felt Brenda's fingers slip inside her. They pumped in and out as her tongue and lips stroked back and forth over her clit, and she humped up breathlessly.

She pressed her own trembling fingers against Brenda's pussy and then slowly and gently drove them up into her, a kind of blossoming wonder filling her mind as she felt the girl's sex squeezing moistly and hotly around her fingers.

She pumped them slowly, twisting from side to side,

so caught up in the novelty of what she was doing she almost forgot the churning sexual firestorm growing in her own body.

Then she began to lick once more, pumping faster and faster until, with another gasp, she felt Brenda's fingers slide out, then something else, something large and solid and thick, slide deep into her body.

A moment later Sean dropped a large pink dildo on to the bed next to her head, and she realised he'd given the same to Brenda. She snatched it up excitedly and pressed it against Brenda, feeling the pressure of her tight pussy lips as she slowly worked it in, using short little thrusts to drive it deeper and deeper, until only an inch remained outside.

She resumed her licking, pumping the dildo just as Brenda was doing, gasping and moaning softly so she could hear the sound of Brenda's own groans of pleasure. She felt pride and joy at the sound, and was hardly even aware now of the two men sitting there and watching.

She wanted to make Brenda come, wanted to make her climax, to make the girl squirm and thrash as she herself had done.

It was an unequal race against time, however. Her entire body was thrumming with sexual energy, her head aching with the force of the pressure inside it as another orgasm hovered over her.

Then it hit her, and she abandoned her efforts, her head falling back as her muscles snapped and spasmed, her body shaking under the waves of pleasure rolling through it.

Allison woke slowly, groaning at the ache in her muscles, especially her thighs. She moved against something and another pair of eyes blinked open.

Brenda smiled softly, then after a moment leant forward and kissed her on the lips.

Allison smiled hesitantly in return.

The night had not run as Sean had planned, she thought somewhat giddily. She realised he had actually planned to keep her bound all night while he, Jeff and Brenda enjoyed the bed. Brenda's interest in Allison had changed that, as had Allison's own highly charged response.

At first he and Jeff had been delighted at the show. The men had become excited, of course, and joined in, but soon worn themselves out while she and Brenda continued. Eventually, she supposed, they had gone off somewhere to sleep.

She wasn't sure how long she and the girl had made love; for hours at any rate.

'Some night,' Brenda said, as if reading her mind.

Allison nodded shyly.

Brenda rolled over, then slid on top of her, and Allison gasped, then reached up, hands going to the girl's shoulders as Brenda leant in and kissed her.

'I'm always horny in the morning,' Brenda whispered.

She kissed her again, and began slowly grinding her body against Allison's. Again, as she had the previous night, Allison felt a wonder at how lovely the other girl's soft flesh felt against her own, how delicious her breasts felt with Brenda's grinding and mashing against them.

She spread her legs slowly, wider and wider, and Brenda did the same. The brunette angled herself in, grinding her soft, furry mound against Allison's bare one, the two sighing softly as the pleasure rose like a wall around them.

Allison's hands slipped down the other woman's back, and on to her buttocks, her fingers kneading the round flesh as she pulled her down and pushed herself upwards. Their tongues slithered together as their soft moans of pleasure filled the cabin.

The door opened and Jeff came in. 'Jesus, are you two at it again?' he demanded in annoyance. 'Couple of right lezzies, you are.'

The two women ignored him, continuing as he fetched a sweatshirt, paused to watch for a long moment, then walked out.

Allison moaned as the fire in her loins burnt hotter and spread throughout her body, as her breasts throbbed in concert with Brenda's grinding motions and her body hummed with lust.

The orgasm hit quickly and hard, and she shuddered below the other woman just before Brenda too hit climax, crying out, cursing in release as she quickened her motions.

'God,' Allison panted as Brenda rolled slowly off and they lay there recovering.

'Just call me mistress, slave girl,' Brenda said teasingly.

'How would you like a spanking?' Allison sighed, eyeing the girl reprovingly.

'Ooo, sounds fun,' Brenda said with a leer, 'Will you tie me up first?'

'Count on it.'

'Come on and get up, you lazy bitches,' Sean said, coming into the room unannounced. 'It's damn near noon.'

They stuck their tongues out at him in unison.

'I feel like laying here forever,' Allison sighed.

'Nonsense. That's what you were doing before, just laying around. Now you're with me.'

'Stuff yourself,' she said with a soft smile.

Brenda snickered and Sean glared, then grabbed her and yanked her out of the bed.

'What you need is a good shower to wake you up, my dear,' he said, pulling her up the narrow stairwell and out on deck.

'Where are we going?' she asked as he led her up to the bow.

'I've always said that one of the things missing from this old boat is a truly spectacular figure-head.'

She had no idea what he was talking about as Jeff came up beside them and the two began to tie ropes to the rings set in her restraints.

'What are you guys up to?' Brenda asked, yawning as she padded up from below.

'We're saluting the gods,' Jeff said.

Then he and Sean gripped Allison's arms and lifted her over the rail, dangling her in front of the ship. They lowered her slowly, as she stared down at the grey water below, her head, then even her raised hands disappearing below the deck.

She felt her ankles pulled back as well, then gasped as the pressure grew, forcing her back tight against the ship's bow, her arms lifted up and back, and her legs pinned back sideways until the narrow edge of the ship was pressed in between her soft buttocks.

She got some of the splashing from the sea now, for her lower body was only a few feet above it, and she gazed ahead of her, at the empty skyline and the sky above, then down at the cold water.

Nothing else was in sight. It felt as if she were alone in the world, and she tried to imagine she really was the boat's figure-head, a carved figure of a woman come to life.

She felt the boat being turned into the waves and now they splashed up around her, dousing her quickly as the bow rose and fell.

The sea was calm, so the waves never actually rose above her hips, but the splashing soaked her, and she gasped in excitement, feeling tingly and alive as the water and waves struck her naked flesh. She imagined herself in a wild sea, the entire front of the ship ploughing through deep waves, her body sliding through the sea before it like some kind of enchanted creature.

She could not hear them up on deck, and was alone with the sea. She moved with the ship, as though a part of it. She felt almost as she had long ago when she'd first dared to open her shirt in a light rain, arch her back, and let the dark sky see her chest as the rain pattered against her nipples. It was not entirely sexual – though that was a part of it – but almost spiritual.

Allison yawned and rolled sleepily out of bed the next morning, untangling her long legs from Brenda's, then padded up on deck. They were moored at a small marina on the edge of the city.

'Oh!' she gasped, drawing back into the stairwell.

'It's all right,' Sean grinned. 'Come and meet David.'

She swallowed a little nervously, then straightened and came out on to the deck, blushing only a little as a strange man looked her up and down.

'Dave, this is Allison.'

'Charmed, I'm most certain,' David said, taking her hand and tearing his eyes off her naked breasts.

'Um, hi,' she said. 'I hadn't realised we were there already.'

'We got a good tail wind,' Sean replied.

She nodded, then smiled at David, a middle-aged, balding man, as he turned slightly away to hide a growing erection.

There was little that embarrassed her any more. Her experiences with Sean, Jeff and Brenda had certainly revised her inhibitions and pride in herself.

Brenda, in particular, had served as an excellent guide. Once Allison's annoyance at the girl had faded she had come to rather like her. True, she was by Allison's standards, somewhat shallow, but then again she was nineteen. But the girl had an insight into men and relationships drawn from a number of years of heavy experience, and in that area she was far, far more experienced than Allison.

She and Brenda had also teased the men mercilessly, showing how much they could please each other without any male help. That had inspired the men to greater feats of endurance and inventiveness. Sean, in particular, had manfully done his best to drive them into exhaustion before they could turn to each other.

The two had competed as well in every manner of sex they could think of, including dancing.

Brenda had won all the early competitions. Her uninhibited strip teases and lewd, grinding dances had been far superior to Allison's more hesitant movements.

After a while, however, Allison became less inhibited, and soon her long legs and grace had her outdoing the younger woman with slower, more erotic movements that highlighted her body at its best. Even Brenda had been impressed.

'So what's on for today?' she asked Sean as she looked out at the city.

'Well, if you can tear your mouth away from Brenda's, we'll all go out and do the touristy thing. At least until nightfall. There are a number of interesting clubs where I want to show you off.'

'Sounds good,' she said with a grin, noting David's eyes widen at the implication she was having lesbian relations.

'I'll er, see you later, Sean,' he gulped, his eyes giving her a final long look before he hurried off down the dock.

'You really are a tease,' she said as she watched the man disappear.

'And you as well,' Sean said, grinning.

'He had a big hard-on just from seeing me,' she said smugly.

'Don't get too arrogant or I'll bend you over and tan your bottom, my dear.'

She snorted in amusement, then went back downstairs to get dressed.

They ate breakfast at a small café, then did the tourist thing at Buckingham Palace, Tower Bridge, the Parliament buildings and a number of churches. Brenda and Allison overruled going to a football match in favour of shopping, so they divided after checking into a hotel and having lunch there.

They had dinner together at the most expensive restaurant Allison had ever seen or even heard of. She was astonished at the prices.

After dinner Jeff and Brenda went to a disco, while she and Sean went to an exclusive club he knew. It was dim inside, though there were bright neon lights running along the walls, and over small round pedestals on which naked girls danced and writhed to the pounding music.

She and Sean sat down at a table near a large stage and ordered drinks. Before long women began to take the stage: strippers, or, as Sean put it, exotic dancers.

Allison would have been mortified before meeting him, but as she watched now she felt no embarrassment, and, in fact, found herself critiquing their performance, thinking of how she would do it different, comparing it to the dances she and Brenda had done on the *Wanderer*.

'What do you think of her?' Sean asked of one big-busted blonde.

'She's OK,' Allison said with a shrug.

Actually she had seemed somewhat clumsy to her.

Sean tugged on her arm and pointed up to a banner beside the stage.

AMATEUR NIGHTS EVERY FRIDAY!

She gaped at him, then closed her lips with a snap. Her heart began to pound and she thought again of how hot she had felt on the little stage at that miserable, squalid little bar back in Braceridge. Yet that had been only topless with just a little shimmying. This was an actual dance, a strip-tease, and everything had to be removed.

She watched the next dancer with growing anxiety,

noting how after she was nude she remained on stage, prancing and gyrating, swinging and swaying, and getting into very lewd positions so that everyone in the audience could, in effect, be her gynaecologist.

It was disgusting!

Yet she was undeniably sexy, hot, trampy, the subject of the lusts of all the men in the room. And as Allison looked around covertly she imagined herself up there naked, imagined the room full of men watching her, thinking of how they'd like to get their hands on her body, their cocks inside her.

'Remember the schoolgirl dance?' Sean said.

That was the last dance she had learnt, the best one. She had already got the blazer, after all, and the blouse, shoes, socks and the little tartan miniskirt had been among the clothes Sean had purchased for her. Adding it to the wardrobe had made her feel both sweet and sexy, naive and coquettish, and she had felt intensely sensual as she'd danced for the other three.

But doing it on stage in front of more than a hundred men was something entirely different. She wasn't at all sure she could work up the courage for it.

She found herself getting jealous of the girls on the stage, however, and feeling contempt for the way some of them performed – and looked. She was certainly prettier than most, she thought, even if she didn't have the big, obviously fake breasts.

Most of them looked fairly cheap, as well. She was certain she could do better.

But every time she thought seriously about it she got a little shiver of heat and fear. The idea of her being a stripper was shockingly exciting, but also quite, quite astonishing.

'What do you think, love?'

'I, uh ... I don't have any clothes for it,' she said hesitantly.

His lips curled up and he waggled his eyebrows, which made her glare at him.

'I suppose you brought some.'

He nodded.

'The schoolgirl one?'

He smiled broadly and nodded again.

'I'm not sure,' she said.

'I know, that was always your problem. You wanted to be sure before doing anything so you did nothing.'

She watched another stripper, and was disgusted, not only by how bored she looked but also by the applause which followed her.

'What are these idiots applauding for? She's awful.'

'I'm sure you could do better.'

'I could!'

He raised his eyebrows and she scowled again, heart fluttering, stomach knotting, indecisive.

She still couldn't do it, couldn't make a bold decision like that, and after a few minutes Sean seemed to realise that. He stood up and took her wrist, pulling her to her feet, then led her around the stage and through a door at the back.

She looked around anxiously but made no effort to pull back as he led her into a small office where a short, rotund man sat behind a desk talking to a sleek young woman in a minidress leaning against the wall.

'Hello, Eddie,' Sean said.

'Sean. How you doing, lad?'

'Quite well, actually. This is Allison.'

Allison blushed a little as the other two looked her up and down.

'Ah, the one you told me about earlier. She's got the body for it. Has she any talent?'

'She did quite well on the way over performing for me and a, uh, couple of others. I think your crowd will take to her.'

'She going to wear that?'

'No, blazer and short skirt. I sent it over earlier. Meghan has it.'

'Schoolgirl thing, eh? Well, she's a bit tall to get away with that.'

'As if that lot out there cares about height,' the woman said with a snort.

'I suppose you're right. You've never done anything in front of a crowd?'

Allison shook her head.

'She won a wet T-shirt contest a couple of days ago.'

'Won a wet T-shirt contest? Well, you've had some public, ah, exposure, at least. You won't turn tail and run off, will you? It really pisses off the customers when that happens.'

'She won't.'

'Don't she talk?'

'When I have to,' she said with a touch of defiance.

'All right then. In twenty minutes?'

'Sure. I'll get her stuff.'

She followed Sean further down the hall where he met a short woman who produced a plastic bag with Sean's name on it. Sean then led her into a small changing room and began to remove her clothes.

'I can do it,' she said in annoyance.

'Want a spanking right here?'

She sighed and shook her head, dropping her hands as he slipped her minidress up over her head and off.

She sat down then, wearing just a lacy white thong and french-cut bra, undoing her high heels as Sean emptied the bag out on to the bench beside her and picked up the blouse.

He slipped it over her shoulders, then began to button it up the front, then held out the skirt and had her stand and step into it, sliding it up her legs and fastening it around her waist.

After that came the white socks, the black shoes and a blue blazer which now had a crest on the pocket it hadn't before.

'You've been busy,' she noted.

'Never let the grass grow under your feet,' he said cheerfully.

'I don't know if I can!'

'Course you can. You're beautiful and sexy and you know it.'

'But in front of all those people!?'

'It'll just make you hotter than ever. You'll probably have an orgasm on stage'

'God!'

'Wait until they see your bare little pussy too.'

'Oh shit! I forgot!'

'Don't worry. They'll love it.'

'I'm sure!'

He stepped back a foot and looked at her, then grinned.

'You look adorable.'

She frowned unhappily.

He stepped forward again and hugged her, then sat her down on the bench, sitting beside her. His lips slid along her neck and up under her chin as his hand stroked along her bare legs, sliding up under her short skirt to her groin.

'Wha-what are you doing?'

He slipped his fingers down the front of her lacy white thong and began to caress her cleft, rubbing gently against her clitoris in a circular motion.

'You think you can get me hot so I won't care,' she gasped accusingly.

He ignored her words, his fingers slipping inside her, his thumb rubbing harder against her clit as his tongue slid up along her earlobe and he nibbled lightly.

The door opened and Eddie came in, halting and then beaming widely as he saw them.

'She about ready?'

'Just about,' Sean said, holding her when she would have twisted away, his fingers stroking harder as the man watched.

Eddie leant against the doorjamb, making no effort to turn away as Allison blushed in embarrassment and lowered her eyes.

Yet Sean's efforts were having a definite effect, and with the strange man's eyes on her the effect redoubled itself. She knew he was watching, even if she didn't look at him, and felt intensely sluttish as his eyes heated her face.

She could feel Sean's fingers moving easily against her moist sex now, slipping back and forth inside her and stroking along her cleft. She moaned softly before she could catch herself, then flushed deeper knowing Eddie had heard.

Sean pulled his head up and turned to the man. 'Come over here a moment, Eddie.'

'Sure,' he said, shuffling over to stand directly in front of them.

Sean slipped his lips over her ears, then whispered, 'Undo his trousers, take his cock out, and suck on it.'

She felt a stab of heat and shock, and her jaw quivered as she raised her eyes slowly. She groaned as Sean's fingers slipped even further inside her and she instinctively pushed forward against them.

'Do it, slave,' he ordered.

She looked up at the man's crotch, which was bulging, then hesitantly leant forward, spreading her legs as she raised her fingers to his zipper. She tugged it down, then slipped her hand inside, feeling for his hot erection, then awkwardly pulled it free and into the air.

She didn't look up at him, concentrating on his cock as she took it into her mouth and began to lick and suck. A heady sexual tide was rising inside her and already she could feel her worries fading, giving way to excitement and anticipation, to arousal over the very thought of doing something so deeply sluttish.

She bobbed her lips up and down on Eddie's slim cock, sucking as he groaned and held her head, whispering obscenities.

It took only seconds, then his seed filled her mouth and she swallowed instinctively. He pulled back and did up his own trousers quickly while Sean slipped his hand out from under her skirt and stood up, pulling her up beside him.

'I think she's ready now,' he said.

'Jesus,' Eddie said, shaking his head.

She followed them up a short flight of stairs and around behind the stage, hardly able to breathe with the excitement and fear warring within her, her insides fluttering as she watched the naked girl already out on stage and saw the reflected light from scores of eyes.

The music halted and Eddie went out on stage. She bit her lip as she heard him announce the first amateur of the night, a young woman from Cornwall, an artist.

The music changed pace and the tune she had danced to on the boat came on. She glanced up at Sean and he grinned and gave her a little push. She closed her eyes briefly, then walked out on to the stage.

The lights almost blinded her at first. Then she heard a chorus of whistles and obscenities scattered amongst the crowd as she reached the front of the stage between two high metal poles.

She froze for a second, then began to dance, swaying in place, loosening her body, letting her neck relax, her head roll, shifting her legs apart.

The fear began to dissipate, the excitement and then pride taking over. She raised her eyes, a look of seductive lust on her face as she began to grind her hips.

Her hands slipped upwards, the tips of her fingers caressing her body, then easing through her hair as she pushed her chest out and began to move more freely.

She danced sideways across the stage, her hot, sensuous eyes flicking over the crowd, then she backed up and abruptly halted, flinging her arms up and back, arching her back sharply.

The blazer slipped over her shoulders and dropped

down her arms to the floor. She twisted sharply, skipping back long the stage, grasping the pole – well, why not innovate? – and swung once around it.

Inside her the heat was building up higher and higher, the very anticipation of getting naked in front of so many people almost making it impossible to keep from climaxing.

She slowed, standing in place, rolling her hips as her hands moved up her body and cupped her breasts. She let her torso sway as she slowly undid one button after another, tugging the front of the blouse wider and wider, her tongue sliding along her lower lip as she pouted at them.

She turned and danced sideways, then shimmied in place, hands moving slowly up and down her body, pausing at her hip to slide the zipper of her skirt down. The skirt loosened and, as she ground her hips, it began to slide downwards.

It dropped to her ankles and she stepped out of it clad in the partly open shirt.

She skipped backwards, stepped on one heel and pried the shoe off, tossing it behind her with a flick of her foot. She did the same to the other shoe, then moved around in white socks, teasing them with flashes of her thighs and buttocks before undoing the last few buttons on the shirt and snapping it off.

There were appreciative whistles and comments as she continued the dance in the bra and thong, and she turned her back to them, rolling her buttocks as she caressed her sides then slipped her hands through her hair.

She undid her bra, then slowly turned, covering her breasts with her arms and hands, carefully slipping the straps off and dropping the bra away.

A crescendo of excitement was building inside her as she teased them with brief glimpses of her breasts, basking in their lust and desire.

She turned her back to them and let her hands fall away, rolling her neck, arching her back, then sliding her hands up above her, rolling her behind and grinding her hips as she turned round.

Gasping for breath, she felt a wave of heat strike her as they yelled in approval. Her face flushed as she bared her breasts to them and resumed her dance, clad now in just the socks and thong.

She had a lot more room here than she'd had in the boat, and her excitement again led her to improvise. She slid slowly downwards, glad now of how Sean had had her build up her dexterity, how he'd massaged her thigh muscles so she could spread them wide, do the splits.

She did so now, splitting there on the stage as the crowd whistled and applauded. She sat there, legs spread in opposite directions, pussy grinding into the stage as she felt the onset of orgasm.

She pulled her legs together and then lay back, drawing her knees up and back, grabbing her socks, then yanking her legs forward and slipping the socks off.

She stood up on bare feet now, swinging her hips, rolling and grinding as she made her way along the stage. She slid her hands up her body, cupping and squeezing her stiff-nippled breasts, then turning and wagging her behind at them.

Then she slipped her hands down her body, caught her thumbs in the sides of the thong, and bent far over, legs straight, as she slipped it right down to her ankles.

More applause, more yells and whistles as she straightened and stepped out of them.

Naked! She was naked! She was so aroused she thought she would explode!

She spread her legs, rolling her hips harder, rolling her torso, grinding at them as they yelled at her and stared at her naked flesh, at her jiggling breasts, stiff nipples, and bare little pussy slit.

She bent forward and dropped on to her hands, body

straight, then arched her back, throwing her head back. She knelt on all fours, crawling across the front of the stage like a cat, body glistening with a sheen of sweat, breasts swinging lightly below as the audience showed their approval.

She came to one of the bars and rose along it, sliding her tongue along the shining steel as she pulled her way up it. She pushed her breasts against it, rubbing them together around the cold metal, then hips swung in, her belly and groin pushing against the metal.

She pushed her legs in, gasping, hanging back now by the arms, rising and grinding herself against it. The smooth pole was cold against her pussy at first, but warmed rapidly, her moistness making it slick as she twisted and ground herself on it.

She felt the orgasm rising like a tidal wave, higher and higher as she clung to the pole with both hands, flinging her head back again and again, rolling it from side to side in a pantomime that was far more real than the audience dared hope.

Then it hit and she cried out, shaking and jerking, rolling around the pole, then sliding down it, thighs clasping it tightly as she arched back even further, hair now sweeping against the stage as she jammed herself against the pole.

Only the pounding music and applause kept her gasps and passion-filled groans from being heard by the audience as they howled their approval and pounded their fists on their tables in applause.

Her fingers slipped free then and she fell back on the stage with a gasp, still grinding against the pole. She arched her back, her hands sliding up her body, over her breasts and then up past her head and along the stage. She rolled her hips from side to side and arched her back repeatedly as the pleasure blasted through her mind and body.

And yet somehow she managed, either through some

hidden presence of mind, or through sheer luck, to keep her shaking and thrashing in time to the music.

She went limp then, but for her heaving chest. And as her mind reassembled itself she desperately sought the strength to rise, climbing to her feet with the help of the pole, then bowing to the wildly applauding audience before stumbling back off the stage.

'Fantastic!' Eddie crowed. 'You were wonderful! Christ! You've never done this before? You're an artist! A fuckin' artist! If you want regular employment I'll take you on in a second!'

'Sorry, Eddie,' Sean said, taking her arm and leading her past him, 'she doesn't want a job.'

'I'll pay her double,' Eddie protested.

'Not interested. Sorry.'

He brought her back to the little changing room and sat her on the bench, where she collapsed wearily against the wall.

'Not a soft cock in the audience, I bet,' he said with a smirk. 'And almost all of them probably thought you were just faking it. If they'd known the truth they'd have rushed past the bouncers and jumped the stage.'

'I – I can't believe I did that,' she groaned.

'I can, though I wouldn't have when we met. Come on, let's . . .'

'Here's her outfit,' Meghan said, handing the pile of clothes to Sean. 'She's got fourteen requests for private dances if she wants to go through with them.'

Sean grinned at her and Allison frowned tiredly.

'What's a private dance?'

'Just what it sounds like,' Meghan said with a shrug. 'She'll do it.'

Allison bit her lip, but was too weary, and suddenly too roused again to argue.

She donned her skirt, blouse and jacket and followed Meghan upstairs to the area set aside for lap dancing. She was filled with doubt, but her body was throbbing with heat. Lap dancing was worse than stripping, in a way, and she'd heard rumours of prostitution, that the men paid extra for it.

The booths were big enough for a chair, a very small table, and not much else. They were the size of public-rest room stalls, with the same kind of doors.

The rules for lap dancing were very simple, as Meghan explained. The client sat in the chair and paid five pounds per song. The dancer ground herself against him but did not let him touch her. She winked as she said that.

The longer she danced, the more money he would place on the table. So it did a girl good, as Meghan suggested, to be friendly.

The man sitting in the little chair was about forty, with a heavy, muscular build. He reached over and slipped a five-pound note on to the table, then pressed the little button that started the music playing from the little tinny speaker.

Swallowing nervously, Allison began to smile and sway to the music, swinging her hips from side to side as she moved closer to him, then straddled him and the chair. She moved her tongue teasingly over her lower lip as she pressed her body against him.

The moment her breasts touched his chest she felt a deep, crackling sexual electricity pass between them, and almost lost her balance. She missed a beat in her dance, then hesitantly began it again, breathing more heavily now as she peeled off her jacket, then her top, exposing her breasts.

By the time she slipped off her skirt and began to slide her heavy naked breasts over his chest the first song was ending.

Without a hint of reluctance the man slipped another note on to the table.

Allison felt her chest tighten. She had read of these kinds of places, of private dancing, read that many of the girls did more than just rub against the clients, that if the client spent enough, – if the dance went on long enough – they let the client grope them, let him sometimes even suck on their nipples or feel their genitals.

It was supposedly against rules in most places but management didn't mind, as long as things didn't go *too* far.

She rolled her hips, rubbing her stiff nipples against his shirt, feeling the heat of his body through it. She pressed her naked buttocks more firmly into his crotch, grinding and rubbing herself down on his lap as her hands gripped the back of the chair.

She rolled her head back, feeling the excitement mounting. The way her legs were spread her pussy was grinding right down against him, and between that and the excitement inside her, not to mention the feel of her sensitive breasts rubbing against his chest, she knew she was on the verge of coming.

The song ended and the man slipped another note down. She gasped, wanting to run, knowing she wouldn't be able to hold off much longer. But her excitement prevented her from pulling back. She continued to grind herself against his body, her breasts, swollen and throbbing now, sliding up and down his chest then, taking things to a new level, rubbing them against his face.

He opened his mouth and she felt his tongue slip out. She groaned but didn't pull back. She was gasping for breath now, grinding and rubbing her crotch against his lap.

When she felt his hand slide down there she gave a short, half sob. Then she felt him extend two fingers. Helplessly she drove herself on to them, feeling them penetrate between her tight, slick pubic lips and slip up into her body. She rode them, feeling her entire body flaring with heat and excitement.

He caught one of her nipples between his lips and bit

down on her breast, sucking headily as she shuddered and trembled and flashes of light blinded her.

She came violently, thrusting feverishly into his fingers, grunting and moaning so that only the pounding stereo beat from downstairs and the loud tinny music coming over the speaker in the booth kept her from being overheard by those outside.

She collapsed weakly against him, laying her head over his shoulder as the song ended. He slapped another note on to the table and another song began. His hands kneaded her buttocks as he bit and suckled on the nape of her neck. She groaned and straightened herself, and he brought his hands back around and grasped her breasts.

His fingers sunk deeply into the thick, soft flesh as he mashed and kneaded them in delight. He licked and sucked and bit all over them, with her hardly moving. Only as the next song started did she once again begin to grind and rub against him again.

She felt his erection through his pants, and watched wide-eyed as he unzipped himself and brought his long, thick cock out through the opening. Meghan had said she should leave if that happened, but her heat was still too overpowering. She stood up, rolling her hips, smiling lewdly down at him as she bent forward and pressed her breasts against his face.

He suckled and chewed again as she seized his cock and began pumping it. Then she pulled free and bent way over, keeping her hips swinging and legs jerking so nobody looking at them beneath the door would find anything amiss. She took his cock into her mouth and began bobbing excitedly up and down. He groaned and gripped her head, running his hands through her blonde hair.

Allison ground herself against him, mashing her breasts around his head and face as he licked wonderingly. His fingers dug deep furrows in her perfectly shaped orbs and she groaned as the pressure and heat grew inside her.

She slipped herself back off his lap and bent way over again, pressing her breasts around his cock, mashing them hard as his cock swelled and stiffened again.

Another note went on to the table, and he groaned as she continued to massage his erection with her breasts. She continued to grind her pussy down against his cock as they kissed deeply, as his hands crushed and squeezed and mauled her breasts with bruising, aching, wonderful force.

His cock hardened, and another note slipped on to the table, then another. She rose up, eyes glassy, body almost radiating heat, then sank down, taking his firm staff deep into her body. His lips crushed hers, muffling her cry of pleasure as an orgasm rolled over her.

She began to ride up and down wildly as he thrust into her, coming again and again and again, mind awash with lust and heat and lewd, wanton desire. Then he erupted inside her as she shuddered in animalistic ecstasy.

Fifteen

She had made almost a hundred pounds for twenty-five minutes work, but that meant virtually nothing to her except as a sign of the lowest she could go. She had, she realised afterwards, prostituted herself.

Perhaps it was only technical, for she hadn't done it for money but for the lust that had filled her, but still, she had had sex with a total stranger and then taken money for it. The very notion amazed, appalled and excited her as she sat silently thinking it over in the car back to the hotel.

'You were certainly in there for some time,' Sean said.

'Yes.'

'That was a long dance.'

She nodded.

He frowned suspiciously but said no more until they were back in the hotel room. Then he ordered her to strip and kneel before him.

'Tell me about what you did in the private booth.'

'I, uh, danced.'

'Did you touch him?'

'How do you mean?' she asked, avoiding the question.

'You know what I mean.'

'Of course I touched him.'

'Did he touch you?'

She nodded, suddenly feeling almost proud of herself. 'He couldn't keep his hands off me.'

'Did he touch your breasts?'

'Yes.'

'With his hands?'

She nodded.

'His mouth?'

She nodded and smiled.

'What else did he do?'

'He fucked me, all right,' she said arrogantly. 'And I loved it.'

'You took money for this?'

'Well, he gave me money for it, yes.'

'You realise what that makes you?'

'The whore you've been calling me since we met?'

He glared and drummed his fingers on the arm of the chair.

'Such impertinence will be punished severely. As will your sluttish behaviour.'

She stared at him calmly, then slowly stuck her tongue out.

He raised his eyebrows, then glared.

'Sorry.' She shrugged.

'Sorry? I don't think that quite cuts it, my dear.'

She shrugged.

'You are a bad girl.'

'Yes, I know.'

'A very bad girl indeed,' he said, 'And what do you think your punishment should be?'

'I don't know,' she said uncertainly. She looked up at him and there was a challenge in her eyes. 'Perhaps you could try singing to me.'

She felt her sex heat rising anew, felt her breasts throb to the beat of her heart.

He growled and pulled on her wrist, slowly, then with a sudden yank that had her sprawled across his lap, belly down.

She gasped as she felt his hand on her behind, flat, stroking her soft skin, following the contours of her buttocks.

The position was so erotic to her that she squirmed as her loins ached, and she fought to catch her breath.

'You obviously haven't the discipline to repress your sluttish instincts. Such discipline ought to have been taught you when you were younger.'

His hand moved over her round behind, squeezing and caressing her pale ivory skin.

'I . . . y-yes,' she whispered.

His hand moved straight down between her buttocks and between her thighs. He palmed her soft, still-moist mound, squeezing gently. She gasped and wriggled as he drove a finger inside her and moved it around.

'And I feel safe in saying that only a right trollop would behave as you have today.'

Allison could certainly not argue with that.

'What you need, I think, is a spanking.'

Even though she knew what he had been leading up to the words made her groan. Despite the powerful series of climaxes she had just experienced at the club she felt her juices flowing again, felt her body tingling with sexual desire and need.

'Do you agree, Allison?'

'Yes,' she said, breathing the word softly.

'Louder.'

'Yes!' she gasped.

'Say it. Tell me what to do.'

She felt her breasts swelling against the side arm of the chair, and her buttocks and sex had never felt more vulnerable as his hands moved over them.

'Say it,' he ordered.

'S-s-spank me,' she whispered.

'Louder!'

'Spank me!'

'Because you're such a bad girl?'

'I'm a bad girl,' she said, her voice breaking, 'I'm a bad, bad girl! I'm . . . I'm a slut!'

His hand slipped away from her sex, then a moment

later it cracked down against her buttocks with sufficient force to make her yelp. It stung, though not badly. The impact itself shocked her more than the pain.

Again his hand cracked down, then again and again, his other hand stroking her naked back as she wriggled helplessly.

The blows started to come down harder, and she gasped and yelped in actual pain now. But she was too aroused, too hot, and the pain was fighting an uphill battle through the pleasure coursing through her mind.

Her buttocks warmed rapidly as she moaned and squirmed. The pain rose to the point where she thought she could no longer stand it, but then faded in the face of the rising wall of heat shielding her buttocks. The sharp, stinging pain from new blows were now softer, duller, and though her behind burned, her insides were burning worse.

'Bad girl!' he said as his hand cracked down. 'Nasty, slutty girl!'

And she was, she thought dazedly. And she loved it. She felt alive and free and truly wanton as she wriggled on top of his lap.

His hand halted and shot between her trembling thighs, seizing her mound in a firm grip and squeezing it. She felt a rush of hot seeping pleasure and groaned, arching her back, pushing herself up at him like the cheapest slut.

'Do you think you can get me hard? Do you think you can do me as you did that man you prostituted yourself for?'

Prostitute.

The word made her tremble, and burned within her swirling mind and throbbing loins. The realisation that she had, in effect, prostituted herself was intensely arousing.

He pushed her off his lap without an answer, holding tight to her arm and hair as he dragged her roughly between his spread legs and jerked down his trousers.

He pulled her face into his groin, rubbing her against his maleness.

'Do it,' he growled.

She took him into her mouth, sucking excitedly even as she tried to rub her thighs together to stimulate the heat within her.

'No!' he ordered. 'None of that! You'll get your pleasure after I've had mine this time.'

He ordered her to spread her legs wide, and she obeyed, her hands massaging him as her mouth sucked and worked over his semi-flaccid cock. His hands moved roughly through her hair and down her back, sometimes squeezing one of her breasts. She continued to work, his cock hardening slowly.

Very quickly, however, he was rigid and her lips were bobbing up and down as she licked at him. She took a deep breath, then slipped his glistening shaft all the way down, taking it deep into her throat. He sighed and squeezed both her breasts, then leant over to slap at her hot buttocks.

Then he sat back, spreading his legs, laying his arms along the arms of the chair, looking arrogantly down at her as her lips and tongue caressed his cock.

She felt used, felt cheap, and her mind swirled with a mixture of indignation and thrilled, wanton excitement. The heat burned within her loins, demanding further satisfaction.

She reached down with one hand, sliding her fingers in between her legs, stroking along her moist cleft, and groaned around his cock as the pleasure rippled up her spine.

Then he yanked her up off his cock, glaring at her.

'What are you doing?' she gasped.

'I think a randy little girl like you needs to be better controlled,' he growled. 'Go and fetch the straps so I can bind your arms together behind your back.'

She stood up, her legs shaky, her head turning from

side to side, then stumbled across the room to the dresser. In one of the drawers there were several straps and she pulled them out with shaky hands.

He stood up and took them from her, then turned her round so her back was to him. She felt his strong hands on her wrists pulling them back, then up together behind her back, pressing them together.

'Hold them in place like this,' he ordered.

She obeyed, her chest heaving as she felt the strap slip round one wrist then tighten. Seconds later it slipped around the other wrist, then began to criss-cross them, binding them more and more firmly.

Her mind was gripped by a sense of sexual exhilaration as he pulled her elbows back and then slipped the strap around them, locking them back. He locked the collar round her throat, then used a small chain to lift her wrists up almost to the point where they were touching the collar, and there he locked them off.

He turned her round, his eyes hot, hungry, as they looked down the length of his nose.

'On your knees, you filthy prostitute,' he said tightly.

She sank down as if in a daze and looked up at him from her knees. He folded his arms across his chest with colossal arrogance.

'Get to work.'

His gall took her breath away, yet it delighted her as well.

She looked at his still rigid cock, then leant in and took him into her mouth.

She knelt there, fighting to breathe as the excitement ran rampant within her body. She tugged weakly at the straps, but they held as she knew they would.

A fire she could not control, did not want to control, was burning within her and nothing could stop it.

She looked up at him as her lips slipped back and forth along his shaft. It was slick again, and her lips moved easily, her tongue swirling across the underside of his cock as her cheeks puckered inwards.

Oh, this is mad, she thought dazedly.

Her breasts throbbed with excitement, her body trembling, her loins aching. She twisted her wrists and arms again and again, moving them almost constantly, feeling a searing excitement.

He reached down then, sliding his hands through her hair, then slowly closing them against her head and holding it tightly in place.

He started to thrust into her, his cock stroking back and forth over her lips, using her roughly. His control of her was absolute, and her mind flared at the thought. She wished she could step back and look at herself.

But that would be just seeing, she thought wildly, like you always used to do. Now you're doing it! Doing it!

He came in her mouth, groaning as his juices flowed, as her mouth took it all in and she swallowed it down.

He cursed, twisting her head from side to side for long moments as his climax shook him. Then he relaxed his grip, finally shoving her so she fell back on to the floor, staggering back himself and slumping in the chair.

She lay there moaning, rolling on to her side, bedraggled and helpless, then he sat forward, and fell to his knees.

He caught at her body, rolling her over, then over again, sliding her up across his legs as he knelt and sat back on his heels.

He caressed her behind again, then gave it a slap before thrusting his hand between her thighs.

'I know what you want,' he growled.

And he did, and she cried out as his fingers were pushed into her sex, as his thumb found her clitoris and crushed it, as the swelling heat exploded inside her and she bucked up helplessly, driving back, her body screaming with pleasure, her mind lashed by wondrous blasts of ecstasy.

That was not the end of her punishment, however, for Sean decided her crime was so indecent, her behaviour so defiant and her lack of remorse so obvious that a more severe punishment was required to teach her discipline.

A small bit of torture, he said, would do her wonders.

He cleared a space immediately next to the big bed, and then hung a long length of rope from the high ceiling overhead. Allison's wrists were locked together in leather restraints and bound to the rope above her head.

He then pulled her ankles apart, keeping her legs straight, spreading them wide and chaining them in place. Clamps were tightened around her nipples and then a small cord was bound to the centre of the chain, leading straight out from her body, and bound to a small hook in the wall. Then she was tightly gagged and the instrument of torture produced.

A feather.

It was a strong feather, a foot long, a goose feather. He pulled a low table over and placed it between her widely splayed legs, then placed the feather on it so the tip brushed directly against her cleft and clitoris. By shoving two heavy books against the feather he braced it in place there, then left the room.

A short time later Sean returned, hand in hand with a tall, exquisite brunette elegantly clad in a designer dress.

The brunette eyed her with a smile.

'This is our audience?' she asked in a rich, beautiful voice.

'This is Allison. She's being punished.'

'I see. Allison was bad, was she?'

Allison's face flushed in the presence of the strange woman. The woman was so beautiful, so obviously sophisticated, and what was worse, she was her own age. That made her worse than Brenda.

'What did the dear child do?'

'She prostituted herself.'

'Ah. Well. We can't have that.'

Allison squirmed under the woman's gaze.

'How much did she get?'

'I found a number of five-pound notes in her purse.'

'Five pounds? Goodness. You'll have to charge more than that, dear, or you'll upset the entire market.'

Allison glared at Sean. He knew full well she had not charged five pounds, nor done it with a lot of men as he implied.

Sean led the woman over to the bed, then they sat down right in front of her.

The woman noted the cord attached to her chain and giggled, reaching up to tug on it, making Allison groan as her nipples were stretched further.

'Oh, you really are being cruel,' the woman said, leaning forward a little and touching the feather.

She began to move it back and forth, and to Allison's alarm and frustration she felt the tickling, the soft brushing, begin to have an effect. She glared at the woman, and at Sean too, then turned her head away, determined to ignore them.

The feather stopped moving and the two stopped speaking. She lowered her head to find them embracing, kissing, stroking each other. She looked away, determined not to get as aroused as she had when he had done this to her on the boat.

She tried to shut out the sound of their lovemaking, but her mind kept slipping back to her dance, to her strip, to her private dance against the man whose name she would never know, and even without the display in the room before her she found herself soon throbbing with excitement and heat.

And then Brenda appeared in the room, giggling when she saw Allison, then growing suddenly shy in the presence of the strange woman.

'Brenda, this is Jennifer. Off with your clothes and join us. Where's Jeff?'

'Passed out drunk,' she said, quickly stripping and climbing into bed.

The two women looked at each other then at Sean. Then the three of them joined together as Allison watched.

Despite all her determination she found herself soon desperately rubbing against the feather, yet its touch was too light to do more than taunt her, and as the three on the bed writhed, twisted and rolled together a sheen of sweat appeared on her body as the heat burned within her.

It was a good three hours later when Jeff shuffled into the room. He came closer, eyed the three on the bed, then ran his hand up and down Allison's back before undoing his trousers and pushing the little table forward to get in behind her. She felt his cock pressing against her anus, felt the pressure mount.

She tried to yell at him, to scream at him, wanting him to touch her clitoris, to squeeze her breasts. But with the gag in her mouth nothing came out. He drove himself quickly up into her rectum and sodomised her slowly, almost casually, grunting with the effort of squatting down to do it.

'Don't touch her pussy,' Sean called from amidst the tangle on the bed.

Allison screamed in frustration as Jeff acknowledged the order. She felt his cock sliding up and down inside her, but even when he raised his hands to cup her breasts and squeeze them he was too soft, too gentle, too slow. He came quickly, then pulled the table back in place and left, still drunk.

When the three in the bed were finished they all sat back to watch her. Allison moaned weakly, legs and arms aching, body still throbbing with the pressure of the sexual need within.

Sean got up and unbound her ankles, slipped the table back and pulled her wrists free.

'There now. You're not bound at all,' he said, 'but you'll still obey your master. You don't need physical bounds, do you, slave?'

Allison trembled lightly and shook her head, barely able to hold her hands back from her sex.

'Speak aloud, please,' he said.

'Y-yes ... master,' she breathed, face flushing as the other two women watched.

'On your knees.'

She almost fell to her knees, staring at his naked manhood, then his buttocks as he moved away.

'On your belly now,' he said casually.

She obeyed once again, gasping as her nipples pressed into the rug.

'Now crawl to me on your belly.'

It was almost too much. Brenda was watching, but far worse the other woman, Jennifer, was staring at her with a look that seemed mildly sympathetic and mildly contemptuous. Allison hesitated, but the fires inside her were too much. She began to crawl across the floor, gasping for breath as she neared his feet.

Then, without even being asked, she bent her lips to his feet and her tongue slipped out, softly caressing his ankle, sliding over the top of his foot. A fire was burning inside her as she demonstrated her submissiveness to the strange woman, as she degraded herself before them all.

He sat down and patted his lap and she crawled up and lay across it, gasping, biting her lips, then sobbing weakly as his hand cracked down against her quickly reddening buttocks.

He halted, then his fingers slipped down between her thighs and caressed her overheated sex, thrusting into her so that she instinctively bucked back with a moan of pleasure.

'Naughty little girl,' he said. 'Are you a naughty little girl?'

'Y-yes,' she gasped.

'Say it.'

'I – I I'm a n-naughty little girl,' she gasped, his fingers making her mind spin.

He pulled back then and pushed her off him on to the floor. 'Go and see Brenda and tell her you've been naughty. Ask her to spank you.'

Allison moaned softly. Asking her to do that was simply too much, she thought. Yet her insides twisted in hunger at the thought of so shaming herself. She obediently crawled over to where Brenda sat on the edge of the bed giggling, weakly kissed and licked at her ankles, and begged her to spank her.

'Sure, slavey,' Brenda said lightly.

Brenda administered it with relish as Allison sobbed and moaned, spreading her legs in an effort to tempt the girl to sliding her hand between her legs.

And then, worse by far, Sean ordered her to go to Jennifer, crawling before her, licking at her feet. With the woman's gracious permission she crawled into her lap, lay face down, and clenched her teeth as the woman spanked her already burning red buttocks.

And when she was finished Sean came over to stand next to her.

'If you want anything else, slave, you'll have to beg Jennifer for it.'

She knew what he meant and whimpered helplessly.

'What could she want?' Jennifer asked as if in surprise.

'Tell her what you want, slave, or I shall bind you spreadeagled on the floor all night with no company but the feather.'

'I – I – I want her t-to help me,' she gasped.

'Help you what? Tell her what you want her to do,' Sean said patiently.

Allison moaned, knowing what she must do.

'Please masturbate me,' she whispered.

'Louder.'

'Please masturbate me, Jennifer,' she said, her voice breaking.

'Goodness. How disgusting,' Jennifer said.

'Do you want to?'

'I don't know. She seems fairly messy. Do I get paid?'

'No, she gets paid,' Sean said with a smirk.

'Darling, I never pay for it.'

'Beg her, slave.'

'Please, Jennifer,' she moaned. 'Please masturbate me! Please! Please!'

It took very little. Jennifer's long fingers slipped inside her and two more began to grind down against her clitoris.

The climax took her breath away, and she was left panting and gasping in a dull haze for long minutes afterwards as Sean saw the woman out.

Sixteen

Allison wore a tight, flowing, full-length black gown which covered her from throat to ankle. Underneath, she wore a narrow gold chain around her waist. Inside her were two large vibrators, buried in her vagina and rectum. The gold chain around her waist also dipped between her thighs, pulling up tightly between her freshly shaved pubic lips.

It was, as she wryly observed, somewhat like a G-string without the G.

An almost identical chain hung from her nipples, the clamps tightly locked around her throbbing little buttons. Because of the thinness of the dress fabric the small clamps protruded very obviously, though most people would probably assume she merely had large erect nipples.

That too was true, of course.

The vibrators buzzed inside her, and within minutes had her moist and squirming as she sat in the back of a taxi cab.

'Do be still,' he finally said.

'I'm sorry,' she whispered.

But she soon began squirming again, her breathing becoming heavier as the heat rose inside her.

'You're squirming again,' he said.

'I can't help it,' she gulped.

'Is that pussy of yours overheating once again?'

Allison glanced at the cabby, a young man with short

hair, and saw his eyes looking back at them in the mirror.

'I can't help it,' she said, feeling a hot flush of excitement. 'You're the one who put the vibrator up me.'

'Perhaps I should take care of you before we reach the club,' he said in a much put-upon voice.

He half turned to her, slipping her skirt slowly up over her knees, then easing his hand up beneath it, sliding it along her thigh as she opened her legs.

The cabby was staring in the mirror now, and she wondered dazedly if they'd have a crash.

Then Sean's fingers found her sex and she groaned aloud, arching her back as he began to stroke her clitoris.

'Oh yes!' she gasped in a desperate voice, playing to the cabby's wide eyes.

Her head rolled slowly and she drove herself against his fingers as she came, her breasts straining against the thin fabric of her dress.

She slumped back, gasping, as the orgasm eased off.

Sean tugged her skirt back down and turned away.

'That should do you for a little bit anyway,' he said casually.

Allison groaned more loudly than she needed to, then almost spoilt it by giggling.

You are the most wicked woman there has ever been, she thought delightedly. Even the sluts at school couldn't begin to compare to you.

The cabby managed to keep the car on the road and pulled up in front of a doorway without a word. Sean paid him, then helped Allison out.

'Do you think he's going to tell everyone he knows about what happened?' she whispered as he led her past two large doormen.

'Undoubtedly.'

She giggled in delight even though her face was flushed somewhat in embarrassment.

They went in past an arrogant-looking man in a tuxedo, walked through a narrow hallway lined in mahogany, then through a large doorway.

The room beyond was lushly carpeted. Immense leather chairs and sofas were strewn about in small groups matched with oak tables. There was a small bar at one end of the room.

There were perhaps three dozen people in the room, the majority men, and most wearing expensive dark suits. The women were all, except for one, young and beautiful. That one exception was perhaps forty, but still beautiful with her short hair, striking features, and full, voluptuous body.

As soon as she saw her Allison knew instinctively the woman was gay, and when the woman turned her eyes on her and ran them over her body she was certain of it.

She also noticed someone else: a young redhead wearing an expensive gown. She also had a gold collar around her throat and a chain that led from the collar to a man's hands.

'Sean, old boy! Delighted to see you again. It's been too long.'

The speaker was a jovial man in a tuxedo, his hair grey, his face a little flabby as he pumped Sean's hand.

'Hello, Harry, how are things?' Sean replied.

'Could be worse. Could be better. You?'

'Rather good at the moment.'

'So I see,' he said with a grin, looking Allison up and down.

'This is a young lady I met while in Cornwall. I've made her my slave.'

Allison blinked at the words, but wasn't embarrassed. She was surprised the man didn't laugh, but took it quite seriously.

'Indeed? Well now. I have to say she's certainly worth the effort to tame.'

'Required very little effort. And actually, she's not all

that tame. I have a feeling she just puts up with me sometimes so she can use me to satisfy her unnatural lusts.'

This time Harry did laugh, long and loud.

'Well,' he said with a wide grin, 'that's the best kind of slave to have.'

He looked down at her breasts then turned back to Sean.

'Nipple clamps?'

Sean nodded and turned to stroke Allison's carefully brushed hair. 'Drop your dress and show Harry, love,' he ordered.

She turned and looked at him in surprise, then at the men around her.

'Oh, don't worry about offending anyone. I told you, this is rather an exclusive club. You won't be committing a *faux pas* here.'

Allison felt her heart hammering. She saw there were several men eyeing her and licked her lips nervously. The idea of stripping in front of so many people was dreadfully embarrassing, but on the other hand the vibrators had worked their magic on her very quickly since Sean's fingers had relieved some of the pressure, and she was filled with excited desire once again.

Still, the room was full of strangers and ...

Sean reached behind her neck and undid the catch. The front of the dress dropped away.

She started to catch it, then drew her arms back down, letting it fall to her waist.

'Very nice,' Harry said admiringly, his eyes moving over her breasts, 'Those look real.'

'They are,' Sean said proudly.

'Lovely.'

He cupped one of her breasts and squeezed it casually, then let it go and tugged at the chain hanging from her nipples.

He laughed and let it go and Sean motioned for her

to pull her dress up again. Face flushed and body throbbing with lust she obeyed, trying to control her ragged breathing.

She wondered what Sean had in mind for her and exactly what kind of club this was. Was she expected to have sex with all the men here? No, that couldn't be it, for there were other girls.

'How come you haven't had her nipples pierced?' Harry asked.

'I may do it tonight, actually.'

'Much better than clamps, though clamps do hold their attention fairly well,' Harry chuckled.

'Well, Sean, this the latest?' another man asked, coming up to join them.

'Stephen! It's been too long!'

They shook hands warmly and grinned at each other.

'This is her. Allison, drop the dress so Stephen can see the goods.'

She swallowed, then reached behind her, undoing the catch and letting it fall to her waist again.

'All the way,' Sean said, eyes gleaming.

She hesitated, then pushed the dress over her hips where it slipped gently down her legs to the floor.

She stood naked but for the chains, the high stiletto heels elevating her rear for the men behind her as her skin flushed in excitement and shyness.

'Oh, very nice body,' Stephen said.

'What've you done, stuffed something up inside her?' Harry asked.

'Two vibrators,' Sean said with a grin. 'She was squirming so badly I had to bring her off right in the cab.'

'Well, a nice tip for the driver no doubt,' Stephen said dryly. 'Are you going to offer her around?'

'That's why I brought her. She's never been done by more than two men in a single evening. Well, two men and a woman.'

'Goodness, her education has been lacking. We'll have to do our best to drown the little tramp.'

He smirked at her, then reached between her legs, fingering her cleft.

Allison gasped helplessly, moaning as his finger slid up and down against the top of her moist slit.

'Hot and wet. Science is a wonderful thing, is it not?' Stephen said.

'Not all of us need mechanical devices, of course,' a new voice said.

It was the tall, broad-shouldered lesbian she had observed earlier, now standing in the midst of the small group of men around her. Next to her was a short, slim brunette with a cute pixie face.

The older woman wore a suit like the men, while the young one was in a long blue gown.

'Alexandra,' Sean said.

'I suppose the little slut has been given the chance to sample more feminine entertainments,' she said.

'Yes, as a matter of fact. She found it both enlightening and . . . quite enjoyable.'

'As well she should,' Alexandra said, glaring at her.

She turned to the younger woman beside her, then roughly gripped her arm and shoved her down on to her knees, pushing her towards Allison.

'Spread your knees, slave,' Sean ordered.

Allison stared at the girl with wide eyes, her mind filled with a hot rush of wanton elation.

She shifted her feet apart as the girl knelt between them and began to lap slowly at her sopping mound.

The first touch made her gasp, and she stared around wonderingly at the group of men watching, feeling a powerful surge in sexual electricity.

The girl slid her hands up her thighs, then around her to squeeze her buttocks as she pushed her mouth in tighter, her tongue lapping harder and faster against her clitoris.

She moaned and shuddered, her hands rising then falling on to the girl's head. She ground her loins in a slow, lewd motion, bucking into her mouth as she arched her back in bliss.

This is me! I can't believe it! I can't believe I'm doing this! I can't believe these people are . . .

She came explosively, a cry of sheerest ecstasy torn from her open mouth as she threw her head back and ground her soft mons into the young woman's mouth.

She slowly eased her head forward, her legs trembling as she gulped in air. She looked around and saw that the circle had greatly expanded, and that she was now the centre of attention for most of the people in the room.

'She sings nicely,' Alexandra said. 'You must loan her to me, my dear.'

'Of course, Alex. I'm always generous with you.'

'Why is she so naked, however?'

'I shall remedy that,' Sean said with a smile.

He turned Allison so her back was to him, then pulled her wrists together behind her back, crossed them, then wound a gold cord round them in a careful, expert, criss-crossing pattern before tying it off.

A gold collar was slipped around her throat and a gold leash attached to it. He then handed the leash to the woman as Allison continued to look around wide-eyed, filled with wonder, amazement and a raw, carnal desire at what she was experiencing.

'I think you need to thank young Emily, slave,' Alex said. Then she turned to the girl beside her. 'Lift your skirt.'

'Yes, madam,' Emily whispered, her voice accented.

She lifted her skirt above her hips to show her own smoothly shaved groin and the soft cleft between her thighs.

A tug on the chain brought Allison to her knees. She eased forward, bending and sliding her mouth along the girl's cleft. She licked lightly, riding her tongue up and down the slit, then easing it up in between, licking harder and heavier as her excitement grew.

Her mind was almost bursting with excitement and lust at the wickedness and daring of what she was taking part in, and she could feel every eye upon herself and Emily as she licked eagerly, thrusting her tongue up deep into the younger woman's sex. She heard the girl's soft groans, felt her grinding into her face, and felt elated at her success, redoubling her efforts.

The girl came with a low whimpering moan and moments later Alex pulled Allison up by the collar and led her out of the room.

Allison was a little nervous, but followed obediently, feeling the eyes of the men trail her as she left the room.

'Oh, don't worry, you little tramp,' Alexandra said. 'They'll soon have at you, jamming their filthy cocks into every orifice and filling you with their nasty cream. But I get you first.'

The girl, Emily, caught up with them and hurried ahead, opening doors for her mistress. They passed several men in the halls, all of whom looked at Allison with interest, and each time she felt a wave of lust, pride and shame as she walked past them.

Then they were in a large, luxuriously decorated bedroom, and Emily was helping Alexandra remove her clothes.

Her body, when naked, was buxom and muscular, and her eyes on Allison were hard and excited.

She reached out and slipped her fingers under the chain between her nipples, then tugged it up, making her gasp, then cry out in pain as she was forced to her toes.

'Only the cheapest, most miserable tart would allow herself to be used and bound by men the way you have,' she said, her voice filled with contempt.

Allison whimpered but she was not about to protest.

'Well? Have you nothing to say?'

'N-n-no, mistress!' she gasped.

Alexandra snorted derisively, then led her by the chain over to a strange-looking piece of furniture. It was shaped much like a saddle on top of a pedestal, and the older woman bent her forward across it. She wound her carefully brushed hair into a tight tail, then tied it to a thick metal ring on one side of the saddle while Emily strapped Allison's legs together at thigh and ankle.

Allison groaned, floods of liquid heat pouring through her body as she ground her behind up lewdly, the vibrators turning her insides to a churning stew even as the woman ran her hands over her buttocks.

'Nasty, filthy girl,' Alex said in contempt.

'Ow!' Allison cried as the woman's open hand cracked down against her behind.

'Are you sorry for being such a vile little cock-loving tramp?' Alexandra demanded.

'I – I . . .'

Alexandra slapped her behind again, and again she let out a yelp of pain.

'Well, you tart?'

'No, mistress!' she cried.

Alexandra's eyes widened, then narrowed. 'Oh, defiance, eh? Well, we'll soon take care of that!'

A steady stream of slaps landed on Allison's behind, turning it bright red. At first each blow sent a sharp stinging pain through her body, but gradually the heat of her punished flesh absorbed the new ache and clouded it.

The vibrators continued to purr within her, and her body only grew more and more aroused. Not only did the spanking not chasten her, but she was almost elated at what had happened to her so far, and what apparently awaited her.

'Foul little trollop!' Alex growled.

She thrust her hand between Allison's tightly bound thighs and cupped her mons, squeezing sharply and jamming the heel of her hand in hard, pushing it against the base of the vibrator and forcing the far end to grind up against her cervix.

The pain lasted only seconds, then a massive starburst of pleasure shook her from head to toe as she climaxed. She shook violently, her head aching as she jerked it up, tugging repeatedly against the pony-tail tied to the ring below.

'More defiance!' Alexandra growled as she watched the blonde shake and tremble.

She eyed Emily, who scurried to a nearby cupboard and withdrew a long thin length of wood. It was more a switch than a cane, but it possessed a certain visual appeal.

Alexandra moved around in front of the blonde. She untied her pony-tail from the ring and used it to lift her head up, spreading her thighs and pushing her sex into Allison's face as Emily began to swing the switch down against Allison's shapely backside.

The stinging was sharper, yet less intense. Allison's backside ached and throbbed, but the sharp little stings only served to make her loins burn hotter as she lapped headily at Alexandra's sex.

Her tongue pushed in deep, swirling around inside the woman's entrance, then sliding upwards against her engorged clitoris. She managed to get her lips against it and suck rhythmically, feeling a wave of elation as the woman groaned in pleasure.

Alexandra cursed and belittled her, yet a minute later she shuddered through a powerful orgasm.

Soon afterwards she unstrapped Allison's thighs and she and Emily took her to bed, their hands and tongues moving everywhere across the naked, tightly bound girl's body.

It seemed far longer than an hour when Sean came to fetch her, and both women were reluctant to see her go. Alexandra even offered an amazing amount of money if Sean would sell her.

Allison wasn't at all sure she was joking either.

Sean led her further down the hall and into a similar bedroom. He removed the cord from her wrists, the chains from her body, and the vibrators from inside her.

He then spread her out in the middle of a massive four-poster bed and used soft gold ropes to bind her wrists and ankles to the corners.

She was then blindfolded and left in place for what she later decided was the most erotic experience of her life.

For a long time she lay there in silence. Then someone turned on a stereo playing soft music: Brahms, she thought.

She felt a weight on the bed, then a hand moving over her body, fingers sliding along her bare cleft, then rolling her throbbing nipples between them.

No word was spoken to her. She didn't know if it was Sean or someone else. And if it were someone else she didn't know if they were alone, or if Sean were there.

The hands squeezed her breasts, caressing them lovingly, and she felt a sharp little spear of excitement as she realised the hands were too small to be Sean's, too small and too soft.

A mouth slipped on to one of her nipples, and a tongue lapped at it as it was suckled. She groaned, arching her back, straining against the bonds holding her as the lips moved over her breasts with eager lust.

She felt fingers at her sex, felt them pulled open, then she groaned as he thrust into her. Again, she knew it wasn't Sean, for it was too slender. Yet she rejoiced in it, instinctively trying to clamp her legs around her lover as the man laid his body on top of hers and began licking and kissing at the nape of her neck.

He made love slowly, his body grinding against her more than thrusting, his cock rubbing slowly across her clitoris in a way that had her nerve endings flaring and her body taut as a piano wire.

She did not climax, however, and after five or six minutes the man making love to her shuddered as he came. He lay on her for a minute as he softened, then withdrew. She did not hear the door either open or close.

She moaned softly, alone again in the darkness. Another weight pushed the bed down, another hand moving over her body, more lips on her breasts, teeth chewing at them as she gasped and whined.

Again she was mounted, and this time she climaxed, crying out her joy as her faceless lover rode her hard and fast.

Three. Five. Eight. Ten. Fifteen ... She lost count as one after another men entered the room and mounted her. Some were so heavy they crushed her into the bed, some very thin and lightweight. Some were hairy, some as smooth as women. Some dropped on top of her to grind into her. Others knelt between her splayed legs, groping her breasts as they thrust into her.

After what seemed an endless time, just after yet another man had climbed between her legs, she felt another weight, this time at the top of the bed. Hands gently tilted her head far back and she felt the unmistakable feel of a penis against her lips.

She opened them and took it into her mouth, licking and sucking even as her body was jarred by heavy thrusts from the man kneeling between her thighs. The man holding her head thrust in and she gulped his erection down, taking it deep into her throat.

The man began to slowly pump his tool in her throat as his hands stroked her head and hair. It took him little time to explode as her throat squeezed down around his tool. Yet another man quickly replaced him.

She took them on two at a time thereafter, exhausting herself with orgasms, her throat aching and raw.

They halted – briefly. Her wrists and ankles were unbound, and many hands rolled her on to her stomach.

Then her arms and legs were spread again and tied to the four corners.

Two more men moved on to the bed. She groaned as a mercifully well-oiled penis slowly pushed into her rectum. At the same time hands lifted her head and another cock was pushed into her mouth, then pushed down her throat.

Her throat became numb as they continued to use her two at a time. She lost track of how many, or even, in some hazy, feverish moments, what was happening, where she was, or even *who* she was.

She was untied again, though still blindfolded. She was lifted on to her knees, her breasts pushing in hard against the chest of a man kneeling in front of her.

He sat back then and half a dozen hands guided her on to his lap. She felt her swollen pubic lips pierced and thrust aside as she slipped down on to another hard erection. Moments later a second pushed up against her anus and thrust deep. Then hands tilted her head to one side and she found another erection pushing through her slack jaws.

It slid straight down her throat as half a dozen hands moved hungrily over her body, squeezing, pinching, caressing. She came again, her head rolling back helplessly as convulsions racked her body, her dazed nervous system tumbling and twisting in the ferocious sensory storm.

After that her mind faded to haze. She felt hands moving over her, turning and twisting and moving her, hard erections pressing against belly, back, buttocks and face, hands at her hair, her breasts, her arms and legs and feet and crotch.

After that, still blindfolded, her hands bound behind her, had come a bath at Sean's hands, then long, exhausted sleep.

Her throat was sore the next day, as were various other parts of her anatomy. It was the first day since she had met Sean which involved no sex, just sightseeing, including a balloon ride.

Seventeen

Jeff had to go home the next day, but Brenda decided to stay. The three of them took a train north to Scotland, to a small castle south of Dundee where Sean lived.

There was a dungeon below, though the devices, for the most part, looked too recent to have been in use centuries earlier.

Some of them were obviously quite old, however, and Allison felt a hot flare of excitement as she imagined virginal princesses held captive and fair maidens tormented on the rack.

'What do you think?' Sean asked, sliding his hand up and down her back.

'I ... don't know what to think,' she whispered. 'Were people really tortured here?'

'I doubt it. My family weren't given much to patience. If anyone ticked them off they just cut their heads off or something.'

'I thought it was the French that did that?'

'The French did it with a guillotine. We just used rusty old swords and axes.'

They paused by a strange steel frame and Allison examined it closely.

'What was this for?'

'Stand against it and I'll show you.'

'I ... wait until I get undressed,' she said breathlessly.

He snorted and shook his head, but nodded as she

stripped off her dress then removed her stockings and shoes. The air felt suddenly chilly but she was warm despite this. The stone floor was cold on her toes, however, as she stepped up against the frame and turned her back to to it.

Sean had her spread her legs more and step on to small metal pedals, then he closed heavy metal shackles against her ankles. He had her raise her hands up and back and closed two more heavy shackles around them.

Then a large metal box swung around and closed over her head, a padded semi-circle at its bottom pressing snugly against her throat. She heard the snap as the box was locked into place, then nothing. She could neither see nor hear a single thing through the box, and the only light was a faint shimmering that came from air holes up above her head.

'How do you like it?' Sean yelled, his voice sounding faint and metallic.

'But what does it do?' she yelled, wincing at the noise.

He unsnapped the box and raised it, smiling. 'After a day or two in it it's said some people went mad. I suppose it was a kind of early isolation chamber.'

'How do you feed someone in it?'

'You don't. I suppose you either open it and give them something to eat and drink now and then or just let them perish.'

'Did anyone . . .'

'No,' he said reassuringly, unsnapping the shackles and letting her out. 'We have much more comfortable versions of this today anyway.'

'Where?'

He took her hand and led her across the room to a heavy work table, then pulled a long leather garment from a deep drawer.

'Sit down here and slide this up your legs. Oh – wait,' he said.

He had her sit on a high stool, then picked up a pair of leather straps and bound her tightly at her ankles and thighs. Then he held out the legs of what looked like a scuba suit. As she slipped her legs down them, however, she found that there was only one leg, and it was quite tight.

Sean tugged on the leather, yanking it up inch by inch until it was below her buttocks. He had her stand then and hold him as he slipped it up around her behind.

Then he turned her and found another pair of straps. He quickly strapped her arms back at her elbows and wrists, then pulled the suit up higher, sliding it over her shoulders. He zipped it up the front and she felt like she was a mummy.

'Not too tight?'

'No,' she whispered.

'Ready for the other part?'

He lifted up a hood and she shuddered then nodded.

He bound her hair loosely behind her, then slipped the hood over her and brought it down beneath her chin. Aside from a small hole for her nose and a larger one for her mouth she was completely encased in leather.

'Open your mouth so I can gag you,' he said.

She opened her mouth wide and felt the thick leather ball-gag pushed inside, feeling her jaw go wider and wider, just to the edge of pain. Then the strap attached to the ball-gag went behind her head and was buckled in place. A moment later another strap came under her chin and pulled up, easing some of the strain on her jaw while at the same time clamping it tightly closed against the gag.

A moment later she felt herself lifted off the floor. She didn't feel any strain on her, though the suit tightened, but she was certain she was hanging in the air.

She wished she had a picture of what she looked like or a mirror. She also wondered what it would feel like if she had thought to have a vibrator or two put inside her before the suit had been strapped together.

She felt a low heat radiating up through her body as every inch of her was squeezed in by the tight leather. She imagined what she looked like, and thought of how helpless, how totally helpless she was. It was far worse than the metal box, she decided. Being unable to move any part of her body even an inch, being unable to even wriggle her toes, soon had her arms and legs aching and cramping up. She tried to twist her weight but found she couldn't even do that.

The heat rose slowly as fantasies played themselves out behind her eyes, and she moaned softly into the gag. The cramps got worse, but were soon accompanied by a hot throbbing between her legs and a tightening of her nipples.

She inhaled deeply and found the pressure tight against her breasts, felt them being squeezed in even harder. She inhaled deeply a second time, then a third, groaning in pleasure as her breasts were pushed in against her ribs.

Her entire body ached from cramps but she inhaled again and again, faster and deeper, until she was light-headed.

She felt the pressure under her chin relax, then the strap around her head was loosened and the gag pulled slowly out of her mouth.

She gulped in air as she felt herself being lowered to the ground. Sean pulled the hood back over her head, and she blinked rapidly in the low light.

'You okay?' he asked.

She nodded breathlessly.

'You were breathing pretty fast. I thought you might have panicked or something.'

'No,' she said.

'Want out of it?'

She hesitated. 'I wish I could see myself, like ... remember with the mirror in my place?'

'There is a hood that has very thin black plastic over the eyes. You can see through it. I don't have one but I can get one later.'

She nodded, looking down at the suit, noting that the straps wound through metal rings going up both sides and set into the side of the hood.

He unzipped the front and she sighed as the chill air hit her overheated skin. She felt her breasts swell, the nipples, which had been squeezed back, jutting out erect as Sean peeled the suit back over her shoulders, then down her body.

'I must have looked so hot hanging there,' she whispered, looking up at the chain above.

'Next time I'll take videos. But – perhaps I can arrange something.'

He unstrapped her arms and she groaned as they came loose. Almost immediately, though, he turned her around and bent her over the stool. His hand slid along the inside of her buttocks, fingers pushing in against her inner thighs and stroking her bare mound.

He pulled back and opened a drawer on the table, then plucked a thick dildo from it.

'A vibrator would be better,' she said breathlessly as she stared at the dildo.

'Don't tell me what you want, slave.'

He rubbed the dildo against her sex, then slowly pushed it in, rotating it and pumping in slow, shallow strokes.

Allison gripped the legs of the stool, bending over further, wishing he would unstrap and open her legs.

Then he pulled the dildo back and she felt his finger probing at the entrance to her rectum. She gasped, instinctively trying to open her legs.

'Are you . . .'

'Shh,' he ordered, slapping her behind sharply.

She felt his finger sliding into her, coated in some slippery substance. It pumped in and out and twisted around inside her. Then the dildo was pushed in. She focused her attention on keeping her anal muscles from clamping down, but every few inches they would anyway. Then Sean would halt, slap her behind, and the sting would distract her, allowing him to slide the thing deeper.

She felt a small cramp deep in her belly, gasping as he tried to jab the dildo further. A moment later he let go of it and reached to the drawer again. This time he drew out a thick vibrator and she squirmed in anticipation as he rubbed the rounded head up and down against her cleft.

She felt her pussy lips stretch and strain as Sean eased the vibrator into her. Keeping her legs closed only made her tighter than usual, and she gasped at the feeling of pressure against her as it bored into her body.

Sean dragged her upright then, and she felt a pleasant twisting inside her belly as the flexible sleeves of her rectum and pussy tunnel squeezed around the hardness of the two thick tubes inside her. He dragged her back a foot or two until she was directly under the chains, then lifted her wrists and clipped them to the rings set into her wrist restraints.

She looked up at them breathlessly, then watched Sean go to the wall and turn a small crank. The pressure tightened on her wrists, and she yelped as she was lifted off the floor to hang with her toes wiggling freely.

The pressure on her arms and shoulders felt deliciously sensual, and she found her breathing coming in ragged gasps and pants as Sean came back to her and smiled. He lifted her legs up and back, then pressed his fingers against the base of the vibrator jutting out an inch or so from her pussy lips. It started to buzz and he dropped her legs so they swung down and back.

He kissed her on the cheek, gave one of her breasts a squeeze, then turned all the lights off but one and left her.

Allison looked down the long length of her body, then up at her arms above. A curtain of sensual pleasure swept around her as she basked in the eroticism of being hung by the wrists. The vibrator buzzing between her legs, still holding her pubic lips back, was making her insides squirm, making her pussy muscles clench and spasm as her legs twitched far below her.

She discovered hanging by the wrists was not as simple as she'd read. She was, she realised, unconsciously 'holding' herself up, using her arms to pull herself rather than just hanging limply. When she relaxed her arms completely she felt a stabbing pain in the muscles at the sides of her chest, and winced, pulling herself up once again.

She twisted her lower body, trying to make the dildo or vibrator jerk inside her, wanting that small extra sensation as her body began to throb with sexual heat.

Her nipples were almost painfully stiff, and she wished for someone to come out, for Sean to chew and suck on them, to pinch and pull them.

She gazed at her shadow on the wall, and imagined she were being whipped by some cruel man. She arched her back as though struck, watching the movement of her shadow on the wall. She jerked again, gasping as though in pain.

She wondered what it would be like to be whipped, and thought about asking Sean. And as she realised with a start that she was actually contemplating it, that she was considering being whipped for real, she felt a crackling sexual heat ripple up and down her spine, and felt her pussy clamp down again and again on the vibrator buried within it.

The orgasm hit her suddenly, she writhed in its grip, throwing back her head and jerking spastically as it poured sensual heat through her body.

Across the room, Sean watched, feeling his erection pressing demandingly against the inside of his pants. He held still in the shadows, watching her go limp, hearing her soft gasps and low groan. She rolled her head slowly, then drew in a deep breath, and he thought he had rarely seen such a beautiful and erotic sight.

He stepped forward then and walked up to her.

'Sean!' she gasped.

He slid his hands behind her head and gripped her thick, golden hair, jerking her head up as he crushed her lips with his. His tongue pushed into her mouth and she moaned against him as he slid one hand slowly down her shoulder and on to her chest, then cupped her breast and squeezed it roughly.

'S-Sean!' she gasped, twisting her head back.

'What?'

'Do you . . . have you ever whipped anyone?'

He sucked in his breath quickly then nodded.

'Could – you –'

'Softly, perhaps. We'll see how it goes.'

He moved behind her and she tried to turn her head to look, but was defeated. Then he came back, holding a strange object in his hands. It had a foot-long solid black handle. Sprouting from the handle were what appeared to be a score of thin leather strips. It looked rawly threatening and she gazed at it in helpless fascination.

'It's only a flogger, not a cat. The braids aren't knotted, and they're fairly light. I never get into the really rough stuff. I mean, there are people who use actual bullwhips on each other. But I don't like it. I think this will serve the purpose for you.'

'D-does it hurt a lot?' she whispered.

'That depends on your definition. It certainly stings. I'll start out light, and you let me know if you think it's too hard . . . or too soft.'

'Here you two are,' Brenda said, skipping out from the stairwell. 'I thought you might be –'

She stared at Allison in delight. 'You look so hot!' she cried.

Then she saw the flogger and her jaw dropped. 'Wow!' she squeaked.

'Come here, you,' Sean ordered.

She scurried forward and he motioned towards Allison. She grinned and ran her hands up and down the bound woman's body, then began to lick and suck at her nipples as her fingers kneaded her breasts.

She licked her way down her body and peered at the vibrator poking out between her taut sex lips, then pressed her lips in and began to lap at her clitoris.

'Oh!' Allison gasped, her head jerking back.

Sean moved slowly behind her, watching her body, watching the play of muscles beneath her skin as she began to tremble and jerk to her body's inner fires. He raised the flog slowly then lashed out, letting the strips slap lightly against the centre of her back.

Allison cried out, more in surprise than pain, and a blast of shocked excitement hit her.

'Too hard?' Sean asked.

'Again!' she gasped.

Sean let the flog lash across her back again, then again, shifting his aim downwards along her back, snapping the strips of leather against her rounded buttocks as she gasped and jerked and moaned.

He struck the centre of her back again, then yet again.

'Harder!' she demanded.

The flog snapped down again, harder, the sound a sharp slap in the echoing stillness of the dungeon.

'Harder!' she cried.

Again it lashed out, the sound angry now as it struck her soft skin. Her body jerked under the lash, and her head jerked back as she came, humping desperately against Brenda's tongue as the brunette continued to lap furiously at her clitoris.

She went limp, gulping in air.

'Y-you have to get a video camera,' she groaned.

'Some things are for enjoyment now, not vicariously in the future,' Sean said.

Brenda stood up, eyes shining. 'I – I want to be your slave!' she cried.

Allison stared at her in shock.

'I already have a slave,' Sean said mildly.

'But you could have two!' she blurted.

He appeared to think about it for several seconds.

'Strip,' he said.

She stripped off her clothes and raised her hands behind her head, thrusting her breasts out for him to fondle and stroke.

He went to the wall instead, lowering Allison to the floor, then unclipping the chains from the rings set into her wrist restraints. She groaned and rubbed her sore biceps, swaying weakly until he unstrapped her thighs and ankles.

Sean approached Brenda and ran a hand slowly over her big breasts, then lifted a chain – a nipple chain, Allison saw. She stroked her clitoris, still feeling a rush of heat within her blood, watching as he slipped the loops of the chain around Brenda's thick, swollen nipples and tightened them until the girl gasped.

'You're sure you want to be a slave?' he purred, holding the chain up with one finger, tugging it up to lift her to her toes.

'Y-yes!' Brenda gasped.

He placed a loose metal collar around her neck. There were a pair of small loops at the back and he forced her arms up high and slipped her thumbs into them, tightening them to hold her hands in place. Then he produced a small piece of cord and tied her two big toes together before turning her to face the cold stone wall.

Allison watched avidly, gasping now as she fingered her clitoris. She slowly sank to her knees, hardly conscious of doing it, caught up in how beautiful and erotic Brenda looked when so tightly bound.

Sean pushed Brenda against the wall, then lifted her nipple chain up and slipped it over a hook set into the wall, making her wince as she rose on her toes.

'Naughty little slave girls require constant discipline,' he said, sliding a paddle out of a drawer. 'Do you think you need constant discipline, Brenda?'

'Y-yes, m-master,' she gasped.

He eyed Allison, who looked on, panting and rubbing herself.

'We'll see.'

He went back to the drawer and came back with a small, wooden paddle. Allison gasped at the sight, holding back her orgasm, waiting and watching as he walked up behind Brenda.

He raised his arm then brought the paddle down against Brenda's upturned buttocks.

Brenda yelped and shook, then moaned softy.

Allison shook as well, her fingers rubbing faster and faster against her clitoris, her other hand cupping and squeezing one of her breasts.

Sean brought the paddle down again, then again, smacking her slowly, the blows growing harder as her behind turned a bright red.

Allison came on the third stroke, breathlessly shaking and moaning as her insides boiled over and a hot, wicked pleasure fountained up in the back of her mind.

After a dozen blows Sean slipped the chain off the hook and had her bend far over to take him into her mouth. He then motioned to Allison, who staggered to her feet and moved behind her, dropped to her knees and began to lick at her moist opening.

It took mere instants for the girl to come, her body shuddering as she bucked back into Allison's mouth.

'Well, maybe I've found another natural,' Sean said, pumping slowly into the moaning girl's mouth.

If Brenda wasn't acting, she had climaxed no less than a half dozen times as Allison licked away at her, especially after Sean began to pump into her throat.

That evening, however, they left Brenda bound tightly at home, laying back on what he called the rack, while he took Allison to a theatre.

'Slave,' he said.

She looked up at him.

'There'll be a special ceremony tonight at the theatre. A graduation ceremony, if you will.'

'What kind of graduation?'

'Yours.'

She blinked her eyes in surprise.

'I believe, after the last week or so, that you've achieved a sufficient maturity and strength to become a true slave. And to proclaim that to everyone.'

'What do you want me to do?'

'Master,' he said.

'What do you want me to do, master?'

'You're going to demonstrate your obedience and how sensual and erotic you are.'

At the theatre they gave her a very thin, lightweight gown to wear, and as the curtain opened she knelt just offstage, heart pounding as she thought of what Sean had told her of the 'ceremonies'. Two men stood on the stage, both in leather from head to toe, leather masks over their faces.

She wore white as she walked hesitantly forward. The eyes of the audience turned to her, watching as one of the men approached. She fell to her knees before him, breathless now.

'Why are you here?' he demanded.

'I – I wish to be a slave,' she whispered.

'Stand.'

She stood shakily and he gripped the front of her

gown with immense hands, tearing it open. The other moved behind her, gripping the back and shredding it. In seconds she was nude, her skin flushing.

Both of them had hard leather clothes and chains, crushing her between them as the audience looked on, their hands moving roughly over her body.

One of them undid his leather trousers, the other opened his leather codpiece. Two hard erections were pushed against her and driven deep inside, almost lifting her off her feet. Hands clawed at her, teeth bit into both sides of her throat. She shook and moaned, the stage silent but for her sounds, no music playing, the audience watching quietly.

The two large men began to work themselves in and out, often in tandem, sometimes thrusting in at the same time, sometimes alternating. She moaned as the heat rose to intoxicating levels, her mind surrounded by a glittering cloud of sexual desire, abandoning all inhibitions to a carnal heat.

But it was only weeks ago, she thought dazedly, I was a shy painter, and now ...

She cried out as the climax hit her, as the two men thrust their loins into her furiously, their strong hands on her thighs and buttocks, tearing her legs up and apart, holding her between them as they used her.

And then she was lowered to the floor, panting, and led across the stage by the arms, groaning as they took her to the centre. There lay a table with gruesome-looking devices of torture. Yet there were no restraints as she was ordered to lay her hand across a high, narrow table and one of the men moved beside her.

He held what looked like a small, gold bracelet, finely made, glistening. A heavy pad was placed around her wrist, then the bracelet, which was open-ended, was put over it. It was closed and an acetylene torch spit fire.

The bracelet, a golden shackle, was welded in place, not to be removed.

She stared at it in wonder, the enormity of the realisation hitting her like a hammer. Never to be removed. To be there always, a sign of her slavery, her sexual submissiveness.

She felt sudden qualms and worries, but then a soaring wave of excitement overwhelmed them. She still thought of herself as a free, independent woman, yet she was to be a slave now, a chained slave at any man's bidding.

The second bracelet was tightly placed over a pad on her other wrist, and again welded together, immovable. Two more rings were slipped around her ankles in a similar fashion, then a final pad was slipped around her throat and a narrow band of gold wrapped around it. Her face was carefully covered but she could hear the torch hiss as it welded the collar together.

The collar was truly breathtaking. The mere idea of being welded into a slave's collar from which she could not escape was enough to make her knees weak and her mind spin. A woman shackled and collared in that manner was the stuff of dreams and fantasies. Before meeting Sean she would hardly have lent credence to the thought such women existed in modern times.

And now she was to be one, a total sexual being.

Cold water cooled her body and the asbestos pads were removed.

An enormous mirror covered the back wall, and she turned to stare at herself as the crowd applauded. The men allowed her to walk back and forth, to finger the shackles and collar and stare at herself in amazement and wonder. She was dazed with excitement at becoming so wanton a woman, so wicked and complete an object of sexual desire.

And still the men were not finished. They ordered her back to the table and there she saw more gold bands, but smaller, much smaller. And she understood with another roiling and fluttering in her belly, that she was to be further marked.

Again they did not bind or restrain her. She stood on a low pedestal, legs apart, and willingly raised her arms up, thrusting out her breasts as she brought her hands behind her head.

A slave, she thought wonderingly, a sexual slave, chained and – and pierced.

She felt the spray against her nipple and closed her eyes, moaning as she awaited the pinch. Then it came. Eyes closed, she did not look, but stood on shaky legs, gasping softly as fingers rolled her nipple.

Then she felt the chill against her other breast, numbing its centre, and moments later another light pinch.

She drew her head forward and looked down to see gold rings hanging gently from her pierced nipples, narrow circles of glistening metal lying flat against her soft, pale flesh.

Then one more, and again she raised her head, closing her eyes, quivering lightly as the spray hit her between the legs. She gasped as she felt the piercing, clenching her teeth for a few seconds before the pain subsided. Another gold ring was slipped into place.

They stood back and she stepped down, turning to stare at herself once again, suffused by a sexual heat that blotted out everything but her own pleasure, and the heated awareness of the strange world of sensual delights she had joined.

Her body fairly glowed in the light, hair tumbling over bare shoulders. Naked, she stood on the stage as the others looked on, gold shackles glinting, collar circling her throat, rings hanging from nipples and clitoris.

Sex, she thought. I am a creature of sex.

The bands were loose, but they could not come off. There were no openings, no locks. They were permanent. Their only adornments were a small round ring on one side and a small clip on the other.

To be used to chain her – like an animal.

She turned then and walked shakily to Sean as he emerged from offstage, kneeling before him. He lifted her up, kissed her, turned her around, then pulled her wrists back behind her, clipping them together.

He turned her around again and she sank to her knees, taking him into her mouth and sliding her lips down to the base of his cock, bobbing her lips slowly back and forth as the audience applauded.

For several days after that they toured Scotland. She and Sean were something akin to honeymooners, while Brenda acted as slave, not just to Sean, but to Allison as well. And Allison was often instructed to punish the naughty little slave girl.

The first time she was able to spank Brenda into an orgasm, her flaming hand cracking against the bound girl's scarlet behind, she felt an intense power and lust. This made her realise there were aspects of the power games she'd been playing that had been left out of her education.

'Naughty little girl,' she growled, her hand stroking over Brenda's soft, red buttocks.

'I'm sorry, mistress,' Brenda whimpered.

Allison's fingers slipped down to caress Brenda's carefully shaved cleft, then as the girl started to grind her hips she again smacked her hand sharply against her buttocks, drawing a cry of pain.

For long, long minutes she alternately spanked and teased Brenda, stroking and slapping her until she was trembling and Allison herself was so hot she could hardly breathe.

Then she forced the girl, arms bound tight behind her back, to kneel while she herself sat back in the chair and spread her legs. Brenda needed no instructions and her tongue was soon lapping eagerly at Allison's buzzing, sparkling clitoris.

She made Brenda lick her to two climaxes before

roughly dragging her across her lap and fingering her to her own shattering orgasm.

They made an odd threesome, with Allison submissive – in most things – to Sean, and Brenda utterly submissive to both of them. In fact, it didn't take long for Allison to realise that Brenda was diving even further into submissiveness than she herself ever had. The girl was meekly obedient at all times, even as she seemed to glow with excitement and heat.

Often the two would kneel at Sean's feet, bound tightly, licking and sucking at his manhood as he stood proudly over them. But other times she was left alone with her own slave to train and enjoy while Sean took care of minor business matters.

It was a lot harder to embarrass Brenda than herself, but Allison knew from her own experience how much excitement came with feeling that flush of embarrassment around strangers. She also knew that it was at its best when mixed with the thrill of not knowing just how far she could go, not knowing what was going to happen or what her partner would do. A little anxiety and uncertainty added wonders to a situation.

With that in mind she acted very cattily to Brenda one night, as if she were jealous. They were in Manchester at the time, staying in a luxury flat owned by a friend of Sean's. After Sean had apparently gone to bed Allison went to Brenda's room.

The girl opened her eyes quickly, not yet having fallen asleep, and obediently crawled out of bed and knelt at Allison's feet.

'I've had it with you, you cheap little trollop,' Allison said with a scowl. 'Sean and I don't need some bigteated cow hanging around, always wanting attention!'

'I'm sorry, mistress,' Brenda said.

'Shut up!'

She removed the shackles and chains from the girl, then ordered her to place her wrists behind her back.

She carefully bound them with rope, then gagged her and pulled her to her feet.

'Come on, you,' she snapped. 'I'm getting rid of you once and for all.'

Brenda's big eyes blinked at her as Allison led her to the door, then opened it and took her out into the hallway.

Allison was taking a bit of a chance but it was late and nobody was around. Brenda squirmed worriedly, though Allison could see that she was obviously aroused being naked in a public place.

Allison called the lift and led Brenda inside, holding her arm carefully, then leant in against her.

'There's a pimp downtown that says he'll pay good money for a white girl with big boobs,' she said. 'I'm going to get rid of you in a way that will no doubt keep you happy forever.'

Brenda's eyes widened and she seemed to tremble, though not with fear. Allison was simply too softhearted to really get away with playing a nasty, vindictive woman, and Brenda knew her too well. Still, the girl didn't know what was going on, and her bare feet danced on the cold floor of the lift even as the bell chimed and the doors opened.

Allison led her out into the garage, both of them looking around warily. 'Come, slave,' she said imperiously, leading the naked girl out onto the concrete floor, then down a line of cars to Sean's Mercedes.

She opened the boot and ordered Brenda inside, helping her pull her legs in, then closed it after her. She scurried around and opened the driver's door as Sean emerged from behind another car, winking, then both of them climbed in at the same time.

They drove through the city to a deserted section of the downtown area where one of Sean's friends owned a shop. Allison parked in the dark alley behind it as Sean hurried inside, then she opened the boot and helped Brenda out.

'Come, slave. The pimp who buys girls lives here.'

Brenda shivered slightly, the chilly night air raising goose bumps over her skin as she let Allison lead her down the alley and up to the steel door at the back of the shop. Allison knocked and after a moment a tall, powerfully built black man in ragged clothes opened it.

'Yeah?' he demanded.

'You Darren?'

'What if I am?'

'I got this slut I want to sell,' Allison said.

The man's eyes moved coldly over Brenda, who squeezed her thighs together and moaned softly.

'Bring her inside.'

Allison brought Brenda in and the man shut and locked the door. Together they led her down a flight of stone steps and then down a dark, damp hallway into a back room.

'How much you want for her?' he asked.

Allison smiled at Brenda. 'Take a look at those breasts,' she said. 'With a body like hers you can make a fortune, easily five hundred pounds a day.'

The black man ran his fingers through Brenda's hair, jerking her head back suddenly to make her breasts thrust out harder.

'I can make money off her, all right,' he said, reaching down to squeeze one of her hot, swollen breasts, 'but it'll take me a lot of effort to keep her in line, too.'

'No it won't. She's a complete whore. She loves sex, with anyone at all. She's also a mousy little slave girl who'll do anything you want.'

She undid the gag from Brenda's mouth and the brunette gasped and licked her lips.

'You'll obey Mr Darren, won't you, slave?' Allison growled.

'I – I – I . . .'

'Answer!'

'Y-yes, mistress!' Brenda gasped, staring up at the man with wide eyes.

'That so?' the man drawled, smirking down at her.

He undid his pants and pulled out a long, thick, semi-flaccid cock.

'Do me then, girl.'

Brenda took a deep, shuddering breath, then slipped to her knees and took him into her mouth. She bobbed her lips up and down his cock, taking more and more into her mouth as he stood with arms folded across his chest. Then, finally, she swallowed it whole, pressing her lips tightly around the base of his shaft.

He groaned and brought his hands down to caress her hair as she slowly eased back.

'This is one talented little slut,' he said appreciatively.

'Just see how hot she is,' Allison said, pulling on Brenda's hair, yanking her to her feet then shoving her over the table as she kicked her legs apart. 'Go ahead. Use her. She'll love it.'

Darren stepped forward and Brenda whimpered, grinding her hips helplessly. He rubbed his spit-wet cock along her shaven opening, then pushed himself into her, drawing a deep groan of pleasure.

'She sure does like that,' he said.

'I told you,' Allison said. 'You can put her on a street corner, then have her stripping in clubs when she's not working.'

Darren's thick organ slid back and forth through Brenda's tight opening as she whimpered and bucked back against him. His hands moved over her buttocks, then down her sides to cup her breasts.

'That true, baby?' he asked.

'Y-yes, m-master!' Brenda gasped.

He pumped faster, his hips slapping against her shapely rear as he rode her.

'I'll give you a couple of thousand pounds for her,' he said.

'Are you joking? You can make that in less than a week.'

'I got expenses.'

'Ten thousand.'

'Too much.'

He altered his strokes, thrusting in from one side, then the other as Brenda gasped and moaned and humped back against him.

'An Arab guy offered me eight just last week,' she said. 'He wanted to ship her to Iran, so I'm not going to take any less.'

'Well, she is nice and snug inside. OK, ten thousand for her.'

Brenda cried out as she came, shaking and jerking as the man thrust in steadily. He pulled out and went to a metal locker, took out an envelope, pretended to count out some notes and handed it to Allison.

She counted it suspiciously, then smiled and thanked him. 'Goodbye, slave,' she said, giving Brenda's behind a hard smack. She turned and trotted away then, leaving the room, but hiding around the corner so she could peek in and watch as he moved once more towards Brenda.

'You belong to me now, girl,' he said. 'You better be worth the money I paid.'

He entered her again, thrusting aggressively, driving her to a second orgasm before finishing.

He had her kneel and suck him erect again, then sodomised her as she bent over the table once more. Finally done with her, he led her towards the door. Allison hurried aside, her own insides squirming with excitement as he led her back down the hall and up the stairs.

'My partners have a place across the alley,' she heard him tell her. 'They'll all want to try you out before we put you on the street.'

He opened the door and led her out into the dark alley – right up to the car where Sean waited.

'There you are,' he said with a grin.

He kissed her on the forehead, winked, then shook hands with Sean and went back inside.

'We decided not to sell you after all,' Sean said.

Brenda giggled and bit her lip excitedly. 'You know, I was just starting to wonder . . . just a little bit.'

'Naughty little slut,' Sean said to Allison. 'Trying to sell my slave.'

'I'm sorry, master,' she said.

'You'll be sorrier when I get you home, slave.'

The two of them sat in the back as Sean drove.

'You know, it was so real I was kind of disappointed it wasn't. I mean, not that I want to be a prostitute or anything but . . . it was just so incredibly hot, you know, to think I had been sold to some big black pimp.'

'Actually he's a florist,' Sean said, 'He owns half a dozen shops. We went to college together.'

Brenda giggled again.

It wasn't often they could risk something like that, of course. But often, just for fun, Allison would order the girl to slump back naked in a chair near the door, using twin dildos on herself, and then order something. When the delivery man would arrive Brenda would, of course, be in plain sight, and his eyes would go huge as he stared. Allison always politely offered her to the man and usually the offer was quickly accepted.

When they were indoors Brenda remained nude at all times save for the chains and metal collar and wrist restraints. She crawled about scrubbing the floor, eating her food and water set out for her and delighting in her degradation. Whenever neither Sean nor Allison wasn't attending to her or she didn't have a chore she would often use dildos and vibrators on herself, gasping pleasure as she drove herself to orgasm.

She wanted to become a true slave like Allison, to have collar and restraints welded about her wrists, ankles and throat, but neither of them would agree to it. She was, after all, still a teenager, and not, they thought, old enough to make a decision like that just yet.

One day Jeff arrived. He was stunned and excited beyond measure to find his former girlfriend now a naked, chained slave girl. He couldn't get enough of her, and delighted in demeaning and ordering her about.

When Allison checked in on them the next morning she found Brenda on the floor, hog tied, as she had been all night, and Jeff sprawled out naked on the bed, arms and legs spread wide. Annoyed, she thought to wake him and give him a few not so gentle instructions in how to care properly for a slave girl, but then his position gave her a startling idea.

The four corners of the bed naturally had straps attached, and no doubt they had been used on Brenda the night before. But now as she crept forward she saw how closely Jeff's wrists were to them and she bit her lip, repressing a wild giggle.

She pulled one down and ever so gently wrapped it around Jeff's left wrist, then pulled it snug and locked it. She moved around the bed then did the same to his other wrist. He stirred and mumbled in his sleep but did not waken.

She lifted his left leg, spreading it wider, then quickly buckled the third strap around his ankle.

'Wha ... what's ... going on?' he asked groggily, lifting his head.

She quickly slipped the final strap around his ankle, then gave his leg a hard pull and buckled the strap tight.

'Hey!' he said, sounding annoyed.

Allison ignored him, going to Brenda and untying her, then massaging her aching limbs and helping her out of the room. A few minutes later she returned to find Jeff scowling at her.

'What do you mean by strapping me down?' he demanded. 'You're going to get such a spanking ...'

'Silence, slave,' she ordered imperiously.

He stared at her in amazement.

'W-what did you call me?'

'Slave,' she said, approaching the bed, then peeling her own nightshirt up and off before climbing in.

He licked his lips as his eyes moved over her body.

'Sure, love. Whatever you say.'

She slapped his face lightly and he frowned.

'Mistress, slave boy. Call me mistress,' she ordered.

'Mistress,' he said, a little embarrassed.

'Again.'

'Mistress.'

'What are you?'

'A-a slave,' he said.

She smiled, sliding her hands up and down his body, fingers caressing him as she leant in and licked along his inner thigh. His manhood rose quickly and was fully erect before she even touched it. She slipped her fingers around it and gave it a thoughtful squeeze, then smiled coyly.

She bent and kissed the head, then took him into her mouth, bobbing her lips up and down slowly as he groaned and pulled against the straps.

But then she pulled back and climbed out of bed.

'Hey! Don't stop now!'

'You don't give orders, slave.'

She found a padded blindfold and quickly returned, sliding it over his face, then went to the toilet and got shaving cream, water and a razor. She sat crosslegged between his spread legs, lathering up his groin as he sighed in pleasure, then began to shave away at his pubic hair.

'Hey . . . what are you doing?' he demanded.

'Shaving you bare, like Brenda and I are.'

'You can't do that!'

She paused. 'Why?'

'Well . . . well, I . . . I . . .'

'You're attached to your pubic hair?'

'Well, no, but . . .'

She continued shaving, carefully removing every hair she could find, squeezing his penis, running her hands up and down it as she moved it around to pull it out of the way. Then when she was done she turned to the penis itself.

Very carefully she ran the safety razor back and forth along it, removing the hairs from the shaft as Jeff gasped in excitement and worry.

A damp towel cleaned him off and she stared at his naked erection in excitement.

'It looks bigger somehow,' she said.

'It does?'

She could hardly keep her hands off it, in fact. She pumped it slowly, delighted by how soft it felt against her fingers. Then she bent and took it into her mouth. Without the hair it seemed even slicker than usual and she quickly gulped it down, swallowing his sperm as he came.

Jeff was so aroused it took little effort to harden him again. This time Allison mounted him, straddling his hips and sliding her own moist sex up and down his silky cock, pausing every now and then to make him beg for more.

After a long, hard ride she unstrapped him and ordered him to roll over. He obeyed, still gasping for breath, and she quickly strapped his wrists together behind his back, then collared and leashed him and led the naked man out of the bedroom and down the hall to where Brenda sat eating breakfast.

Brenda was astonished but very clearly excited to see her boyfriend so bound. He knelt before her and meekly apologised for keeping her tied so uncomfortably all night; then, with Allison prodding him, begged her to spank him.

Brenda was hesitant but again Allison was in charge

and she quickly took Jeff across her lap and began to spank his bare behind.

Satisfied, Allison left them to it, then went out in the garden to find Sean examining a blocked outlet in one of the fountains.

'Hello,' he said, giving her a quick kiss.

'Hello. The others are up.'

'That's nice.'

'We have another slave.'

He peered at her in surprise. 'Excuse me?'

'Jeffrey is at this moment naked, his hands tied behind his back, and bent over Brenda's lap being spanked.'

'Is that a joke?'

She giggled and shook her head.

He made a face. 'Disgusting.'

She glared and he quickly continued, 'Not that there's anything wrong with being a slave, of course, if that's the way one is inclined.'

'I think you would look very good in handcuffs,' she said thoughtfully.

He chuckled and shook his head. 'Oh no, my dear. If you want a little male slave that's up to you, but my interests lie on the other side of the chains.'

'But you'll do it anyway, won't you, for me?' she pouted appealingly.

'No.'

'Please?'

'No! Absolutely not.'

'Just once? Pretty, pretty please?'

'Allison,' he groaned.

'That's mistress to you, slave boy,' she said, beaming.

NEW BOOKS

Coming up from Nexus and Black Lace

Nexus

Educating Ella by Stephen Ferris
August 1997   Price £4.99   ISBN: 0 352 33189 5
When young journalist Emma is asked by Paula, her editor and lesbian lover, to follow up a story about Miss Doyle's bizarre sex club, she becomes addicted to the strange practices that go on there. For breaking the rules she is handed over to the Master, to undergo the Rites of Correction at the Temple of Pleasure.

Secrets of the Whipcord by Michaela Wallace
August 1997   Price £4.99   ISBN: 0 352 33188 7
Jo discovers a mysterious old book that has an intense aphrodisiac power over any woman who reads it. A hidden cult steals the book and plans to use it to lure young women to their organisation to satisfy their bizarre lusts, but she is determined to thwart them. In order to get the book back, however, she must join the society by undergoing five humiliating yet strangely enjoyable ordeals.

There are three Nexus titles published in September

Amanda in the Private House by Esme Ombreux
September 1997   Price £4.99   ISBN: 0 352 33195 3
When Amanda's housekeeper goes missing, she travels to France in an attempt to find her. During the search she meets Michael, who awakens in her a taste for the shameful delights of discipline and introduces her to a secret society of hedonistic perverts who share her unusual desires. Amanda revels in her new-found sexual freedom, voluntarily submitting to extreme indignities of punishment and humiliation.

Bound to Submit by Amanda Ware
September 1997   Price £4.99   ISBN: 0 352 33194 1

The beautiful submissive Caroline is married to her new master at a bizarre fetishistic ceremony in the USA. He is keen to turn his new wife into a star of explicit movies and Caroline is auditioned for a film of bondage and domination. Little do they know that the film is being financed by Caroline's former master, the cruel Clive, who intends to fulfil a long-held desire – to permanently make her his property.

Eroticon 3
September 1997   Price £4.99   ISBN: 0 352 32166 0

Like its predecessors, this unmissable collection of classic writings from forbidden texts features some of the finest erotic prose ever written. In its variety of people and practices, of settings and sexual behaviour, this exhilarating anthology provides the true connoisseur with the flavour of a dozen controversial works. Don't miss *Eroticon 1*, *2* and *4*, also from Nexus.

BLACK lace

There are three Black Lace titles published this month

A Volcanic Affair by Xanthia Rhodes
August 1997   Price £4.99   ISBN: 0 352 33184 7
Pompeii AD79. As the volcano rages, Marcella and her priapic lover Gaius begin their affair. Their escape from destruction only strengthens their love, but in the ensuing chaos they are separated from each other. Marcella loses herself in the perverse world of decadent Rome in a vain effort to recreate the pleasure she felt with Gaius, but soon becomes tangled in a bizarre web of deceit and sexual revenge.

Dangerous Consequences by Pamela Rochford
August 1997   Price £4.99   ISBN: 0 352 33174 7
After an erotically charged conflict with an influential man at the university, Rachel is under threat of redundancy. To cheer her up, her friend Luke takes her to a house in the country where she discovers new sensual possibilities. Upon her return to London, however, she finds that Luke has gone and she has been accused of theft. As she tries to clear her name, she discovers that her actions have dangerous – and very erotic consequences.

The Name of an Angel by Laura Thornton
August 1997   Price £6.99   ISBN: 0 352 33205 0
Clarissa Cornwall is a respectable university lecturer who has little time for romance until she meets the insolently young and sexy Nicholas St James. Soon, her position and the age gap between them no longer seem to matter as she finds herself taking more and more risks in expanding her erotic horizons with the charismatic student. This is the 100th book in the best-selling Black Lace series, and is published in a larger format.

Bonded by Fleur Reynolds
September 1997   Price £4.99   ISBN: 0 352 33192 2
When the beautiful young Sapphire goes on holiday and takes photographs of polo players at a game in the heart of Texas, she does not realise that they can be used as a means of revenge upon her cousin Jeanine. As the intrigue mounts, passions run ever higher – can Sapphire hope to avoid falling prey to the attractive young Everett, or will she give in to her libidinous desires?

Silent Seduction by Tanya Bishop
September 1997   Price £4.99   ISBN: 0 352 33193 3
Bored with an unsatisfying relationship in her home village, Sophie enthusiastically takes a job as a nanny at a country estate. She soon finds herself embroiled in sexual intrigues beyond the furthest reaches of her imagination. A series of passionate encounters begins when a mysterious, silent stranger visits her at night, and she sets about trying to discover his true identity.

Nexus

NEXUS BACKLIST

All books are priced £4.99 unless another price is given. If a date is supplied, the book in question will not be available until that month in 1997.

CONTEMPORARY EROTICA

THE ACADEMY	Arabella Knight	Oct
AGONY AUNT	G. C. Scott	Jul
ALLISON'S AWAKENING	John Angus	Jul
BOUND TO SUBMIT	Amanda Ware	Sep
CANDIDA'S IN PARIS	Virginia LaSalle	Oct
CANDY IN CAPTIVITY	Arabella Knight	
CHALICE OF DELIGHTS	Katrina Young	
A CHAMBER OF DELIGHTS	Katrina Young	Nov
THE CHASTE LEGACY	Susanna Hughes	
CHRISTINA WISHED	Gene Craven	
DARK DESIRES	Maria del Rey	
THE DOMINO TATTOO	Cyrian Amberlake	
THE DOMINO ENIGMA	Cyrian Amberlake	
THE DOMINO QUEEN	Cyrian Amberlake	
EDUCATING ELLA	Stephen Ferris	Aug
ELAINE	Stephen Ferris	
EMMA'S SECRET WORLD	Hilary James	
EMMA'S SECRET DIARIES	Hilary James	
EMMA'S HUMILIATION	Hilary James	
FALLEN ANGELS	Kendal Grahame	
THE TRAINING OF FALLEN ANGELS	Kendal Grahame	Dec
THE FANTASIES OF JOSEPHINE SCOTT	Josephine Scott	
HEART OF DESIRE	Maria del Rey	

HOUSE OF INTRIGUE	Yvonne Strickland	
HOUSE OF TEMPTATIONS	Yvonne Strickland	
THE ISLAND OF MALDONA	Yolanda Celbridge	
THE CASTLE OF MALDONA	Yolanda Celbridge	Apr
THE ICE QUEEN	Stephen Ferris	
THE INSTITUTE	Maria del Rey	
SISTERHOOD OF THE INSTITUTE	Maria del Rey	
JENNIFER'S INSTRUCTION	Cyrian Amberlake	
JOURNEY FROM INNOCENCE	G. C. Scott	Nov
A MATTER OF POSSESSION	G. C. Scott	
MELINDA AND THE MASTER	Susanna Hughes	
MELINDA AND THE COUNTESS	Susanna Hughes	
MELINDA AND SOPHIA	Susanna Hughes	
MELINDA AND ESMERELDA	Susanna Hughes	
THE NEW STORY OF O	Anonymous	
ONE WEEK IN THE PRIVATE HOUSE	Esme Ombreux	
AMANDA IN THE PRIVATE HOUSE	Esme Ombreux	Sep
PARADISE BAY	Maria del Rey	
THE PASSIVE VOICE	G. C. Scott	
THE SCHOOLING OF STELLA	Yolanda Celbridge	Dec
SECRETS OF THE WHIPCORD	Michaela Wallace	Aug
SERVING TIME	Sarah Veitch	
SHERRIE	Evelyn Culber	
SHERRIE AND THE INITIATION OF PENNY	Evelyn Culber	Oct
THE SPANISH SENSUALIST	Josephine Arno	
STEPHANIE'S CASTLE	Susanna Hughes	
STEPHANIE'S REVENGE	Susanna Hughes	
STEPHANIE'S DOMAIN	Susanna Hughes	
STEPHANIE'S TRIAL	Susanna Hughes	
STEPHANIE'S PLEASURE	Susanna Hughes	
SUSIE IN SERVITUDE	Arabella Knight	Mar
THE REWARD OF FAITH	Elizabeth Bruce	Dec
THE TRAINING GROUNDS	Sarah Veitch	
VIRGINIA'S QUEST	Katrina Young	Jun
WEB OF DOMINATION	Yvonne Strickland	May

EROTIC SCIENCE FICTION

RETURN TO THE PLEASUREZONE	Delaney Silver	

ANCIENT & FANTASY SETTINGS

CAPTIVES OF ARGAN	Stephen Ferris	Mar
CITADEL OF SERVITUDE	Aran Ashe	Jun
THE CLOAK OF APHRODITE	Kendal Grahame	
DEMONIA	Kendal Grahame	
NYMPHS OF DIONYSUS	Susan Tinoff	Apr
PYRAMID OF DELIGHTS	Kendal Grahame	
THE SLAVE OF LIDIR	Aran Ashe	
THE DUNGEONS OF LIDIR	Aran Ashe	
THE FOREST OF BONDAGE	Aran Ashe	
WARRIOR WOMEN	Stephen Ferris	
WITCH QUEEN OF VIXANIA	Morgana Baron	
SLAVE-MISTRESS OF VIXANIA	Morgana Baron	

EDWARDIAN, VICTORIAN & OLDER EROTICA

ANNIE AND THE SOCIETY	Evelyn Culber	
BEATRICE	Anonymous	
CHOOSING LOVERS FOR JUSTINE	Aran Ashe	
DEAR FANNY	Aran Ashe	
LYDIA IN THE BORDELLO	Philippa Masters	
MADAM LYDIA	Philippa Masters	
MAN WITH A MAID 3	Anonymous	
MEMOIRS OF A CORNISH GOVERNESS	Yolanda Celbridge	
THE GOVERNESS AT ST AGATHA'S	Yolanda Celbridge	
THE GOVERNESS ABROAD	Yolanda Celbridge	
PLEASING THEM	William Doughty	

Please send me the books I have ticked above.

Name ....

Address ....

....

....

.... Post code ....

Send to: **Cash Sales, Nexus Books, 332 Ladbroke Grove, London W10 5AH**

Please enclose a cheque or postal order, made payable to Virgin Publishing, to the value of the books you have ordered plus postage and packing costs as follows:

UK and BFPO – £1.00 for the first book, 50p for each subsequent book.

Overseas (including Republic of Ireland) – £2.00 for the first book, £1.00 for each subsequent book.

If you would prefer to pay by VISA or ACCESS/MASTERCARD, please write your card number and expiry date here:

....

Please allow up to 28 days for delivery.

Signature ....